THE
LAST
TESTAMENT

JAMES HOLMES

First paperback edition May 2020

Book design by Adam Hall
Edited by David Gatewood
Interior Layout Kevin G. Summers

ISBN 978-1-7343698-3-0 (paperback)
ISBN 978-1-7343698-2-3 (ebook)

www.jamesholmesauthor.com

Then destruction will come upon them suddenly like birth pangs upon a woman with child; and they shall not escape.
—Paul, 1 Thessalonians 5:1

It's not easy facin' up when your whole world is black.
—Mick Jagger

Science doesn't mean you can't believe in God or gods. That's not ruled out.
—Physicist Brian Cox

CHAPTER I

Rachaiya, Lebanon
Ten Days After Event

The Earth and the womb were bleeding.

John Sunday knelt on a blanket of snow, the pine trees above crackling their ice branches, the cold around him a numb mask. The sky was an inky black churning in the heavens, a spilt drink sopped up by the clouds. It made the world seem like it had been cast into an eternal eclipse, drained away colors until everything was gray.

Yet still he could hear the chattering of crickets—insects that should not have been here.

Because they didn't belong in this world.

He and Kat had climbed over the peaks heavy with snow, then trekked down into the valley. They'd stuck to the woods, avoiding the roads, which were choked with dead cars and hid evil things. Now, from his hillside perch, he gazed down at the small town tucked in the shadow of Mount Hermon. But he didn't have binoculars—or, for him, a monocular—and the only way he was truly going to see if it was safe was to get closer.

And it really didn't matter whether it was safe. One way or another, he'd have to go down there. Kat was losing a lot of blood. She'd told him what he needed to do—what he needed to get. And if he failed, their blood—hers and the baby's—would be on his hands. Blood that would never be washed.

He wished she were here with him now, but it was too dangerous. She was limp on the horse, and if she toppled, she and the baby would be hurt. So he'd left her tucked among pine trees about a mile back.

Jesus, it's cold.

He had to move, get his blood flowing.

He stepped down the snowy slope, removing the M4 from his shoulder sling and bringing it around. It was light in his hands. He had one magazine with eleven rounds left. Another ten in the 9mm on his hip. Kat had the Winchester, which had more ammo, but was a slower reload.

Not much of a last stand.

His boots crunched snow as he moved low. More snow was falling, whipping around him like ice flies, and with that cover and the eternal dark, he made it across the open ground without being spotted. Or so he hoped.

He moved against a building and around the corner, through an alley of snowdrifts, and he saw them. The snowdrifts had covered some of the gore, but not all. He saw scattered parts of bodies, pieces of bone, bits of torn flesh, skin flailed and peeled, blood frozen in ice. Dead children. And babies. They bothered him the most. Some had likely been killed by their own parents, and he wondered what kind of god would allow that.

He tried not to look as he crept past the dead, through the valley of cold bones, to what looked like a main street—or what passed for a main street in this small desert town. As a bitter wind howled past, born of a thing he had not yet seen—he wondered if it was watching him now—he scanned the Arabic signs that hung over open shop doors and shattered windows.

He spotted what he was looking for: a red cross. At one time it would have been illuminated to shine its message of aid, but now it was just cold plastic partially buried in snow.

He checked his angles and saw no one. Either the town had been abandoned, or they were waiting for him. Waiting to kill him. And if he died here, she would die there, frozen beneath a pine tree, and then all would be lost.

He closed his remaining eye and did something that once had been foreign to him. Now he found it came more easily, because now he believed there was someone actually listening. Still, the words felt like wood in his mouth.

Please, God.

He turned the corner and raced down the street, past a decapitated man leaning against a car, a crimson ice splatter against the door, his gray-bearded head in his lap like he was offering it. Halfway to his destination, Sunday tucked behind an abandoned car. He checked to make sure no one was coming down the street for him, but all he saw were the dark, empty storefronts, white drapes in a broken second-story window flapping in the breeze and longing to be set free. To his surprise he also smelled a stale rot, of either food or the dead, drifting past. He had assumed the cold would have kept the smell at bay—but with so much death here, maybe even ice couldn't compete.

That's when he heard the crickets again. Louder now. Closer. Like he was stepping through tall honey grass on a sun-filled field in June, and the crickets were chirping because he was near.

And that's how he took the sound.

As warning.

Yet he didn't have a choice. He had to keep going. They were out of food. She needed to eat.

Sunday rose fast from his spot and moved down the road, his boots slipping a bit in the snow. The chirping increased—as if to say, *There he is!* He increased his speed and practically raced down the sidewalk, the chirping becoming a caterwaul as he darted through the broken glass door of the clinic.

He scanned the dark lobby with the M4, panning it over the counter where there once would have been a receptionist. He saw nothing but tipped-over chairs and splatter of frozen blood in the snow dust.

He moved past the lobby and stepped down the narrow hallway at the back, checking each of the little rooms where sick children had been treated for sniffles and coughs. Every room now looked like a crime scene—cabinets open, glass jars scattered, cotton tufts floating in blood lagoons. He searched some of the cabinets but saw nothing he could use.

In the back room, an office, a young doctor lay on the floor, her white coat soaked red. She was frozen stiff, her hands clutched at her neck. It looked as though she had repeatedly jabbed her own throat with a pen that still rose from her jugular. She was missing an arm and half a leg, and her chest had been hollowed out by someone or something, but she had taken her own life before anyone else could.

Sunday had still not wrapped his mind around it all. Around the idea that there was an alien world here now. A world that the books of the ancients had foretold, but science had never imagined possible.

A bookshelf stood behind the doctor's desk. He set his rifle on the desk and went through the volumes, picking them up one by one and flipping through them, all of them in Arabic. Finally he found one with the information he sought.

There was a scuffle in the hall.

Sunday quickly stuffed the book into his backpack, grabbed the rifle, and moved cautiously to the doorway, ready to fight. Or to run.

But all he saw was a dog, half-starved, its prominent ribs like fingers crushing the organs within. It was a shepherd, its eyes empty and black, fur thick and matted with dried blood.

Sunday wondered if dogs were vulnerable to the possession, too. He hoped not; he didn't want to risk the sound of a gunshot on a dog.

He stepped slowly into the hall, not wanting to startle the creature. But as he moved slowly past, the dog merely stared, eyes wide, showing no signs of hostility despite its hunger. It sniffed the air in Sunday's wake, followed by a tender whine.

Sunday continued back through the lobby and outside into the eternal night.

He scanned the street again and knew where he had to go. A grocery store down the way. He hoped it had something left that was still edible.

A crunching sounded behind him. The dog. It was following him.

That's when Sunday noticed it: the crickets had stopped. All he heard was falling snow, a whisper of fluttering ice.

Why so quiet? Where was everyone?

* * *

Kat Devier lay beneath the trees, wrapped in a saddle blanket, yet still as cold as the snow on the branches above her. She looked to the horse standing nearby, now stained along its sides with a crimson red streak. Blood. *Her* blood. It had dripped and dribbled down the saddle and painted the sides of the horse. She wanted to wash it off, as if the animal would be embarrassed, but instead she turned away.

The weight of the baby was sitting on her bladder, so she hiked her thobe and squatted. The yellow of her urine mixed with red and burned a bloody hole in the snow. She was dying. She knew that. There was only so much blood left. The world was spinning, and the trees around her began to dance—she could hear their sway.

And then she saw him, standing watch beneath a tree: her father.

He looked just as he had when she saw him last, at the age of six. In fact the man before her was not much older than she was now, though he'd grown a mustache to make him look older. He wasn't sick—the hollow of the cancer had yet to claim him—and he even graced her with a smile. Strangely, the falling snow didn't touch him; the flakes moved around him, their trajectories warped.

Kat stood and adjusted her thobe. "Daddy?"

Her voice was swallowed in the emptiness of the orchard.

He can't really be here, she thought. Or could he—now things that could not be, had become?

He reached out a hand toward her and gestured for her to come closer. And that was when she knew. He was her collector. The one sent for the crossover. For some, she figured, the boatman is known.

No. It's not time.

She heard the distant crunching of snow. The horse lifted his head, his ears back, and searched the trees.

She was not alone. And it was not her visions that had spooked the horse.

* * *

The dog paused at the entrance to the grocery store, hesitant, perhaps smelling danger in the air. Sunday noted the warning but had no choice. Kat was starving.

He crossed the threshold into the darkness, careful to mind the crunch of broken glass, doing his best not to breathe in the stench of dank rot festering somewhere within. He stepped around a register with its drawer open, the money now an artifact, and moved down an aisle, past spilled bottles of pink antacid and squished tubes of toothpaste, searching first for the items she had requested. He found the sanitary napkins and tucked two plastic-wrapped packages into his sack. Then he turned the corner of another aisle, searching for food.

Sunday stopped when he saw the old man. He was on his haunches, squatting near the meat counter, his back to Sunday, tearing into some kind of meat. He paused a moment to sniff the air like a dog, then continued feeding without turning. Perhaps what he was eating had come from the butcher. Perhaps it *was* the butcher.

Sunday raised the rifle, but was still hesitant to use it because of the sound. Instead he stepped back softly, quietly, away from the old man, and found his way to the canned goods, sacred tins, grails of preserved food. Most were scattered on the floor. He picked them up and slipped them into his backpack. Baby corn. Beans. Peas and carrots.

He moved a bit farther down the aisle, and saw a man sleeping on one of the bottom shelves, tucked into the shadows like a hornet under a stair. Sunday wondered if he could swipe more cans without waking him. But in his mind he saw her face, the dark anemic circles under her eyes, and knew he had to try.

Slowly, quietly, he grabbed a can of tender mushrooms he could almost taste, placing it in his sack as carefully as though it were a Faberge egg. Then a can of asparagus and another of beets. These were foods that in the old world he would have passed up, but here, now, they were trophies, caloric prizes, where the winner lives another day.

As he added another can to his sack, the contents shifted, the cans clanking dully from within. The man on the shelf shifted slightly.

Sunday froze.

Don't roll over.

The man didn't move, but a shuffling step sounded behind Sunday.

He turned.

The old man from the meat aisle had appeared almost right next to him, staring at Sunday with hollowed-out eyes. Sunday had the feeling that it wasn't the man who stared at him, but something else deep within those recesses, as if the man's flesh were a suit to be borrowed and worn.

Sunday brought his weapon around to fire, but the man swatted it away with such force it flew from Sunday's hands. The old man then grabbed Sunday by his jacket with one hand—his other hand was nothing but a bone hook—and pressed him toward the sleeping man on the shelves. Except the man had rolled over and was no longer sleeping, if he had ever been.

Sunday tried to break free, but the old man was strong, far stronger than he had any right to be. Before Sunday could reach for the 9mm on his hip, the man on the shelf had risen and grabbed hold of both of his arms.

The old man then stepped back, looking Sunday up and down, assessing him, bloody pieces of rotten meat clinging to his lips and beard.

"We remember your smell," he hissed. His mouth was open, but his lips didn't move when he spoke. The voice seemed to come from somewhere inside him. "Where is the pregnant whore?"

With a sudden burst of violence he ripped Sunday from the other man's grip, slammed him onto the floor, and pinned him there, hovering above, his mouth open and his breath rank.

A clicking came from the end of the aisle, and both Sunday and the old men turned their heads to look. A woman was crawling on all fours toward them. But not a woman. Her limbs were wrong, bent the wrong way, like an insect, and her hands and feet lacked flesh, just jagged bones *tick tick ticking* on the linoleum.

The old man waited, as if he had been expecting her.

She came close, until her face hovered just above his. She smelt earthen, of blood and decay and the abandoned dead he'd known on the battlefield. There was enough left of her to see she had been young, maybe even pretty. But no longer. When her mouth opened as if to speak, white-clawed fingers emerged from her throat like long, knuckled tentacles.

Here was a creature that made no sense... yet Sunday felt the memory of her. She was similar to the beasts he had seen in the coma dreams. Creatures that had hovered in the shadows. Yet they no longer waited for an invitation, because the door had been left wide.

And now they were here. In the land of men.

He felt a terror growing inside him, because of all the deaths he had ever faced, this one was the most unknown. And being dead would not end it.

The two men held him down as the hand from the woman's mouth traced his flesh, up his face to his scalp. Fingers like bone nails clamped down on his skull. And then, from her mouth, moving down to her fingertips, he saw a dark rank fluid coursing through her translucent veins, bound for his head.

They were going to taint him somehow. Fill him with something. Possess him.

A sudden chirping of crickets sounded nearby. The woman-thing paused just as suddenly, searching for the source. From the next aisle over came more sounds. A spinning bottle. A soft, padded step.

The dog came around the corner and stepped into the aisle.

It growled, then let loose with a barrage of barking. Darting forward, it locked its jaws on the old man's arm and yanked him away from Sunday.

Sunday seized the opportunity. His right arm now freed, he grabbed the 9mm from his hip, fired into the shelf man, knocking him back into the rack, then slipped free of the woman's grip on his skull, scooted quickly back, and pointed the gun at her.

She hissed with a whisper that almost sounded like, "Please."

Sunday fired.

As the woman-thing fell back—injured? dead? he didn't know—he put a bullet in the back of the head of the old man, snatched up his backpack, and ran for the entrance. The dog scampered close behind.

At the doorway he saw more people coming down the street from his left, perhaps forty or more. Too many—Sunday didn't have enough rounds to kill them all. And yet if he ran back to Kat, they'd follow him, endangering her.

The dog stood at his side, barking madly, the starved creature bravely holding its ground.

"Come on!" Sunday shouted—and together they ran.

* * *

Five men crossed through the snow, guns at the ready, their purpose violent. The one in the front, an Arab with broken teeth, stopped and pointed. There in the snow was a blood trail, its crimson dots as clear as an arrow.

They tracked the path, leading them right past the horse, which huffed and moved away from them as they approached. Perhaps the horse sensed that these were not men. They wore its skin, but that flesh was a lie.

* * *

Sunday raced down the street, his boots slipping in the snow, the dog at his side. Yet the horde of once-people who followed behind were just as fast, though the condition of their bodies suggested they had no right to be. And Sunday didn't know where he was going. Where to run. He was just pushing it, full-out, hoping to get some distance, someplace to escape to, someplace to hide.

It wasn't working. His knees clanked like bone hinges as he pushed on, down another street. He was weak from not eating. Weak from the cave and the coma and the torture in the bunker. And they were gaining.

Then he saw it: a cross on a tower steeple. Snow blanketed the dome tower itself, but the cross jutted out like a lighthouse on a dark island.

Sunday ran toward this holy place. Not because it was a place to hide, but because he harbored a small, desperate hope that God was watching. That He would offer him sanctuary.

But the door was locked. Sunday rattled the bronze handle and threw his shoulder into the wood of the door, but it wouldn't budge.

So much for sanctuary.

The horde was closing in. Beside him, the dog growled and its hackles rose. It was ready to fight.

Sunday took his cue from the dog. He raised the M4, took a knee right there in front of the locked church, and thought of Kat. He pictured her as he'd left her, beneath that pine, snow ice jewels in her hair, her body failing. He had wanted to save her. To prove he was worthy of her.

He opened fire. He didn't have nearly enough ammo, but he hoped that maybe a few shots would scare the rest off.

The first round tore through the head of a young man, too young, his beard still somehow pre-pubescent in its thickness. He would never reach the age when it would fully form. Sunday fired again. Another hit. Nine bullets left. Eight. Seven, six.

They kept coming.

Five. Four. Three. Each a shot to the head, center skull, his desire for a double-tap overruled by the need to conserve ammo.

Two. One.

Click.

He heard the trigger tap empty, a sound that haunts every soldier's heart. Then he reached for his hip, that split-second draw drilled into him, and pulled the 9mm. He fired again, the horde practically on top of him.

As he fired, again and again, his mind drifted beyond the tart of the gunpowder fog, beyond the bullets that tunneled through snowflakes and into the flesh of the taken. He drifted back to her again, and the smile she had given him before he left. It was small, barely there, the first hint of inner joy he'd seen since they'd been reunited. She had ridden the mountain in silence, a human vapor, and had he not seen her still bleeding, he would have thought her already dead. But the smile, faint as it was, had given him hope.

The sound of thunder boomed across the dark heavens above. As if God had suddenly awoken to judge, to clear the earth of the sins of man and beast. But it wasn't thunder that echoed down to him along the snow-covered street—it was calibrated, a bullwhip crack.

The blasts turned semi-automatic, and Sunday knew the sound. An AK-47. He'd heard that particular weapon fired at him many times through the years. And now it was being fired by someone up there in the cross tower.

Sunday wanted to look up, but instead he kept firing, using every sacred, remaining round in the Walther. The horde of not-humans fell before his shots and those from the shooter above, until only one remained standing. An old woman. She did not approach, just stood alone among the dead, a tichel covering her head of decaying flesh. She raised a bony finger in his direction and hissed with great fury.

"*The sow shall not bear.*"

Another gunshot rang out from above, the crack echoing in the cold street, and the old woman's body dropped to the snow.

* * *

The men crept through the white forest, their breath—though it was not their lungs that did the breathing—catching the winter air. The blood trail led to a horse blanket lying near a stand of trees, its shape round and fetal, someone hiding beneath it. The bottom of a pair of boots stuck out at one end.

The men circled the blanket, raised their weapons, and fired. Wool dander mixed with the falling snow.

The lead man leaned in to raise the blanket and look, but before he could, a round tore clear through his skull. It knocked him to the ground with such fury that the other men stood stunned. Even as they looked to see where it had come from, another round rang out through the trees, a rapid crack, and a second man dropped.

The remaining three fired wildly into the trees, not knowing where they were shooting, just hoping to get a lucky hit or at least force this sniper down while they got their bearings.

Two more men fell. Their attacker was unfazed by their suppressing fire.

The lone man left standing was no man. He was a boy. Sixteen years old. He looked at the dead men around him, and saw they'd been shot in the tops of their heads, their hair blown back to reveal the skin craters. That's when he realized the shooter was above them. He looked up.

Too late. A round tore through his forehead, splitting one side of his brain away from the other.

Kat slowly, carefully, climbed down from her pine tree perch, her protruding belly keeping her from clutching the tree with anything other than her hands and feet. When at last she dropped down, her bare, swollen feet sank into the snow, and she crossed back through the cold to the circle of dead men. She double-checked that they were indeed dead before sitting on the blanket to put on her boots.

These things aren't dumb, she thought. *They tracked me. Used weapons.*

The snow fell softly from above. With the echo of the gunshots cleared from the air, it was again a peaceful place.

CHAPTER II

Deep Run, Maryland
Two Days After Event

Eve McCallister woke on the cold gravel, her face speckled with a dozen hollow points, as if she'd fallen asleep on a waffle iron. She sat straight up with a jolt, and looked into the darkness for the man who had run up the path pointing a gun at her.

He was still there, beyond the chain-link fence, slumped awkwardly in a hump, face down like he was bowing.

"Hello?"

She slowly stood and moved closer to the fence. He didn't move. His face was partially submerged in the snow, but she could see the dried blood on his neck and the snow around him.

Snow? Why is there snow?

She wondered how long she had been out. It was dark outside. And cold. And... *snowing.*

Eve moved back toward where she had awoken. Around the outline of her snow silhouette were the remains of a dried, milky molt. She reached up to her face and found that some of it still clung to her. She caught a crispy flap of it, peeled it away from her cheek, painlessly, like the skin of a sunburn, and looked at the husk.

No.

She'd seen this before. In the mirror after the car crash. Her skin dried and flaked around her ears. That was when her face had first changed.

Did it happen again?

Then it hit her like a night bus.

"Daddy?" she called out. Except the voice that came from her throat didn't sound like her.

Oh God. That's not my voice.

She moved toward the bunker entrance. From up ahead, she heard what sounded like hungry dogs. She trudged through the snow, turned a corner... and saw them.

A feast of turkey vultures, their red heads rapidly flicking and tearing and pulling upon her father. There were a half dozen of them, their raspy snake-like hisses laying claim to their stake.

She ran at them, screaming, swatting, and they squawked and spread their black wings and eventually rose to the sky, acting more annoyed than alarmed by her presence.

Eve dropped to her knees next to her father's frozen body and struggled to roll him over. He landed with a crunch on the ice—and she drew back.

"Daddy..." she said, because even though she was twenty-two and they had exchanged harsh words, she still called him that. She reached out, wanting to touch him, but she couldn't bring herself to do it. His face was nearly gone. The winged collectors had plucked and pulled off their morsels until he looked more meat than man.

A lump rose in her throat.

This man, she thought. This man had raised her when her mother died and it was just the two of them. This man had taken her to countless museums as a little girl, dragged her until her little blue Converse sneakers flopped on her feet, just so she could learn a little more about the world. This man had worked relentlessly so he could provide her with every little thing she ever wanted, because he said he loved her.

And this same man...

She knew what he did. She had judged him for it. Because although he sought her love, he was an author of men's deaths, and of the ends of families and children. And though he worked all those long hours away from her, all she ever really wanted was his time, not his money.

Yet despite his sins, despite everything, she still called him *Daddy*.

She thought she should drag him inside the bunker, to be close to him—but she knew the body would grow rank. Instead she straightened his collar and zipped his zipper—because it was cold—then nestled upon the soft pillow of his jacket and his bloat and rested there, her tears falling upon him, the snow blanketing them both.

* * *

It wasn't until his jacket started to shift beneath her resting head that she realized something was wrong.

She lifted her head, slowly unzipped the jacket, pulled open his shirt... and jerked back in horror.

A pair of hands were moving within the skin of his chest, rolling around inside him, swimming to the surface.

She pushed away, vomit rising in her throat like a rat crawling up a sewer pipe.

His body shifted in the snow, and for a moment she wondered if her father had what she had. The ability to come back. But he didn't molt, and he didn't change. Instead his body arched and lifted, just as it was, bloated and half-eaten. His dead head shifted and turned to her, and his single remaining eyelid flopped open, revealing a half-eaten eye.

"Daddy?"

But she knew this thing that now stared at her was not her father. She felt it. It was something far away, yet it was also here.

And she needed to get away from it.

She looked to the bunker and wondered if she could make it to the door. She rose to her feet and turned to run, but his hand clamped down on her ankle, pulling her toward him, his body lurching as if he had a palsy.

Eve screamed.

She kicked him square in the face, her foot sinking into the bloat of his flesh, and he released her. She ran full speed, slipping in the snow, to the door of the bunker. The cold steel handle felt like heaven in her hands, because she was close to escape.

But it was locked.

She looked back—and he was there. Standing in the snow shallows right behind her. He looked down at her, his face tattered and torn, and he smiled. Then he pulled back his jacket, and there, dangling from his belt, was a set of keys. He flicked at them, the silver clinking like little chimes, and Daddy moved toward his little girl.

CHAPTER III

Rachaiya, Lebanon
Ten Days After Event

Sunday heard the jostling of the lock, and the wooden door of the church creaked open. In front of him stood a little boy in a dark-brown fur-tipped parka. He was no more than ten, his dark hair matted with dried blood, his face streaked with dirt. Despite his age, he clutched a Kalashnikov in his small hands as if it made him a man.

The boy said nothing, just stood aside, and Sunday and the dog stepped into the church.

It might once have been a beautiful place. The ceilings were vaulted, and stained-glass windows adorned the sides. But the blue paint above was peeling, many of the windows had been broken, and the smell of charred smoke hung in the air. The pews had been knocked over and toppled, and the altar had been pressed up against a far door.

And then there were the bodies.

In the center of the room lay the burnt body of one of the creatures, its limbs singed in a circle of black. Next to it lay the burnt corpse of a dismembered man.

And all around, scattered among the toppled pews, were more bodies. Dead humans. A battle had gone down here, in this holy place, and for the humans, it had not gone well.

But at least Sunday knew these creatures could be killed.

A gray-haired priest lumbered down the stairs at the back of the church. He was easily three hundred pounds, his gut a cauldron beneath his black robes. Around his neck dangled a wooden crucifix, and from his shoulder hung an AK-47.

The priest stopped several feet from Sunday. "You alone?" he asked in Arabic.

"Yes," Sunday answered.

The priest looked to the dog. "That your dog?"

"It is now," Sunday said.

The priest assessed his guests through narrowed eyes. Then he switched to English, his accent producing a slight upward tilt at the end of each word.

"We can't stay here," he said. He turned and moved toward the back of the church. "We have to go. Now."

"Why?"

"Because those things outside... they aren't done."

* * *

As Kat sat on the horse blanket tying the laces on her boots, one of the dead men made a crackling sound. She spun to face him, and had to suppress a scream when a narrow bone claw jutted from the dead man's gut and split him open from the inside.

A creature with long bone appendages crawled out of the wound in his stomach. It had a human-like shape, but far more stretched out, and its pale face was recessed into a fleshy neck like some kind of half-molted insect.

Kat knew she should move, fight, run, but for a moment she simply froze in shock and fear. It wasn't until the adrenaline kicked in that she reacted. She grabbed the rifle off the blanket, leapt to her feet, and stood over the creature. Before it could fully emerge from the man's dead body, she fired, cocked, and fired again, the .44-caliber rounds tearing off chunks of the creature's head. When the creature opened its mouth, as if to speak, she blew off its jaw.

From all around her, she heard more crackling and peeling. All of the bodies now shifted in the snow, as if being pushed and jostled from within.

By the time a jagged bone burst from the gut of the second dead man, she was already racing back through the snow forest toward the horse.

* * *

Father Simon led the boy and the stranger and the dog to the back of the church. On the way, he grabbed a roll of duct tape from among a pile of supplies beneath the altar and tossed it to the stranger with one eye whose life he had just saved.

"For your wound," he said, nodding to the stranger's stomach. The man's shirt was wet with fresh blood.

As the man taped his bleeding gut, Father Simon took a moment to look him over. In addition to the missing eye, the man's face was covered by a criss-cross of scars. He looked like he'd been fed through a shredder. And clearly he'd seen battle before today. He was good with a gun—excellent, in fact. Simon had watched this shooter at his doorstep firing his 9mm with perfect accuracy even while under duress. Simon had known men like this, back in Beirut.

The priest turned to the child. "Give him your rifle."

The child did not speak of course, but indicated his protest by shaking his head.

"Please," Simon said again, doing his best to sound paternal.

The child relented. He handed the scarred man his rifle—slowly, reluctantly, as if parting with his security blanket.

The stranger flicked the magazine release, checked the ammo, and then loaded a round into the chamber, something the child had failed to do.

"Where are we going?" the stranger asked.

"There is a house a few kilometers up the hill. The man there has guns. Many guns."

"I have someone in the woods. I have to get her," he said.

Father Simon frowned. "You said you were alone."

"I am. Here."

"We cannot wait. Those things are waking, and then they're even harder to kill."

The stranger shook his head. "I don't have a choice. Without me, she and the baby will die."

"Baby?"

"She's pregnant. And bleeding."

The boy reached up and tugged on Simon's robe.

Yes. Yes, I know.

Father Simon mulled for a moment, his tongue tracing the inside of his teeth. Finally, he sighed. "Where is she?"

* * *

Kat sank in the snow as she ran, the powder pulling her down, her breaths frosting in the air. They were catching up to her, clicking like crickets as they moved through the dark trees. She no longer even knew which way she'd come, which way she was going, only sought to get away from those things.

And then she spotted it. Her own blood path, crimson spots dark against the white. Finding her second wind, she turned and followed them, racing back to the clearing. She wanted to look back, to see how close the creatures were to catching her, to lay eyes on them fully in morbid fascination, but instead she kept running, sinking into the snow, collecting her footing again, and running some more.

The horse was still there. She grabbed its reins and climbed up into the saddle. Only then did she risk a glance back.

They were a hundred yards out, more spider-like than human in their movement, able to cross the snow more easily than she because their long bones had been stretched to spread their weight. Plus they weren't weak, starving, bleeding, and pregnant.

"Hiya!" she said as she kicked the horse, but the animal was already moving, not waiting for her permission.

* * *

Sunday and the priest, the boy and the dog, crossed an alley that led onto a side road. As they moved, Sunday heard the collapse of the wooden church door behind them and the scooting and slamming of furniture. Those creatures were inside the church, and they were searching. For him.

The road the group moved down was littered with cars, and Sunday's eyes scanned each vehicle for a potential threat. Then they turned onto another road, this one strewn with bodies, all of them split open as if pillaged for parts, the carcasses left behind like blood flowers to blossom in the snow. Sunday scanned these as well. In this world, nothing could be trusted.

He wondered if, in fact, he could trust this priest. Where had a man of God gotten guns, and where had he learned to use them?

The street they followed came to a dead end marked off by a chain-link fence. The priest slung his AK over his shoulder and began to climb. Sunday would not have thought this giant mass of a man could manage it—and in fact the chain groaned and stretched as if it were equally disbelieving—but he pulled his belly up, not without a struggle, and eventually landed on the other side with a thud. The boy scrambled over next, nimble as a monkey, and then Sunday looked down to the dog.

He debated leaving the animal here, on this side of the fence, because he didn't need another mouth to feed. But the dog would likely be killed. Or it would starve.

The dog looked up at him as if it realized the decision that was about to be made here.

Sunday sighed.

He wasn't sure how the dog would respond when picked up, so he went in slowly and scooped it low. The dog didn't resist, and Sunday wondered if the dog understood it needed to get over that fence to survive.

He carried it with him as he climbed, clutching it to his chest. Once on the other side, he set it down again, and the four of them ran for the trees, running flat-out through the snow. Behind them, Sunday could hear the creatures in the streets, ransacking buildings and cars, looking for them.

* * *

Kat's heels kicked into the sides of the horse, although the animal didn't need her encouragement. The horse was already hopping and running with sweating intensity through the soft snow, galloping with wild force and an equal desire to live. She bounced hard as they galloped, the baby inside jostling, as did the blood between her legs that slicked the saddle and threatened to slide her off the horse.

Even over the horse's heavy breathing and her own, she could hear their pursuit, their cricket sounds a *tick tick tick* in her ears.

From the corner of her eye, she saw one closing in on her left side. It hopped across the snow next to her, nine, maybe ten feet tall, all sinewy and stretched with abnormally long arms and legs. In its abdomen it carried faces, a melting of humans molded together into a fleshy clay, all trapped within, their expressions reflecting the agony of being owned by this thing.

At that moment the horse passed under thicker canopy, and its hooves found harder ground barely touched by the snow. Its pace picked up dramatically, and they tore through the dark forest with such speed Kat feared some unseen tree branch would knock her off. She lowered herself until her face was right up against the heat and beating veins of the horse's neck.

She thought once more of the faces trapped within that creature's belly. Like her, they were mere riders at the mercy of their mount. The difference was, she was free to get off at any time—and those who chased her could not.

* * *

Sunday looked up sharply as a creature came tearing through the trees at them. The priest raised his rifle to shoot it.

"No!" Sunday shouted.

The white spotted horse came galloping into sight, Kat on its back. "They're coming!" she said, pulling to a stop beside them.

The priest looked up at her. "Please! The boy," he said.

Sunday nodded that it was okay and Kat lowered her hand and groaned as she pulled the child onto the horse. He slipped into place behind her.

"How many?" Sunday asked.

"Four or five." She reached into the saddlebag and grabbed a box of cartridges. Steadying her Winchester rifle on the saddle horn, she reloaded.

"What are you doing?" Sunday said. "Go!"

She continued to reload. "We do this together," she said firmly.

He started to protest, but it was too late. The creatures burst from the darkness of the trees, closing in fast.

Kat steadied the horse, raised the rifle to her shoulder, and opened fire. Her blast buried itself into the spongy flesh of the lead creature, but it kept coming. Sunday and the priest opened fire as well, and Sunday squinted against the orange bursts of gunfire, a new light in this dark place. Their rounds tore chunks of flesh and bits of bone. These creatures were not of this world, but their bodies could be broken. Could be stopped.

When it was done, the creatures' rank sulfur fouled the air. Sunday stood over one, still quivering, its twisted flesh a sick gray against the white snow. Beneath its skin swirled a mass of body parts, faces screaming in agony, arms and legs of not just one human, all of it merged and melted together. This thing was alien and human, insect and man, demon and damned all in one.

Among the tortured faces was that of a young girl. "*Aidez moi*," she said, her voice one long exhale.

Sunday hesitated. *Aidez moi?*

He looked up as Kat, who had urged the horse closer. "She said *aidez moi*. What does that mean?"

"It's French. It means 'Help me.'"

Sunday raised the rifle and pointed it at the girl's face. It was the only way he knew of to end her suffering.

CHAPTER IV

Tel Aviv, Israel
Day of Event

Ayelet Tal lay in a hospital bed, the room full of Shin Bet security, waiting for the impromptu ceremony to begin. She shifted uncomfortably beneath the blanket that covered her legs. She didn't want any more recognition. She didn't want any more visitors. Particularly not the deputy prime minister and his entourage.

And particularly given the nature of her injuries.

She'd been split open at her seam. Front to back. The saw had sliced open her perineum, torn through her vaginal and anal muscles, and would have sliced into her intestines had the raid not happened when it did. It was torture to now lie here with everyone in this room knowing full well what injuries lay beneath her blanket, everyone whispering about it because it was so awful, and can you imagine.

To have visitors was insult, not accolade.

But she did what she so often did: she lay back and took it.

Deputy Prime Minister Benjamin Rudik came to stand beside her bed while another man stood in the corner snapping pictures with a cell phone camera. Rudik held out his hand, she obediently took it, and he clutched her hand tightly with both of his, like he was about to seal the deal on a used car.

He leaned in close enough that she could smell the coffee on his breath.

"You are an honor to the homeland, and to God," he proclaimed loudly—for her, the room, and God to hear.

She nodded, wondering if she was expected to thank him. Thank him for his presence. For the photo op. Would she end up in some monthly newsletter, or would these men just show her picture around their office cubicles and say, "Can you believe it? This woman was split open right between her legs." And then there would be some crude jokes about other ways to split apart a woman. And when they saw her again, they'd all treat her like she was some kind of fragile cripple.

She didn't thank him.

When the photo op was over, the men lingered a little more, as if waiting for snacks and punch. More men came over and shook her hand, and thanked her for her service…

The lights flickered. There was a pumping sound in the fluorescents, the mercury vapor gasped for breath, and then the room went dark. No generator kicked on. No emergency lights. In a matter of seconds, the room, the hall outside, all of it was without light and power. The background electrical hums and beeps she had forgotten were there were now notable by their sudden absence.

Ayelet looked to the window, the only source of light. And yet even there a darkness grew. A great cloud was unfurling across the sky, faster than any storm she'd ever seen, a rolling vapor, an oil spill draining black across the heavens.

What is *that?*

"Move! Move!" shouted one of the men on the deputy prime minister's security detail. In seconds, they'd gathered the deputy prime minister beneath their wing and had pushed him out the door, apparently sensing as much as Ayelet did that this was no mere power outage.

The door closed and clicked behind them, and Ayelet was alone once again. She watched the shadows creep across her blanket in the vanishing sunlight. She half expected a blast wave to slam against the window, shattering the glass and tossing her across the room. That would almost make sense—a bomb. Though it was like no bomb she knew of.

The other possibility, the one that lurked deep in her mind... did not.

That possibility involved an apocalyptic group breeding little Jesus babies, a group of pregnant nuns in a church in Rome, and Ayelet being tortured in unthinkable ways to find out what she knew, because Silas Egin and all the others had a plan they needed to protect.

And maybe that plan was now coming to fruition.

A Bible verse appeared in her head like she was reading it on a sign.

The trumpet will sound, the dead will be raised, and we shall be changed.

That was what Egin had said in the church.

A scream sounded in the hall outside her room. It was answered with two gunshots.

Ayelet knew then that she had to move. Something was coming for her. No—something was already here. She pulled back the blanket and looked down at the bandaged diaper that wrapped her lower torso. She was in no condition to stand. Not now. Not for a long time. Maybe not ever. But the wheelchair was across the room, tucked in the corner. She had no choice.

Painfully, awkwardly, she swung her legs off the edge of the bed and pushed herself to a standing position. She shuffled across the floor with the tiniest of steps, careful not to tear the stitches that held her together. Even so, with each step she felt a little tug on the strings, a pull on her injured flesh, the rough ends of the stitches scraping between her legs, and she wanted to cry from the pain.

More gunshots—farther away but still close.

She quickened her pace to a sliding shuffle.

When she made it to the chair, she sat, her movements cautious. She wondered if the stitches had held because she could feel something damp between her legs. She wheeled over to the door, cracked it open, and peered into the hallway. Light from her window, and from other open doors, generated faint illumination, but the darkness outside was coming faster now, an eclipse creeping over the hall.

Another patient stood in a darkened doorway. An old man who looked like he'd just been woken from a dementia dream. "What's happening?" he asked. His voice weak and drifting, as if his old lungs were unable to muster enough strength to stretch his vocal cords.

"I don't know."

Ayelet wheeled into the hall, but there was no one else around. No patients. No nurses. No staff.

Where is everyone?

She smelled something in the air. Burnt ozone— the smell of electrical sparks after her kitchen blender had worked too hard.

She pushed open a pair of double doors and rolled herself along an empty corridor. She was about halfway down the hall when the doors opened behind her, and she looked back. The old man stood there, his eyes wide.

"Please," he said with a sob.

Suddenly he dropped to his hands and knees and slammed his head into the tiled floor, repeatedly. The sound of his skull knocking against the marble echoed against the bare walls.

Oh my God.

She knew then. Knew there was something here with them. Something that had a power over them. And that scared her more than the darkness that was closing in around her.

Before she could decide what to do, the old man was back up to his feet, his face broken and bloodied, and racing toward her at full speed, with the gait of a far younger man.

She reacted then, spinning her chair and rolling away as fast as she could, but he was already too close and there was no way she could outrace him. She heard his thumping bare footsteps behind her as she spun the big wheels round and round with a fury.

The double doors in front of her opened, and a big man in a suit appeared.

Oh God. There's someone else. Coming for me.

He raised the gun and pointed it at her.

This was it. And for a moment, Ayelet was grateful that it would all be over quickly. She'd already said her prayers and begged for forgiveness back in the bunker when the men produced the saw. And then they sawed anyway. By her math, her slate was clean.

The man fired, and the bullet whizzed over her head. She turned and saw that the old man had taken a round to the center of his chest. Blood was rapidly blossoming on the front of his hospital gown. But it didn't stop him. Didn't even slow him. He kept coming.

No.

The big man fired again, putting two shots in the old man's skull. His head snapped back with each impact, but even now he kept moving forward as if being pushed by an invisible hand. It took three more shots to the head and another to the chest before he finally fell to his knees and collapsed to the floor.

Ayelet's mind was racing. This didn't make any sense.

She turned back to the big man in the suit. The man who had just saved her life. She realized she recognized him; he was from the deputy prime minister's security detail. Someone had come back for her after all.

"I'm going to pick you up," he said, and he wasn't asking for permission. He holstered his sidearm, cradled her beneath her thighs and under her arms, and scooped her up like a baby. Then he lifted her up and over onto his shoulders, drew his weapon again, and went straight for the emergency-exit stairwell.

Without windows, it was almost completely pitch-black in here, but he raced down into the blackness with her slung on his shoulders like a sack of feed. She feared something could be hiding for them around the corner, or at the bottom of a turn, and they'd never know it. They'd just run smack into it, and she wondered what she would see then.

At the bottom of the stairs he burst into the lobby, which was now a killing field. Bodies lay scattered all around, twisted in pools of their own blood. Ayelet didn't have long to look at them or determine how they had died, because her human transport was already out the hospital doors and into the street.

The rest of the security team, along with the deputy prime minister, had taken cover near three black SUVs.

"Engines are dead!" shouted one of the men.

"Go!" shouted the man who carried Ayelet. "The bunker!"

They surrounded the deputy prime minister and moved in a fluid mass, weapons ready, down the sidewalk. The day had turned to a hazy twilight, rolling black clouds thickening over the world, and Ayelet could hear distant screaming. The entire electrical grid was offline. The stoplights were out. The buildings dark. But then Ayelet realized it was more than just wired electricity. People stood outside their cars, checking under their hoods as if to see if there were an issue with their battery.

"Back!" shouted one of the men on the security detail, but from Ayelet's position she couldn't tell what he was shouting about. "Back! Back!"

Two gunshots. Then another. And once more.

The man who carried her said nothing, only grunted as he kept moving forward.

They passed a Hassidic Jew lying on the ground face up, a double-tap to his skull. Had the security officer just shot this man? But as they moved on, she watched the man slowly, carefully get up again, as if he'd merely fallen. He immediately ran after them with the speed of an Olympic athlete.

"Behind you!" Ayelet shouted.

The big man carrying her stopped, spun around, and fired, hitting the man again and again in the head, correcting his aim to compensate for the kickback of the man's cranium as it filled with rounds. There was only tenderized meat and bone left when the man at last fell face-down onto the sidewalk.

Ayelet heard the words in her mind, in a voice that was not her own.

The trumpet will sound, the dead will be raised, and we shall be changed.

As they continued to run, she saw the street around her erupting into chaos. A group of young women spazzed and seized, banging their heads into the asphalt just like the old man in the hospital had done. A fat balding man in an apron, some kind of cook, tackled a woman and stabbed her repeatedly in the face with a fork. Another man chased a woman fleeing with her baby in her arms, but as he closed in on her, Ayelet closed her eyes. She didn't want to watch that one.

They turned a corner, and a voice shouted, "Oh my God!" It sounded like the deputy prime minister.

More gunshots, then they were surrounded, and Ayelet felt strangers tugging at her hospital gown. She couldn't see anything through the mass of bodies, but there was screaming and shouting, and gunshots, and she was being pulled in multiple directions, and the man who held her started to let her go.

No, please don't! she thought. If she fell, that was it. She'd be devoured by this mob, torn apart.

He adjusted her on his shoulders and fired until his weapon clicked.

Another member of the security team collapsed beside them. He fell to his knees and began slamming his head repeatedly into the concrete.

Oh, God, it's happening to them too. It's going to happen to all of us!

The man leapt up again and attacked one of the other members of the detail. He jumped on his back, clawed and bit at him like an animal, then pulled him to the ground and slammed his partner's head over and over into the pavement with such force that Ayelet heard his skull crack.

"Go!" she shouted to the big man carrying her.

He pushed through the crowd, grabbed the deputy prime minister's arm, and dragged him along with them. Somehow breaking free of the mass of people, he sprinted down the street, through a set of empty guard gates hanging open, and toward a metal door on a plain concrete gray building. He pulled on the door, but it was locked. He banged hard, the sound of metal reverberating beneath his fist, then looked up at a camera above the door.

"I have the deputy prime minister!" he shouted.

He set Ayelet on the ground and leaned her against the wall, then tossed his empty gun aside and turned back to the camera.

Sitting upright, Ayelet could see much better now. Not that she wanted to. The rest of the security detail was mixed up with the mob, but only one of them appeared to still be himself. And he didn't last long. A little old lady grabbed his arm and ripped the limb from its socket with seemingly no more effort than a child would use to stretch apart putty.

The big man banged again on the bunker door and shouted to whoever might be listening. He dragged the deputy prime minister into view of the camera.

"I have the Eagle! Do you hear me? I have the Eagle!"

The door remained locked.

He kneeled next to Ayelet as the mob closed in on them. He looked at her, and she at him, and he gave a faint smile—as if in relief that the mystery of how he would die was now known, and thus the mystery was no more. He reached for her hand, and she gave it to this stranger.

Then she heard the sound. A clicking from the bunker door. It swung open, and two soldiers stepped out, armed with CTAR-21s. They laid down cover fire as a third soldier emerged, grabbed the deputy prime minister by the back of his shirt collar, and pulled him into the bunker.

The big man scooped Ayelet up again, and a second later they were inside, the metal door slammed shut behind them.

"Mr. Rudik, are you hurt?" the big man asked.

The deputy prime minister didn't answer. His face was chalk white.

"Ben!" The big man put a paw on the deputy prime minister's shoulder. "You need to answer me. Are you hurt?"

"No, no," he said.

He turned his head toward Ayelet. "You?"

"I'm fine," she answered. Though she was anything but.

Outside, the mob banged and scratched and clawed against the metal door. It was only then that Ayelet noticed what was strange about this place: the lights were on. Faint yellow lights, stretching down a long corridor.

Electricity?

They descended deeper into the bunker. Exhausted, Ayelet rested her head against her savior's big shoulder. He carried her like a bride, deep into a hole dug by men to wage war.

CHAPTER V

Caesarea Philippi
Two Days After Event

Silas Egin woke with a start, recoiling from a bullet that had long since sailed its trajectory through his skull. He couldn't see, so he reached up and wiped his eyes, half wondering if his pupils would still be in his skull when he touched his eyelids. They were, thank God, but his face was covered in some kind of cold, gelatinous mesh. He wiped the gunk from his face, and he could see.

White. Everything was white. And cold.

Snow.

He was lying on his side. A deafening metallic throbbing in his head jarred his teeth and ears. He felt around to see if his skull was still split open. It wasn't. He had healed.

I'm alive!

I have my father's power! To live, die, and be reborn!

Egin's mind immediately turned to the power that such an expanse of years would bring, to the might his own father wielded and what he had been able to accumulate with such a gift. Money and land and resources. Egin's father had run the world; the world just hadn't known it.

He collected himself, pushed to a sitting position, and looked around. And there it was—emerging from the cave. A giant plume of black smoke, as if the cave were a great furnace filling the sky with night. The smoke churned and swirled, a beautiful dark tornado.

It had come. They had brought this into the world.

And as Egin watched that twisting spiral radiate skyward, he wondered if *He* had come as well. They had told the followers of the Way that it was Christ who would return, that the Baby Jesus would come and save them. But that was never the plan. God had abandoned them long ago, for their wicked ways—had turned His back on them.

But there was another.

The Antipodal.

Because in all his father's time walking the earth as a pilgrim of the Way, the only Holy One who'd ever proven Himself was Him. And His existence, unlike God's, was truly known, because His work was proven every single day. Sure, modern humans chose to deny it; they said that evil was not the work of some ancient entity, but that there were just a few bad people out there. Egin knew better. He knew the world was full of His seed, all humans tainted with it, and now He'd risen to claim His stake in them because the children of God were His.

As Egin gazed up at the dark clouds filling the sky, he felt mighty and strong. He was a lieutenant in this war, and he would be welcomed—because he had played his part in fulfilling the promise made by his father.

Where is my father?

He rose to his feet, his legs weak as if every movement was new again, and scanned the mountainside. It was too dark to see far. Yet as he looked, a shadow formed, as if solidifying from the darkness itself. It was ominously tall, and slender, and black. At first he thought his new eyes were playing tricks, for it did not move, just stood very still, as if it were part of the rock of the mountain. But then the shadow shuddered and in an instant it was standing right next to Egin.

And Egin knew. Though he looked at an empty shadow, he knew that this was the Everything. His mind filled with the knowledge that this, this too-tall shadow before him, *this* was the source of all evil, of all things that burn dark in men, of all crimes, all sorrows. The blackness here was a thing that could not be seen, could not be peered into, but it was *felt.*

And the feeling was wrong.

This is not how it was supposed to be, Egin thought. *I was supposed to be lauded. Championed. Welcomed.*

Instead he felt his mind being owned. And though he saw only blackness, he could smell wet muddy earth within himself and the sizzling of his synapses. He wept and urinated down his leg and screamed and begged God's name… but there was no answer in the heavens. He had never known such vast emptiness, for he truly saw now the scale of this being's dark, cold, uncaring origins.

A moment later he was on his knees and slamming his head repeatedly into the snow and the hard ground beneath it. He wanted to stop. He wanted so very much to stop, because this was not how it was supposed to be, but his body just wouldn't listen. He fought to regain his mind, but his limbs were under another's sway. He felt his breath leave him, a vise clamping down over his muscles. It was consuming him. Climbing inside him. To wear him as a suit.

His final thought, before it all went to black, was that he could not die. That whatever this thing did to him, it could not truly kill him. Because he would be reborn. Because he had the power, and he could beg for forgi—

The thing within silenced his petty thoughts, and there would be no more, because *There are far worse things than death, child of dust, and you shall pray for death, but you will not find it. You will seek the one you have forsaken, but the light is dead to you and in the darkness you are forever mine.*

CHAPTER VI

Rachaiya, Lebanon
Ten Days After Event

Sunday led the horse, with Kat and the boy upon it, through the dark, icy wilderness, bound for a house that the priest told him belonged to a drug lord. He and the priest had exchanged names, but in his exhaustion, Sunday had already forgotten.

"That's how we got the guns," said the priest. "The boy's older brother," he nodded at the child on the horse, "had them in his trunk. The two of them were stuck in the city and came to the church for refuge."

"Where is he now?" Sunday asked.

"Back at the church," the priest said, sinking deeper than the others into the powder.

The priest looked up at Kat. Sunday knew what he saw. Her face was sickly pale, her eyes drifting, and she was swaying heavily with the rhythm of the horse.

"She needs help," the priest said.

"She needs a C-section," Sunday answered.

"Maybe someone at the house knows these things. He has many resources."

"This guy is just going to let us walk right up to his front door?"

"He should," said the priest. He gestured again to the child on the back of the horse. "That's his son."

Sunday looked up at the boy, who was helping keep Kat in the saddle. "You did a good job back there," he said. "Not a sound."

The boy smiled.

"He does not speak," said the priest.

Sunday nodded, but it was harder walking now because he felt like he had his foot in his mouth.

* * *

The dark house stood on a snowy hill, not a single light visible inside, outside, or above. Sunday and the others stood outside the gate that led to a narrow drive. The gates had been ripped from their hinges, the iron twisted and bent.

Sunday looked up at Kat on the horse. She was still fading. He didn't know how much farther she could go. If she couldn't find help here…

He turned to the priest. He was going to have to trust this man. "I need someone to stay with her. I'll take the boy and check the house."

"I will keep her safe."

Sunday hoped that was true.

The house was a ranch-style home tucked in among desert scrub and olive trees. Not a sound drifted from it as Sunday and the boy moved low and fast up the drive. Close to the house, they crouched behind a low wall and peered over.

Two bodies lay face-up in the front yard, guns clutched in their frozen hands, bullet holes in their heads, blood splattering the snow like red seed.

The child's face was white, his eyes wide. These people were obviously known to him.

Sunday touched his shoulder, and the child slowly turned. They made eye contact, and Sunday nodded, indicating he knew, he understood. Then he pointed to the house to remind the child he had to keep going.

They crossed around the low wall and into the yard, past the bodies, and up to the porch. Sunday checked the front door. Locked. He thought to knock, but if there were still creatures around, he didn't want to alert them. He was starting to move off the porch to check for another door when the child pulled a key from his pocket, slid it into the lock, and opened the door like he'd just gotten home from school.

The child then pulled from his pockets a stubbed church candle and a lighter. He flicked the lighter and lit the little candle, and was about to step through the door. But Sunday put a hand on the boy's shoulder and gestured for him to stay behind him. Raising the rifle, Sunday led the way into the darkness.

If the child could have spoken, Sunday figured he probably would have called out. To shout to see if his mother or father were home. Maybe a brother or sister. But instead, in the flicker of the candlelight, Sunday could see the boy's head frantically scanning back and forth. Sunday once again put a hand on his shoulder to ease him, to keep him from suddenly running off.

Sunday checked his corners as he stepped through a living room filled with cold, stuffed birds, their shadows dancing in the candlelight. There were quail and plovers, created by God, but formed in death by another's hands.

They moved down a long hall, stopping in at an office where three wooden gun cabinets stood wide open. There were still two shotguns and several hunting rifles, plus two M4s stacked and ready—a drug dealer's insurance, one that might have already been cashed in.

They continued on, through a huge kitchen, and then into a dining room.

The long table was covered in snow. Above it was a hole in the roof about four feet wide; snow continued to flutter through the opening. Dozens of shell casings, a shotgun, and two AR-15s lay cold and still on the floor, among congealed puddles of frozen blood.

Where are the bodies?

The attackers had come in from the roof—had ripped it wide open. The creatures Sunday had seen thus far were fast, like hounds, and though they were strong, this had to be something different. A different kind.

As Sunday was distracted by the hole, the child suddenly darted off. Sunday gave chase, lest this child stumble into something that would swallow him whole.

The child ran to the end of a hall and opened a door. Sunday came up fast behind him. The door led to a bedroom, empty but for a large canopy bed. Bloody footprints led to a bathroom, and the child followed their trail, his breath quickening, filling the cold air with the fog of his lungs.

The child stopped in the doorway to the bathroom, frozen. Then he spun around immediately and buried his face in Sunday's jacket.

Sunday held the child a moment, then moved forward, rifle ready. There were two bodies in the tub. A little boy in dancing monkey pajamas was curled up in his mother's lap. His neck was slashed, her wrists sliced and drained of life. Above them, a symbol was scrawled in blood on the white tile.

A protector. A symbol of old conjured to ward off an ancient threat.

It hadn't worked.

CHAPTER VII

Deep Run, Maryland
Three Days After Event

Eve McAllister stood her ground, and her dead father stood his. She couldn't understand why or how he stood before her, but she knew she needed to get away from him. But her back was against the door to the bunker, with snowbanks on either side.

He stepped forward, his face drooping, the skin slipping from his cheekbones, and lunged for her.

Instinctively she leapt to one side and scrabbled up the snowbank, slipping, stumbling, but, for the moment, avoiding his grasp. He climbed after her, moving strangely like a crab climbing over a dune, but she found her footing across the embankment and ran in the dark toward the chain-link fence that surrounded the bunker. She jumped onto it and practically threw herself over, just avoiding his outstretched hands as he grabbed at her ankles.

Dropping to the other side, she ran toward the dead driver whose head was half buried in the snow. She scooted around him, using his body as a berm, and fished in the snow around his cold, black fingertips.

She found what she was looking for and raised the 9mm.

Her father climbed the fence, landed with a thump in the snow, and came toward her. She didn't wait, she simply opened fire, just as Daddy had once taught her. The slugs entered her father, but he kept coming.

"Stop!" she screamed, as if the word had more power than the gun.

She fired again, this time hitting him square in his jaw, knocking his head sideways. He recovered from the impact and ran full-speed toward her. She fired. Again. And again.

Finally he collapsed in a skid, feet away from her. She stood over him and fired again into the back of his skull until the gun was empty.

Then she raised her head toward the dark sky in search of answers. She felt warm tears on her cold cheeks, before they too were chilled by the cold.

She might have stayed there and continued to sob, but the body of the half-buried driver convulsed in the snow next to her.

"Motherfucker," she said.

She reached down, ripped the keys off her father's belt, and raced back toward the bunker. She scaled the fence, then chanced a look back. The driver, his face black from pooled blood and frostbite, was on his feet and chasing after her.

Eve ran to the bunker door, sliding over the snow-bank and down into the little ravine. She fumbled with the keys at the lock, unsure which key to use, her hands shaking so much she had to steady herself with her other hand.

She could hear the driver climbing over the fence. She slid in a key, then another, but neither worked. Footsteps thudded across the snow toward her. *Goddammit! Which key is it?*

Another key, and this one slid right in, and she turned it. A second later she pushed open the bunker door and slammed it shut behind her, just as the driver came banging down on top of it.

She felt the door in the darkness for the handle, and found instead a wheel. She spun it even as the man jarred the handle on the other side. Only when she was sure the door was sealed tight did she dare take a breath, standing there in the cold dark, the man still banging on the other side of the door.

She was safe, for the moment. But from what, exactly? And for how long?

She felt around and found a light switch, but when she flicked it up and down, nothing happened. She was trapped in the dark, a dark so black she might as well be blind.

Putting one hand on the wall, she felt her way deeper into the bunker, down a set of stairs. She had no idea where she was going, or where anything was, and she felt like she was trudging along the bottom of the ocean. She passed through a doorway and fumbled her way forward, keeping her hands in front of her, wondering if she was going to run into something down here, something waiting for her, something that would drag her deeper into the darkness along with it. Her breathing was rapid and her heart pounded, because her mind was dumping imaginary things into her eyes, and she felt for sure there was something in the bunker with her.

Eventually she bumped into a shelf with some boxes, and she opened each, trying to decipher blindly what was in each one. At last her fingers found what she had been hoping for above all else.

A flashlight.

Thank God.

But when she slid the switch, it didn't turn on. She flicked it back and forth, back and forth, and it would not shine, and she threw it across the bunker and screamed in rage.

She dropped to her knees, beaten, and in the darkness, she sobbed and cried.

Please.

She said aloud, and then again, so it could be heard by the one who should have been listening.

"Please. Help me."

There was no answer.

CHAPTER VIII

Rachaiya, Lebanon
Ten Days After Event

That night, Sunday moved them all into the house, because despite its broken roof, it offered more protection than sleeping outside. He even brought the horse in through the front door, so it could get out of the cold. It milled around the living room like it was looking to buy the place.

There was a decent reserve of canned food in the kitchen, which at least allowed them to eat more than beets. The dog and the horse seemed perfectly delighted with canned carrots—in fact the dog wanted more. Sunday limited each to one can, not enough, but more than he could spare. He ran his hands over the dog's ribs as he fed him.

"Sorry, boy," he said. "That's all I've got."

Away from the eyes of the boy, he and the priest dragged the bodies from the tub outside into the snow, lest they somehow come back to life in the middle of the night. They laid them near a stack of firewood and covered them both with a blanket, then the priest said a prayer.

"For I know that my redeemer lives, and that He shall stand at the latter day upon this earth. And though after skin worms destroy this body, in my flesh shall I see God and mine eyes shall behold Him, and not another…"

When they were done, Sunday searched the house for supplies. He returned first to the office with the gun cabinets, where he packed up the guns and ammo. He searched the desk drawers, finding a compass, but the needle spun without pull, and he wondered if what had come into this world also held power over the poles.

Atop the desk stood a framed photo. It featured a man, the woman from the tub, the mute child, and the boy who'd been wearing the monkey pajamas. They were all smiling and happy. The father had draped his arms around them, as if to protect them.

In a laundry room he scored needle and thread, and in the bathroom medicine cabinet he found alcohol wipes. Steadying himself on the toilet, he stitched the open wound in his gut that had come courtesy of the old man in the grocery.

Afterward, he got Kat a clean dress from the closet of the boy's mother and gave her one of the packages of sanitary napkins. He had her use another bathroom instead of the one in the master bedroom where blood still caked the tub. When she was done, she climbed into the canopy bed, and the dog hopped up and curled up on the covers at her feet.

"Where's the boy?" she asked him.

"With the priest," he said.

"Do you know their names?"

"No."

She nodded, her eyes hazy, drifting.

He started to leave, but she reached out and grabbed his wrist. She pulled him back to the bed, placed his hand on her belly, and rested it there.

The baby moved inside her, a life still foreign to this world.

"Feel that?" she said.

He did. He did.

* * *

That night, Kat awoke to find the boy tucked into the bed beside her and the priest on the floor of the bedroom, snoring with reverb. The boy had wanted to sleep in his own room, but John had insisted everyone be in one area so he could guard them effectively. She couldn't see or hear him, but knew he stood watch in the hall.

She pulled the covers up around the boy, and he rolled away from her. He wasn't sleeping either.

A few minutes later, in the dark of the bedroom, she felt the boy trembling. His breath caught and his body shuddered. He curled into a little ball and cried.

Kat thought how strange it was that even children who can't speak still make sounds when they weep.

She was hesitant to touch him. But she did, her fingertips on his shoulder, and he rolled back toward her, tears rolling down his cheeks. She wiped his face and spoke to him in Arabic.

"*Hunak makan 'afdal , yantazirun hunak,*" she said. *There is a better place. They wait for you there.*

He wept more, an ugly sobbing, as he mourned the people who had died in the bathroom just yards away. Her attempt at wise words had not worked, and she wondered if she would fail as a mother. But she pulled him in, and he let her, and that was how they fell asleep together. The child in the woman's arms, the faint smell of his mother in the dress that she wore.

* * *

At night the dreams came, as did the demons.

Father Simon sat up on the floor and searched the room. The pregnant woman and the dog slept on the bed, but the boy was gone. Simon rolled awkwardly to his feet, like a rising buoy.

Where's the boy?

He lumbered into the hall, searching for John Sunday, but did not see him either. From outside the house, he could hear crickets chirping, as if the insects were somehow related to these creatures. He moved down the hall into the front room and found the boy staring out a window, a shadow against the white of the night snow.

The windows were shuttered. Did he open one?

The priest approached slowly but made certain he was heard, not wanting to startle the child. The boy remained still, and Simon half expected him to slowly turn his head and stare up at him with cold dead eyes.

When he arrived at the boy's side, the boy simply pressed his little pointer finger against the cold glass. The priest looked out into the darkness, afraid of what he would see. Perhaps the boy's mother, there in her nightgown. Or the little boy in his little dancing monkey pajamas. Instead he saw nothing. He didn't know what the boy was pointing at, and the boy certainly couldn't tell him.

"Come," the priest said. He pulled the boy away from the window and gently put an arm around him to guide him back to bed.

As they passed back down the dark hallway, the little boy paused outside another door—the door to the boy's bedroom. He looked to Father Simon, his eyes asking for permission.

The priest understood. "You want to sleep here tonight?"

The child nodded.

Simon opened the door and checked inside. He wondered if the boy could be trusted to sleep alone, or if he'd wander off in the middle of the night in search of dreams he couldn't catch.

"All right," he said. "But I'm going to sleep on the floor."

Father Simon took an extra pillow and blanket from the bed and settled in, while the child lay down in his own bed. They had been there only a minute when the scratching began.

The priest looked over at the boy. He'd heard it too—his face white with fear. There was something in the room with them.

The scratching continued. Simon traced the source to a closet door.

He stood and gestured to the boy that it would be okay.

He grabbed a trophy from the child's desk and held it like a club as he moved toward the closet. From behind the door came the clicking of hooves on stone. He hesitated, then flung open the door.

He saw nothing.

He turned to the child. "It's okay," he said. "There's nothing to be afraid of. Come. See."

The child shook his head.

"Come on," he beckoned. "It's okay."

The boy slowly rose and moved to the closet door.

Father Simon placed one hand on the boy's shoulder. "See?" he said, moving some clothes around inside. He patted the back wall of the closet. "Nothing."

With that, the priest pushed the boy into the closet and slammed the door shut.

The mute child sobbed and cried and banged and tried to escape. But Father Simon leaned his mass against the door to hold it shut, and soon it fell silent within.

Then the priest sank to his haunches and wept, because he had fed the boy to the beast.

* * *

He woke with a start, his body covered in sweat, and looked around the bedroom. The woman and the dog and the boy were still asleep.

Just a dream. Just a dream.

This had been his second dream now with the boy. The first had been in the church. While they slept in a corner, the smell of the dead lingering in the vestibules and the pews, he had dreamt he saw the cold marble statue of the Mother Mary come to life. She turned her stone head and stepped from her granite perch, moving toward him down the aisle like a bride, and as he curled into a ball, too scared to move, he looked over at the child. The boy, too, was staring at her, as if he shared the same dream. Or was it a vision?

The marbled Mary approached him, and as she turned, he saw that she was heavy with child. She kneeled, her stone fingers extended, and touched the boy. The boy placed her hand in his, and the priest could see then that she was dripping blood from beneath her stone robe.

She then turned to face Father Simon, but as she did, the rock of her face began to crumble. First her nose, then her cheeks and eyes, as if she cried silt. When she was decayed to the point of horror, he woke.

Now he lay in the dark, trying to make sense of both dreams, wondering if the boy had again shared his dream, and if the boy had seen the terrible thing he had done.

* * *

John Sunday sat in a chair down the hall, the spot chosen so that he had line of sight to both the bedroom door and the dining room, which was still exposed to the sky. By the light of a dying candle, he let his gaze travel over the various photos on the wall. Pictures of the boy, his brother, his mother and father. Together. Smiling. On a beach somewhere. Blue skies. Blue water. The sun so bright it could have left the photo and filled the room.

The boy's father was a drug lord, but his house was just a home. A room full of toys for each of the boys. Nice clothes in the closet for the wife. Two nice cars in the garage. Sunday's own father had done far nobler work as a carpenter—legitimate work—but as a father, he regularly beat his son. The dad in these photographs meanwhile made a living feeding poison to people, and yet he seemed to be a loving father.

Sunday shifted in the chair to keep the blood moving. Beside him sat the medical book he'd taken from the clinic. It included a section on performing a C-section, complete with diagrams. Where to make the cut, how to pull apart the muscle, slice the uterus, and remove the baby by its head. He'd have to fish around in there a bit. He wasn't a doctor, but there were no doctors anymore. And he figured he could close her good enough.

The problem was he had no way of sedating her. He'd found nothing at the clinic, nothing here at the house. He wished the drug dealer had kept at least some of his product in his home. But he'd have to find a way to put her under somehow, because a C-section was a necessity. There could be no natural birth; she'd bleed out long before that.

He was scared. Scared that she'd die by his hand. Their journey over the mountain together had rekindled something in him. Seeing her in this state, so weak, so in need… He wanted to make up for not being there the first time she'd been pregnant. She was becoming again the woman he wanted to protect. The one he wanted to watch over.

He shifted again, the cold wearing into his muscles. He'd eventually wake the priest, switch shifts, and get some sleep. A few hours. He was used to going for days on end, only a few hours here and there, until his body felt like he perpetually had the flu. He hadn't slept much in the last ten days. He wasn't sure he'd really sleep tonight either.

He replayed what he knew, what he could decipher as truth in this new world that made no sense. All the electricity was off. The cars were all dead. So were the batteries. Flashlights didn't work. Anything that could generate or hold power… didn't. Whatever had burst out of that cave, it had done something, sent out some kind of pulse perhaps, that fried the entire planet, sending it back to the dark ages.

And there *was* something in the air; he could feel it. Beyond the snowflakes, the atmosphere felt charged, like the coming of an electrical storm or when you're near a transformer substation and the particles are revved.

Is that why things don't work?

And then there were the creatures. These things— or were they all one thing?—that had crossed over, had taken over the bodies of the living and the dead. Kat had said the men who attacked her in the forest even had guns, so they, some of them at least, must have held on to the skill and knowledge of the humans they possessed. Others of them were built up in grotesque ways, humans and parts of humans glued together, and the more humans assembled, the harder they were to kill. Flesh as modeling clay. Perhaps that was the only resource these things had.

But whatever it was that had come here, Sunday knew it was dead set on finding Kat. The old lady had told him that much. They wanted Kat dead, because the baby was a threat.

He took up the tattered red Bible Kat had grabbed from the farmer's house. He'd never thought much about God on the battlefield, because God had never been more than a distant idea to him, but now... now He seemed much closer. Or perhaps not God, but something. Something was closing in.

He picked up where he'd left off. He'd been reading Revelations, because Kat said it explained some of what was going on.

"Then the kings of the earth, the princes, the generals, the rich, the mighty, and everyone else, both slave and free, hid in caves and among the rocks of the mountains. They called to the mountains and the rocks, 'Fall on us and hide us from the face of him who sits on the throne and from the wrath of the Lamb! For the great day of their wrath has come, and who can withstand it?'"

If he's real, why doesn't He come?

If this unholy thing was real, then why not the other? Surely some all-knowing, powerful being was aware of what was happening here. Surely He could release his army of Angels and cleanse the earth. So why didn't He? Why were they alone?

He rolled his neck and remembered there was coffee in the kitchen. He picked up the candle, slung the rifle over his shoulder, and walked down the hall.

On the kitchen bar were the duffel bags that he'd packed with the food and the guns and ammo. He sifted through one and pulled out a tin of instant coffee. Boiling water was a problem since he didn't dare light a fire, but he mixed the instant and sipped it cold.

And out of the corner of his eye, he saw it.

Someone passing outside the bay window in the front room.

Shit.

He put down the mug and resumed the rifle's ready position. He moved out of the kitchen, the swirl of the breeze blowing around the room so much it rattled the pots and pans hanging from the rack like wind chimes. He stepped into the front room, neared the window, and looked through the slats in the shutter.

In the snow, outside the window, were footprints. Someone was out there. Someone had been looking in.

He searched the dark snow beyond. There. Beyond the low wall. A shadow standing under a tree.

He wondered if this was bait. A ploy to get him out of the house. Lure him to leave, only so he could be ambushed. Maybe it was survivors, someone looking for food. Maybe it was the things that wore people as skin. His best bet was to stay put, to keep Kat...

A knock sounded on the front door.

Sunday moved, rifle ready, wondering if in the next moment someone would come bursting through the wood. The breeze in the house from the hole in the roof swirled around him, sending snowflakes fluttering, and his breath hung in the air. He pressed himself against the side wall, fearing whoever this was would fire through the wooden door. He wondered too if they possessed tools to break the lock.

From outside, he heard shifting in the snow. Back and forth. Whoever was on the stoop, they were cold. Another knock.

Sunday's curiosity would not get the better of him. He knew better than to open that door. Good or bad, this newcomer needed to move on. There was no way Sunday was going to open that door.

Then he heard a small voice, meek from the other side.

"Sir, please." The accent was Arabic. "I have something for the baby."

CHAPTER IX

Tel Aviv, Israel
Day of Event

The big man carried Ayelet to a small corner bunk of some unknown soldier's room and sat her carefully, gently, on the edge of the bed.

She looked up at him. He was tall, with streaks of gray peppered through his dark hair. He opened a cabinet, searched through it, and pulled out a pair of camouflage pants. He looked at her, assessed the pants again, and handed them to her.

"What's your name?" she asked.

"Jonah," he said as he fished through the cabinet some more. He pulled out a belt and a pair of boots and handed them over.

"Thank you," she said. "For coming back."

He nodded.

"Why did you?" she asked.

Her question implied plenty. He had risked his life to save hers. But more than that, she knew he had violated his training and protocol when he left the Eagle— the deputy prime minister—and returned for *her*. She suspected why. Suspected his ulterior motives, because she'd only known men to want one thing from her.

Doesn't he know my injuries? Isn't he in for a surprise?

"I honestly don't know," Jonah said. "I heard a voice in my head telling me I needed to get you. Clear as can be." He looked at her and smiled. "So I did." He turned and hovered in the doorway. "Can you dress yourself? I can go find a woman, maybe, to help you."

"No, I'm okay."

"I'll see if I can get a wheelchair or something. Otherwise I'll come back to carry you."

She nodded again, although she was less than pleased to be human cargo.

He closed the door behind him, and she was left alone in the room. Someone else's room. Taped to the bunk wall was a photo of a man with his wife and daughter on a beach. She wondered if they were all dead.

Is what's happening here happening everywhere? Is it part of their plan?

She remembered that Bible verse again like it was an ecclesiastical earworm. Was it Egin's voice she kept hearing in her head?

The trumpet will sound, the dead will be raised, and we shall be changed.

Was that what was happening? Did they succeed somehow? Did they really know how to bring about the end?

She believed they had, because it was the only real explanation now. That the world had ended not from famine, or virus, or war, but by the Hand of God.

She hoped it was true. Because the alternative was that He was present but not participating—and that whatever was happening outside would be left up to humans to resolve without His divine intervention.

Have we been abandoned?

She struggled to get dressed. She had to be very careful not to tear the stitches as she pulled on the camo pants. But she did it, then tightened the belt and slipped into boots that were too big for her feet.

When she went to the door, Jonah was waiting outside.

"I couldn't find a wheelchair," he said. "Do you want a lift?"

"No," she said, hobbling into the hall. "I got it."

CHAPTER X

Rachaiya, Lebanon
Ten Days After Event

The girl at the door was still waiting.

"Please," she said. "I know you can hear me. My grandmother is out here. She's very old. We're cold. And hungry."

Sunday was not swayed. He could hear her shifting on the porch outside, her feet stomping up and down to stay warm, crunching the snow beneath her feet.

Sunday looked down the hall. Kat was up and walking toward him with a candle, her face pasty pale even in the candlelight. At her side was the dog, as if she now commanded it. She came close to the door and listened.

"Please," the girl outside repeated. "I hear something."

Kat pressed her ear against the door and listened. Sunday did as well. There *was* a sound outside.

The crickets. Their chanting had increased.

"There's something out here," the girl said, her voice frantic. "Please."

Kat looked questioningly at Sunday. He shook his head. She reached out anyway to unlock the deadbolt, and he grabbed her hand.

"We don't know who she is," he said with a harsh whisper. "She could be one of those things."

"We don't know who *anyone* is," she said.

"*Please!*" the girl cried from outside. "There's something! I see it!" She banged on the door now.

Motherfucker. This girl was going to alert everyone within six miles that she was standing outside this door.

"Please!" shouted the girl, pleading.

Kat shook off Sunday's hand, unlatched the lock, and opened the door wide.

On the doorstep stood a teenaged girl and an old woman, both wrapped in snow-caked scarves and skirts. They darted inside like they were running from a crime. Sunday looked past them, out into the yard, searching for any sign of what they had seen. There was nothing.

And he wondered who had just been let inside.

CHAPTER XI

Langley, VA
Three Months Before Event

Lincoln Pierce sat outside the office of the CTC director, wondering if this was his chance. He should never have been passed over in the first place. Sure, he was still young, but he was older than she was. He had the qualifications and the skill set, which meant there was only one thing that had prevented him from being promoted: his race. That worked against him in an agency still run by gray-haired or balding white men. White men dead set on keeping the keys to the castle to themselves. White men who publicly promoted affirmative action and diversity, but behind closed doors or at family get-togethers, with bourbon in hand, commiserated with one another about what had happened to America. A woman could sometimes slip through. Like his boss. But she was pretty—fit their standards. She was allowed through just so they could look at her.

He adjusted the folder and glanced at the secretary. Older. Hispanic. *A checkmark in their token box.*

He was qualified, dammit. But it had been this way his whole life.

Only black kid in my private school. Only black kid at Dartmouth. Only brother on the sailing team, for damn sure.

But there is an opening...

The secretary looked over at him and told him he could go in.

... and it's mine.

He approached the door, knocked, and heard a single-syllable grunt that sounded faintly like "Come." He stepped into the office.

Sitting at his desk, behind his computer, was Tom Ferguson. Lincoln had never been called to the man's office, wasn't even sure where it was, and he was pretty sure that up until a month ago Tom Ferguson didn't even know Lincoln's name. Which meant this was an opportunity. Do what Tom Ferguson asked, do it well, and Lincoln just might get somewhere. Lincoln needed to do what Master said to make it in the white man's world. And Tom Ferguson was the Master.

"Give me a second," Ferguson said, typing.

Lincoln sat. There was a tattered American flag in a frame hanging on the wall behind Ferguson's head and a window that overlooked the forest outside Langley.

Lincoln's own office didn't have a window. Nor did he ever much leave the tiny space. He worked hard, filed his reports on time, did what he was asked to do. Found things others had missed. He felt he was meticulous. Precise. He liked his books, and his artifacts, because they didn't judge. Not like people did.

He was more skilled than she was.

Ferguson turned away from the computer and spun the swivel chair so he could give Lincoln his full attention.

"Show me."

Lincoln opened the folder and pulled out several sheets of paper. "This is the first page I've been able to recover since the initial find. A rather tedious process. The pages were stuck together with a lime gesso plaster. I had to peel it away without losing any of the ink, so I used a special mixture of acetone and Planatol. Then I—"

"What does it say?"

Lincoln slid his report across the desk. "Aramaic. Same as the first page."

Ferguson read the translated text out loud. "*The Savior spoke then in sadness of what was to come next. 'A great darkness shall be loosed upon the Earth that will hollow the hearts of men and wear them as its flesh. Men will wander a new wilderness, hunted by beasts they once called kin. And as in the time of Herod, they shall hunt me.*

"*'I have trusted you with the key to my resurrection as I have trusted the Keys of the Kingdom of Heaven, the Key of David, to the first and last disciples. And when held by one pure in the Holy Spirit, only then can you unbind the Gate to God. Without it, the Synagogue of Satan shall destroy me, and us all.'*

"*When done, the Savior—*" Ferguson looked up. "It just ends? Are there any more pages?"

"Yes. But the more I peel, the worse it gets. Right now I only have a handful of random letters."

"Have you told anyone about this?"

"I kept it confidential, like you asked."

"Good." Ferguson picked up his pen and tapped it on his desktop. "What do you make of this? The keys he's talking about?"

"Well, Christ gave the keys of the Kingdom of Heaven to Peter. That's the basis for him being the first pope. The symbol of papal authority."

"And he was the first disciple, right?"

"Well, possibly. His name is mentioned first throughout the New Testament."

"Who was the last?"

"I don't know."

"Could these keys be real? Could Christ have given him a real key?"

"I believe it's more symbolic, sir. Any time you see Peter portrayed in paintings or sculptures, he's holding a set of keys, but the real keys weren't supposed to be physical—just a symbol of his power to lead the Roman Catholic Church. Maybe what this is saying is the key to that power will be passed from the first disciple to the last, giving each the same authority."

Ferguson pursed his lips and nodded. "Pierce, you've done great work here. Really. With Kat... out..." He seemed to drift a second, then corrected. "You've done a fine job stepping in for her."

"Thank you, sir."

"I've got something else for you. Do this, and your future here? Very bright. Very bright indeed."

"Sir?"

"Find these keys."

Lincoln shifted in his seat. "Um, again sir, I don't think... I think this is talking metaphorically."

"I heard you," Ferguson said. "I want you to track down any and all candidates for keys, circa first century AD, that are still in existence. Museums, private collections, black market websites. Any key from the first century. Roman. Egyptian. Hebrew. Greek. I don't care. If it still exists, and it's from the time of Christ, I want to know where it is."

Lincoln nodded. "Yes, sir."

Ferguson pointed at him with his pen. "You report only to me. Just like you did with the translation of the text. I mean that. Complete list of every key. In particular any key that could be symbolic of Christ, the early church, the apostles."

Lincoln nodded again. "Sir."

"Good. Good. You can go."

Lincoln stood and headed for the door. Before he left, he turned in the doorway.

"Any word, sir? On her?"

"None. We've got our top people on it though. But if, God forbid, something happens to her, we will need a replacement."

The thought was wrong. Lincoln knew it. For him to move ahead, something had to happen to Kat.

And yet, as he stepped outside, he was surprised by how comfortable he was with the idea of shoving someone else off the ladder—or at least watching her fall—in order to move up himself. *He* didn't order her to go to Jordan. He didn't kill her, if she was dead. His hands were clean.

And *somebody* had to run the division.

Besides, it should have been him running things all along.

He was almost to the elevator before his mind shifted to the absurdity of the assignment he'd just been given. Was his promotion really dependent on this? On a key?

Why in God's name would the head of the counter-terrorism center for the CIA be so interested in finding something that didn't exist?

CHAPTER XII

Rachaiya, Lebanon
Ten Days After Event

John Sunday studied the women who had entered the house. Even with the bundles of clothes and backpacks and snow upon them, they were small. The older one was probably mid-sixties, her brown skin cracked like a windblown Sherpa. The girl was maybe eighteen, paler, her eyes sunk fishing bobbers, her face gaunt like she hadn't eaten in a week.

By now the priest and the boy were up and coming out of the bedroom. The dog sniffed at the women, and Sunday wondered if his nose was reliable. But it was Sunday who barked.

"Who are you? What do you know about the baby?"

The girl turned. She rolled her shoulders and winced and pressed her ribs with her elbows as if in pain. Her left arm was wrapped in a cloth sling. Instead of answering Sunday, she turned to Kat.

"Please," she said. "My grandmother is starving. If you feed her, I'll tell you."

Kat looked to Sunday, who shook his head.

She ignored him too. "Follow me," she said.

Now Sunday remembered. Kat always did do whatever the hell she wanted. At least their relationship was getting back to normal.

In the kitchen, the girl did not eat, but the grandmother was ravenous. Sunday made damn sure she had the can of beets.

The girl's name was Samiher. She could speak English, but her grandmother could not. After the old woman ate, Kat sat them on a couch in the living room, and the grandmother put her feet on the coffee table and dozed as the others spoke in a language she could not understand.

"We have walked very far. We are from Rafid," said the girl. "We are Dom."

The priest explained. "The Dom are like... in English, you say... gypsies?"

"How did you know I was here?" Kat asked. "That I was pregnant?"

The girl pulled her backpack over from the corner of the couch. As she reached inside, Sunday leaned forward in his chair, the rifle ready in his grip. She pulled out a small black case, placed it on the coffee table, and opened it. Inside were a pair of syringes and a spoon, their cleanliness in question. Next to it she placed a small twisted baggie of white powder.

"It is mine," she said. "The last of it. But if I bring this to you, and I give my offering, then... then maybe it will end."

"What will end?" Sunday asked.

"The dead who talk."

* * *

It was eleven days earlier when the girl, Samiher, had awoken on the bathroom floor, the syringe still stuck in her arm. She looked around, trying to remember where she was. Then she saw her forearm, still tied off with pale tubing, the area around the syringe pooled with a spider's web of dark, dead blood.

She groaned as she slid the syringe out of the vein, and the blood trickled with it.

She pressed it with some toilet paper, then stood, her arm limp like it was dead, and shook it. It did no good. The arm had begun its death, and perhaps it would creep through her, tiptoeing beneath her skin. She'd loused it up good and needed a doctor, but she knew there were none to be found.

She wandered around the apartment, trying again to remember where she was. She recalled men. A party, if that was what it could be called. The place was small and dirty, stacked with dirty plates and rank food. There were bottles on the floor, and cigarette butts, and clothes so filthy it seemed the cotton had begun to rot. The shutters were closed, but through the cracks she could tell it was getting dark outside.

"Hello?" she called, her voice weak from thirst.

There was no one here.

On a coffee table littered with garbage sat a little plastic baggie, twisted and tied like a present. She looked around once more, shocked that someone would leave drugs on the table.

Why didn't anyone take it?

She plucked it up and put it in a pocket of her skirt.

A car honked outside. Frantic, repeated, and then sustained. It was followed by a gunshot that startled her so much it made her do a double-take.

She moved toward the window, hesitant, but drawn to know what was happening. Peering through the wooden slats, she saw a policeman with a gun down on the street. He fired repeatedly through the windshield of a parked van. Samiher instinctively ducked, as if the bullet would somehow bounce skyward and hit her, before rising back up to look through the slats once more.

The policeman moved around to the driver's side, fired four more times through the glass, then opened the sliding door. From her viewpoint, she could see into the back seat. There were two children inside.

The policeman raised the gun and pointed it at them.

"Don't," Samiher whispered.

He shot them both.

He then raised the gun to his own temple, turned his head away, as if he could not face the bullet, and fired one final time.

Samiher looked up and down the street, the slats of the shutters limiting her view. No one came. No one ran to check on the family in the van to see if they were alive. No one came to inspect the dead policeman.

No one came.

She stumbled to the door and stepped out into a dirty gray hall filled with more garbage. As she walked the corridor, people shouted and screamed from behind closed apartment doors. Then loud banging, like someone was slamming doors or hammering something. *Whack. Whack. Whack.*

As Samiher reached the stairwell, a young woman opened an apartment door beside her. In her arms she held a baby. The woman stepped out into the hall in silence... and threw the baby over the railing of the stairs as if she'd just tossed out a bag of trash.

From below there came a soft thud.

"No!" Samiher cried.

The woman returned to her apartment, unaffected by her actions, and closed the door.

No. No. No! What is going on?

Samiher was panicking now. Something was very wrong. She ran down the stairs, past the infant. There was no saving the baby—one look, and she knew. The door to the outside was open, and she stepped out onto the stoop. Dark black clouds stretched across the sky. She couldn't tell if it was dawn or dusk because the clouds blotted the sun.

The streets were empty.

Is this real? Or am I still high?

She felt a sudden urge to run home. A place she hadn't been in six months.

And that's what she did. She ran the whole way.

* * *

Sami was gasping for breath as she stumbled up the trash-strewn sidewalk to her little house. She'd been running full-on for twenty minutes, which she was in no shape to do. She passed the graffiti wall, turned the corner of the courtyard, and stopped.

The dirty brown front door was already wide open.

She had seen things as she navigated the city to get home. Things she couldn't get out of her head no matter how fast she ran. Things she feared she might never get out of her head.

A man bludgeoning an old woman to death with a rock.

A police officer using his club on a little boy.

A pregnant woman jumping off a rooftop and landing on her belly on the sidewalk.

Samiher wanted to cry for them. Cry for the old woman, the little boy, the pregnant woman, the baby thrown down the stairwell. She wondered if perhaps she herself was really dead, that the drugs had killed her, and her body still lay on a dirty bathroom floor.

And now, as she stepped up the narrow, scuffed brown tile steps and into the little house, her nerves were burning wicks.

"Papa?"

That was a name she hadn't used in a long time. It reminded her of a man she loved, but hid from, ashamed, because Papa had a real job as a taxi driver and had worked hard to move them out of the shanty. He had provided them this house made of concrete and not corrugated metal, with a hard floor and not dirt. Papa had told her he would do whatever it took so she didn't have to dance in the cabarets because that's what Mama had done after she divorced him and he'd never let that happen again. He had done all this for his family.

But she, she had brought him shame, because she did not stay and raise her brother and sisters. She had turned from him, choosing the easy way, filling the blood of her kin with the bite of the serpent.

Now only the wind, whistling with cold, answered her as she called through the house. And as she stepped down the hall, she saw drops of blood on the peeling brown linoleum near the open back door. Just a couple of drops. Just a little bit. But...

Holding her breath, she walked to the back stoop. She so wanted to feel the sunlight on her face, to hear her brothers and sisters playing in the back courtyard. To perhaps hear her father strumming the rababa. To smell the orange blossom or vanilla of her grandmother's namoura in the kitchen.

Instead the air was cold and metallic, the world silent, the back courtyard empty.

There was no one here.

Clothes fluttered on the line outside, the little shirts and dresses of her brothers and sisters dancing in the wind. A chill ran through her as she stood on the stoop, because she feared something bad had come into her home. Something... evil.

She closed the door and locked it, and looked again through the little house. But there were only two rooms and a bathroom, and her search was over quickly. She stepped back out the front door, the sun fading out completely, the light draining from the world. And in the darkness, she could hear distant people screaming.

* * *

She had sat down at the kitchen table to wait, because *they'll be home soon*, but eventually she had fallen asleep.

When she woke, it called to her.

She stirred, the wound in her arm throbbing, and stepped into the dark bathroom. Outside the wind howled with such force it scraped ice across the window glass. She checked the needle mark on her arm; it had soured and was a spiraled black.

Her solution was to sit on the toilet seat and produce the little black case and baggie. She set up shop on the edge of the sink and was able to get enough dripping water from the tap for her spoon. She used the lighter to cook the junk. Then she searched her other arm for a fresh, ripe vein and tied it off with a shoelace from one of her sisters' pink sneakers. She watched herself in the cloudy mirror that hung on the back of the bathroom door as she slid in the needle.

A moment later she had scooted from the toilet and was pressed against the cold of the tub, leaning her head back and staring up at the ceiling. There were leak stains there, dried and brown, marks of past floods from the upstairs apartment.

Outside the bathroom door, she heard them. The voices of her brothers and sisters.

"*Sami*," they called.

She stood, the last surge of adrenaline before the drug sludged through her legs, and threw open the door. She stumbled through the house, calling their names, slurring their names because they were home again, but there was no one there.

"*Sami*," they whispered.

"Few are yooo?" she called into the dark house.

A movement caught her eye, and some dark thing darted past her, moving like a child in the darkness. Her stomach dropped as she heard its shadowed feet, and she wanted to run, but her muscles were syrup, and she collapsed on the floor, pulled down to the brown linoleum, and she was forced to crawl, her body weak, dragging herself back down the hall, as behind her a shadowed thing in the shape of a child came up behind her. She dragged and dragged, pulling herself across the floor, her arms heavy and slow, every action so, so slow, and she made it back into the bathroom. She could hear the sound of crickets in her ears, and she kicked to close the bathroom door, her foot weighing a hundred pounds, and she hit nothing but air, then kicked again and again until she connected with the door and closed it.

She could hear it out there, scratching at the wooden door, clawing with little fingers, and she didn't know if it was drug or dream or demon.

She pushed away from the door and rested against the toilet, her arm itching like there were bugs in it, and she unwrapped some of the gauze so she could scratch at it. She looked down into the black, open wound, and there… there was something sticking out. She thought it was the broken tip of a needle, so she stuck her finger into the bloody flesh and tugged at it, her eyes closed because even the drug could not dull the pain.

She plucked it from the wound.

It was long and metal, flat on one end. It looked like an old rusted nail.

It's not…

Her mind couldn't finish, but some part of her knew it wasn't real, because that would be impossible. When she tossed the metal onto the floor of the bathroom, it made a little *ting* as it struck.

"*Sami*," the voices whispered.

She covered her ears and shouted for them to stop.

She caught a glimpse of herself in the mirror on the back of the bathroom door, and nearly screamed. Although she was sprawled on the floor, the Sami in the mirror was standing. Standing and staring down at her. And this reflection, this Sami, it was not her. It was not her, and it was watching.

"*Sami*," the voices beyond the door hissed. "*Saaammmmiiii.*"

The Sami in the mirror shouted. "*Stop!*"

They hissed in response, and the Sami on the floor watched as her reflection turned and looked behind her and there in the mirror was a shadowed man on a cross on a hill, a dark orange sky moving rapidly behind him. The Sami in the mirror moved up the hill toward the cross and examined the bloody nail pinning his feet to the wood. She kneeled before the cross, and there, at the base, rested a small basket. She pulled back a little blanket, revealing a baby within.

The mirror Sami fished through her pockets and pulled out the little bag of heroin. She tucked it gently into the basket with the baby. Then she rose to her feet and looked down the hill into a valley, where stood a lone house.

Sami, the Sami sprawled on the bathroom floor, drugged out and terrified, recognized it. It was the house of the man for whom she worked. The man who provided the drugs for her to sell to the Dom.

* * *

When Sami woke again, it was to someone shaking her. She opened her eyes, but couldn't focus.

A hand smacked her hard across the face. That brought her back. She looked up to see an old woman, her hand raised her strike her again.

"Grandma?"

The woman lowered her hand. "Sami."

Samiher looked around. She was still on the floor of the bathroom. "Where is everyone?" she asked in Domari.

"I don't... I went..." She sighed. "I don't know." She leaned in closer and whispered. "Is he here?"

"Who?"

"The shadow man."

The question made Sami realize it was not the drugs, nor was it a dream. The things in the shadows were real.

"I... I don't know," Sami said. And the tears began to fall.

She reached out for her grandmother. She was afraid the gesture would not be reciprocated and she would be judged for leaving, but her grandmother collected her in her arms, and Sami nestled in, and they held each other there on the bathroom floor. It had been so long since she'd been held in love, in true love and not the kind that uses, and if she had not been so overwhelmed by that love, she—

What was that?

She thought for sure she'd felt something move beneath her grandmother's skin. But that couldn't be. Her grandmother was here, holding her.

And she was safe.

* * *

John Sunday watched the girl carefully as she told them her story. He searched her face for any tell she was lying. Plotting. Planning. He looked to the baggie on the coffee table and wondered if the drug was good or if it would kill Kat as soon as it broke the skin.

Why are they here?

How did a drug dream tell her so much?

He wondered if the dream was sent by God, using Old Testament visions to communicate. But if so, why the hell didn't He just show up and take care of this Himself?

Why was it John Sunday's responsibility to protect this baby, all alone, in a world that had gone completely to shit?

CHAPTER XIII

Messina, Italy
October, 1347

It had rained for six months, and it was rare to see the sun, so Father Giovanni Vicario was taking the opportunity to tend to the garden. He was clearing the aphids from the hazelnut leaves, a task that was probably fruitless, because they had hidden so well in the recesses and shadows, and despite his cleansings and the constant rain, there was no washing them off. Yet today, today was a rare bright day, and Father Vicario hoped he could spend it saving what was left of the meager garden.

Ah, he found one. A plump, meaty green devil that had nestled under the curl of a leaf, shaded from the sun, hidden from his view.

A servant girl raced up the hill and shouted at him from beyond the stone wall of the churchyard. She was frantic, and sweaty, and pasty white.

"*Per favore, Signore,*" she said, out of breath at the stone wall. "*Ultimi riti!*"

Father Vicario held the aphid between his fingers, contemplating. He knew his duty, but some of the trees had slipped and toppled over in the mud, and he wondered if Father Liccio could go in his place so he could tend to the garden.

The girl shouted again. *"Per favore! E il duca!"*

That changed things.

Duke Lorenzo Eligos was a man of means. He owned mines of silver, copper, and gold; he dealt in arms and furs, jewels, brocades, and wool. A broker. A banker. A farmer. The trade of the country rested upon his shoulders. His home was a fortress filled with art, and statues, and collections from all over the world. He funded wars and oversaw fleets of ships coming from China and Greece and Africa.

Father Vicario had solicited him many times over the years for funds to help build the Palais des Papes. But the palace was in France, where the pope was, and the duke had no interest in helping Avignon. Nor did he have an interest in paying to repent for his sins or to buy his way out of purgatory.

And now he was dying and sought last rites.

Perhaps in his final time of need, Eligos would desire entrance into heaven, and see fit to finally bequeath his vast fortune to the church.

The winds shifted, the dark clouds began feasting on the sun, and the sky rumbled. He squashed the aphid beneath his thumbnail, and by the time the priest had traded his straw hat for his walking stick and scarf, the rain had returned.

* * *

As the priest navigated the wagon-wheeled ruts of mud on foot, he wondered if he should have brought a cart instead to load up any items Duke Eligos might want to donate in his final moments. Perhaps a statue, or a heavy chest.

But he was getting ahead of himself.

When he walked up the path to the manor, he was surprised to find he was alone. There were no workers in the fields or among the rows of olives. Perhaps they were just getting out of the rain. Yet when he arrived at the house, up on a hill overlooking the dark, gray sea, the front door was sitting open and untended.

Where are the servants?

"Signore?" he called out.

Only his own voice answered in echo.

He stepped inside and found that the manor had been upended. Cabinets had been cleared of plates and silverware, and the front room was littered with broken shards of a vase that had apparently been too heavy to pilfer. He had a selfish thought—that he was too late and all the good stuff had already been taken and there was nothing left for God.

He called out again, then went upstairs, past empty bedrooms. And then it was his nose that led him. The air was tart, the smell sour. Someone was dead, or dying. But there was another odor, too, beneath the scent of death—an even filthier foulness, shit mixed with the entrails of a slaughtered animal left in the midday sun.

A cloud of thick black flies filled the hall ahead. For them, the stench was a feast.

He might be far too late for last rites.

Raising his scarf up over his mouth and nose, he swatted at the flies as he pushed through into the bedroom at the end of the hall. And there they both were: the duke and his wife. Both dead.

She was laid on the bed, her hands neatly folded, her fingers curled and black, her eyes open but shriveled to the size of raisins. Her skin was overrun with large black boils. Her neck was sickly distended and bloated like she'd choked to death on two apples, and her flesh had filled with something that looked like it waited to burst forth. The flies buzzed and crawled all over her.

The duke was next to the bed, sitting in a chair, leaned back with his head tilted skyward, his mouth twisted in a near scream, his fingertips curled around his chest. He too had boils on his throat. But he had died much more recently, perhaps just hours ago.

The priest stepped back, aware there was a pestilence in this home. The air, the smell… it was as if the pit of hell had opened and swallowed these two souls. Perhaps that was what this was. A curse from God Himself, to spite this man who had spited Him.

The priest stood in front of the duke and raised his hand to begin the ritual. He kept the scarf over his mouth as he spoke the words.

"Dio amorevole e misericordioso, affidiamo nostro fratello alla tua misericordia…"

Loving and merciful God, we entrust our brother to your mercy…

The duke's head suddenly flopped forward, his eyes wide open, and the priest in his fright nearly stumbled backward onto the bed with the dead woman.

My God. He's alive.

Vicario collected himself and adjusted the scarf over his mouth.

"Bless you, my son. Do you wish to confess your sins?"

The duke let out a long breath, filling the air with more rank, and shook his head, but it was his eyes that indicated he would not be confessing anything today.

"The kingdom of God is close, brother. Do you not wish to wash your soul before you step through His gate?"

The duke gagged and made a whooping sound. But after a moment the priest realized he wasn't seizing for air—he was laughing.

Laughing at him. Laughing at *God.*

Even on the brink of death, this man mocked Vicario's institution and his faith.

The priest turned to face the dead woman on the bed. She would provide no such mockery. Ignoring the minor exhaling from the duke that might be interpreted as protest, Father Vicario delivered the last rites over her.

When he was done, he turned back to the duke, wondering how long it would be.

"Do you wish me to stay with you, brother?"

The duke shook his head, barely. But Vicario persisted. He was here for a reason, after all.

"What then, sire, shall we do with what is left of your possessions? The church could surely put them to use."

The duke shook his head again, this time with more intent, so that Father Vicario imagined this was the non-verbal equivalent of a shout.

He had journeyed all this way, and for what?

Father Vicario nodded once. He had nothing more to do in this room.

He decided instead to check out the rest of the home. While the duke lay dying upstairs, the priest scavenged the manor, partly out of curiosity, partly because he was secretly shopping to see what the servants hadn't already swiped.

In the kitchen he found a small door that led to a cellar. There was a heavy lock on it, but the priest put his shoulder into it and was able to crack the frame and push through. It led to a narrow, dark stair, and he fetched a candle before descending into the darkness.

In the candlelight he found a room filled with artifacts from another time. Egyptian masks, ancient Roman scrolls, old paintings. A treasure trove from the past that had not been swiped by the peasants.

By mid-afternoon, he had fetched the cart after all. By evening, he had loaded a heavy Roman vase from the cellar, several chests of ancient coins, and hundreds of scrolls and paintings. It was past nightfall when he finished. But before he rode out, he once more ascended the stairs to check on the duke.

In the flickering light of the candle, he assessed him again. Truly, the priest thought, he was dead now. Though strangely, there was a white webbing growing along his neck and face, like the fuzz on a mushroom in the forest.

Despite the duke's requests, the priest blessed him anyway.

When the rites were complete and he lowered the candle, he saw something in the Duke's twisted, curled hand. Gently unfurling the man's hardened black fingers, the priest uncovered what was in the Duke's grip.

A key.

A half circle on one end, three metal fingers on the other. It was old, ancient. Perhaps it too would fetch a price.

He pulled the key away, only to find it was attached to a necklace around the duke's neck. The priest pulled harder, snapping the chain and shifting the neck so that the duke's head seemed to be nodding in agreement.

At last the priest held the key in his hand. It had been important to the duke. Perhaps his most precious belonging.

But what does it unlock?

CHAPTER XIV

Rachaiya, Lebanon
Eleven Days After Event

Kat settled the two women in the boy's room. John prepared to resume his post in the hall, but the priest had told him he'd take over. John didn't put up much of a fight. He was tired. Exhausted.

The boy and the dog once more settled next to Kat on the bed, and John lay on the floor on her other side. As they lay there in the shadows, the soft sound of snow falling outside, her mind tried to piece together what was going to happen to them. What options they had. What life even was in this new, shadowed world.

"What's your plan?" she whispered into the darkness.

"Get you someplace safe," John said, his voice already starting to fade.

"Where's that?"

"Don't know. Higher ground. Maybe the mountains."

She hesitated. Because she didn't want to know the answer.

"Do you think they're after me?"

"Yes."

"Do you think they know I'm here?"

"I don't know."

She wanted to ask him more, but his breathing slowed and thickened, and she knew he was out. She remembered that sound, of his breathing next to her in their nights spent sleeping in the warmth of a home that had long since vanished, the hearth cold, the fires out.

She rolled toward him. She couldn't see him in the darkness, but in her mind she pictured him there. Scarred now, all across his body, across his face. He was a tattered patch of human. The people who had done that to him, had done it well.

Perhaps she was to blame for some of those scars as well.

She got up from the bed, the baby shifting inside her, and pulled a blanket off a chair. As she laid it over him, she hesitated for a moment, searching her mind for the reason they had divided. For the emotion that had so filled her with acid that she had felt compelled to punish him.

He wasn't there.

That was the reason.

But he's here now.

She knew he would do whatever it took to keep her safe, and although he snored lightly on the floor, some part of him was always up on that ridge looking to protect her.

She placed the blanket gently over him and returned to bed, hoping to find sleep, while she felt the baby inside her was most certainly awake.

* * *

Despite being on watch, Father Simon also dozed in the chair in the hall. He had tried hard to stay awake, but he'd slept so little in the church, and he'd walked more this day than he had in many years.

The dreams returned. And in them he heard the bedroom door open softly at the end of the hall and saw the little grandmother, her long gray hair down around her shoulders, step out into the darkness. She crept past him and quietly opened the front door, searching the threshold of the night, and he wondered if she was about to let someone else inside. Instead she left, stepping right out into the frigid cold and trudging through the snow in her bare feet.

He rose from his chair and followed her, watched her and she searched the ice forest.

She found what she sought.

A dark shadow that stretched across a row of dead trees. A shadow no different than any other, but when she faced it and stood there, he heard whispering from the darkness.

His bowels dropped as his mind was probed by a voice he could not unhear. It was infinite, and his mind could not understand that, because his religion and science had only given him a letter, and this thing spoke in books.

It was everything he had hoped his God would be, but this was not his God, this was His opposite, because all things have a positive and negative. And the priest wept, his mind broken and owned, never again to see the light, to long for it, but to be stolen from it forever.

The old lady approached the shadow and knelt before it. The priest did the same, falling to his knees as the crickets chirped around him in the dead forest.

* * *

Kat dreamt too. She dreamt that she was home again, a little girl in her little pink bedroom. Her father lay on his belly playing dolls with her in front of the dollhouse. They were pretending together. She was having a "spot of tea" with her girl baby doll, and he was the daddy doll, and soon they would share a dessert of fine plastic ice cream.

He stopped playing and put his boy doll down.

"Keep playing, Daddy," she said.

He stood and looked down at her. "I have to go."

"Go? They still have to have ice cream."

He knelt again with a groan and gestured for her to come closer. She scooted in, and they were the same height, and she could smell him, no scent in particular but the one she knew as the smell of her father.

"Even when I'm not here, Kit Kat, I'm here," he said as he touched her heart.

"But I want you *here*," she said, handing him back his doll.

He smiled. "You have to go too," he said.

"Where?"

"Away. They're coming, Kit Kat. For you."

The sky outside darkened, and there was something at the window. A tree branch tapping against the glass. She turned her head to look at it, and when she turned back again, her father was gone.

"Daddy?"

"Run, Kit Kat."

The tree branch was a long bone hand and it tapped against the glass as if asking her, ever so kindly, to be let in.

CHAPTER XV

Tel Aviv, Israel
Day of Event

As ominous as it sounded, the "war room" was nothing more than an eight-hundred square foot conference room with three tables arranged in a U-shape, and computers and phones and television monitors set up to feed a constant stream of information from the field. It could have been called "the information room" or "the decision room" or even "the basement," but the men who sat in this room bred war, and it was always in their lexicon.

There was a time in this room when there would have been live updates coming in from front-line soldiers fighting in Gaza. Or Syria. Or Iran. Some was real data. Most of it was hypothetical, phantom enemies born in countless exercises and fantasies, like war porn.

Ayelet sat in a chair and leaned her head against the back wall, trying to recover from her walk here. But she found it difficult to find a comfortable sitting position, and soon she was leaning forward again to assess the room and listen to the men discussing what was happening and why.

The bunker had electricity, which was something she hadn't seen in the city, perhaps even the rest of Israel. Maybe the rest of the world. Jonah had explained to her that the electrical miracle was courtesy of an EMP shield around the bunker. The whole place was encapsulated in a kind of Faraday cage, and within that cage the generators were able to work. Which meant that whatever had happened outside, it certainly had an EMP component to it.

Is that what devils use? The physics of the universe against us?

But despite the electricity, and the frantic human energy of the men in charge, the war room was still more dead than alive. The monitors on the wall were on, but showed only a stagnant blue signal. The phone banks were silent. The computers were working, but dark. There was no communication with the outside world. They had electricity, but no one to talk to.

Deputy Commander Yonatan Berg listened as a captain finished his status report. There were forty-seven people in the bunker, the captain said. There had been sixty-four, but seventeen soldiers died when they went topside to defend the front and back gates before the bunker doors were closed for good.

"Could it be some kind of virus?" asked the deputy prime minister.

"How would that affect the electricity?" asked Berg.

"Some kind of bioweapon with an EMP component?" hypothesized another officer.

"If it's a virus, why aren't *we* sick?" Jonah asked, gesturing to himself and Ayelet. "Why not the deputy prime minister? We came from up top."

"I don't think it's a contagion," said a man with cropped gray hair and round glasses. He wore a white coat with a nametag: Dr. Ari Geller. "I think it's electrical. We know it's disrupting electrical signals. Perhaps this EMP is also disrupting the electrical signals in people's brains. And we're not affected because the EMP shield is protecting us."

"Is that possible?" asked the deputy prime minister.

"With our technology? No," Geller said, adjusting his glasses. "But researchers have used electrical pulses to trigger hallucinations in the cortex. People see things during electrical storms. So theoretically, an EMP *could* trigger mass hallucinations. Make people see things that aren't there. Make them violent."

"I think it's something more," Ayelet said softly.

The men looked over at her, as if having forgotten she was there, and no doubt ready to dismiss whatever she said because she was wounded. Or a woman. Or because of what she was about to say.

"I think it's *melekh mashiach*. The coming of the Messiah."

"Puh," spat the commander.

"You read John Sunday's report," she continued. "What happened to the Jesus cult?"

Berg shifted in his seat. "They tracked them from Egypt to the Banias Nature Reserve. There was an attack there. But we don't even know if they're related to this. They seem an unlikely group to possess a weapon powerful enough to cause all this."

"I don't think it was a weapon," Ayelet said. "I think you have to consider the possibility that this is a punishment from God."

Some of the men shifted in their seats now.

Berg shook his head and turned back to the doctor. He wasn't going to deal with her. Because if what she said was true, there was something out there that was more powerful than men and their war rooms.

"If it is EMP making people go crazy, how do we test that?" Berg asked the doctor.

Geller frowned. "We could find someone up top who's affected. Bring them down. See if the EMP shield here is able to break the signal."

Berg nodded. "Then we send a team topside."

"Wait—what if he's wrong?" asked the deputy prime minister. "What if it's viral? You bring someone down here, they'll infect us all."

"If that's the case, sir, then you're already infected," Berg answered coolly. "And we have nothing left to fight."

Then I gazed upward and saw the Spirit saying to me, "Paul, come! Proceed toward me!". Then as I went, the gate opened, and I went up to the fifth heaven. And I saw my fellow apostles going with me while the Spirit accompanied us.

Apocalypse of Paul

CHAPTER XVI

Rome, Italy
67 CE

Beneath the candle, Longinus sat at a desk in a room scattered with artifacts. Around him were blocks of fig and oak, portraits of the dead, and rolled scrolls. He had collected the wares from the woman's house in hopes that something here would give him an indication as to where the key was hidden, but they offered only paint and prose.

He had presumed the little girl who took off with the portrait would seek out her kin. He had the surrounding villages scoured for her, had rounded up the followers of the Christ, and had even offered a reward for any burial portraits, but all he ended up with were useless piles of painted wood.

His mind flickered as much as the candle flame. He needed to find her. The child. Something was hidden in the portrait she took, some tell, the gospel of the woman who tended to the Christ. Some clue for him to unravel, some word that would lead him like a map to treasure.

Instead he sat in a room filled with pictures of the dead, looking outward with eyes that were unsympathetic to his plight.

A knock sounded on the door.

"Come," Longinus called.

A soldier stepped into the storage room. "Sir, the prisoner is here."

Longinus nodded and rose. He brought the candle with him, leaving the room in darkness as he closed the door behind him.

* * *

Down the narrow stone steps to the carcer floor, the scent of piss filled the air, and the stone walls wept filth and dirty water. Longinus waved the torch around the various cells until he saw the man chained in a corner. The guard unlocked the iron gates, and Longinus stepped into the cell.

He cast the torch near the prisoner's face. The man had aged much since Longinus had last seen him. The large hands were still there, but time had skinned his muscle closer to the bone, and his gray whiskers were caked with filth and mud. The narrow tendons in his arms strained as the chains held his wrists wide above his head, but he hung limply, in body and spirit. Perhaps he knew this was the pit from which the condemned did not rise.

Longinus turned to the guards lingering near the cell. "Leave us."

The guards departed, leaving Longinus alone with the prisoner.

Longinus leaned in close. "I see that despite all your miracles, God still sees fit to clock your years."

The old man raised his head. "All things have a season, brother."

"It would seem yours is winter."

"Are you here to speak in lyric, or do you tell me what you seek?" asked the prisoner. "Why have you dragged me here? Has my case not been cleared by Caesar? Can I not be a citizen of both Rome and of God?"

Longinus smiled. His face had changed several times since they had last met, and he could tell that the old man did not recognize him. "I followed your ways, Paul of Tarsus. Preached it in places God himself had abandoned. Saved the souls of many in cells like this. And still my wife suffers."

Paul's eyes widened, searching the centurion's face. "Longinus?"

"The name is no longer important. Have I not earned His pardon?"

"It would seem not. Was Cephas not here as well, in this very tomb, perhaps in this very chain? Did he receive your grace?"

"He, like you, sent me in circles."

"Did he not give you what you sought?"

Longinus turned and looked out through the bars. All around him in the dank carcer, other men were chained to cell walls.

"Aye. I crossed the gate, into a world that could not keep me. And they tortured me for a thousand years. But where is the key that opens that door for good?" Longinus turned back to the old man. "She deserves peace, brother. Is my quest not just? To free her from her suffering? In the night, I hear her screams upon the wind. And so this, this world, becomes my true hell. Where is the little girl who carries the Gospel of Mary? Do her words not contain the location of the key I seek?"

Paul shook his head. "Brother, for one who preached the way, you should have heard its word. The Lord gave the Keys of the Kingdom. *Keys.* There is more than one. Two, to be precise."

Longinus studied the man's face. He saw no sign of deception there. "Then where is the other?"

"Here. With us now."

Longinus rolled his eyes. "Do we speak in parables again? Is there some word or sign or symbol, some wicked clue for me to decipher now?"

"No. It is here. Somewhere in this prison. The guards took it from my neck upon my arrest."

"And what does this key unlock?" Longinus asked.

Paul smiled. "A place so bright, it blinded me."

* * *

The apostle's belongings were searched, revealing a small leather pouch containing a tarnished green-hued key. On one end was a half circle, like a setting sun, and on the other end were three prongs. It was heavier than most, but looked like any other, and Longinus wondered if he was about to be deceived again with some story of miracles and magic.

He returned to the cell and held the key in front of him.

"What is this?"

"That is obvious, brother."

"Bah. Where does it go? What does it open?"

Paul stretched his palms, the chains digging into his wrists. "Unbind me and I shall show you."

Longinus eyed the priest. The centurion had read Paul's letters while he'd been under house arrest. He had seen his word, his calls for the end of the world. His visions of heaven. Such a slick tongue.

Seeing Longinus's hesitation, Paul nodded to the cell that still contained him. "Where am I to go?"

Longinus called for the guard, and moments later, Paul stood unshackled. He rubbed his wrists and massaged the tendons in his tired arms.

"So?" Longinus said, holding up the key.

Paul reached out and took it. "The key will take you to a place beyond this world. But to stay there, you must be one with the Spirit. The gate does not open if your mind and your body are not cleansed in the word of the Lord."

"Show me what this does and *then* we'll gauge my purity."

Paul walked over to the iron bars of the cell. He held the key up like he was wielding a hammer and whacked it hard against the bars. Then he turned and smiled.

"Do you hear it?"

Longinus leaned in, listening. "No. I..."

And then he did. A low rumble at the edges of his awareness. A rapid heartbeat wobble that rattled something deep inside his skull. He looked to the floor and saw rats scurrying across the stone, their heads rising and bobbing as if in a trance.

He tried to focus on Paul standing before him, the key still in his hand, but could not. The cell bars shimmied and disappeared, and the walls around him vibrated as if he stood at the epicenter of an earthquake. All around him swirled colored lights that pulsed and drained away from the point where Paul held the key.

"What is this?" Longinus said, his voice trailing behind him.

"The gate," Paul said, his answer finding its way to Longinus in the same trailing manner.

Paul waved for him to move forward, but there were many Pauls, each a vibration of the next. "Come," he said, and as the old apostle stepped forward, he was drained away by the light. His body turned orange, then red, and then he faded away completely.

"Paul?" Longinus called, his voice now even farther from his ears.

He moved toward where the bars had been, his feet moving with ripples, and reached out his hand. His fingers turned orange, then red, then disappeared completely. He stepped the rest of the way forward, and lights danced around him.

Longinus sensed that he was no longer walking. Instead he was being carried, lifted, escorted by hands that were not his own. And when it ended, he stood in a field of flowers outside the filth-stained wall of the carcer. The flowers contained shapes he'd never seen, their petals continually emerging and disappearing all while dancing in a gentle breeze.

Paul stood next to him in the field, and he also fluttered in and out of sight.

"What is this?" Longinus asked.

"A place always here. Just beyond our grasp. Where all things have been and shall be. Look." He gestured in one direction and then the other. "Do you see it? The tunnel? All things, in all directions. All options, all worlds, all possibilities."

Longinus saw only the flowers outside the eternal wall. "I see no such thing."

"Do you not? See? There? The orange shores of Malta. At sunrise. And there? The cliffs of Rhodes from my boat."

"I see only a wall."

Paul paused and looked at him. Then he nodded.

"That means you go no farther."

"What? I've only just begun."

"And so say us all when we step through the gate." Paul moved away from him, drifting in and out of view.

"Wait, brother!" Longinus shouted. "Take me!"

Paul smiled. "It is everything." And he vanished as thoroughly as if he'd stepped behind a curtain Longinus could not see.

Suddenly the lights around Longinus went out, and he heard a slam, and he stood back in the dark, dank carcer. Yet at the same moment he was struck by a brilliant flash of white, so bright that his pupils burned. He covered his eyes, but there was no escape. It felt like there was burning sand inside his head, scraping his eyes raw, red hot pokers gouging out his vision. The pain was excruciating.

It was too late.

When the pain subsided enough for him to open his eyes again, he was blind.

"What is this?" he screamed, flailing against the bars of the cell. "What has happened?"

He tripped on something and fell. He felt around, and his fingers found the whiskers of the apostle's beard.

"What have you done?" Longinus shouted, shaking the apostle. "You have blinded me!" he wailed. "Answer me!"

But there was no answer.

In a rage, Longinus pulled his sword, grabbed hold of the apostle's hair and pulled it backwards to reveal his neck, and struck true with the blade. Over and over the metal fell until he felt the warm blood on his knees and hands on the cell floor, and knew the deed was done.

He fell back against the cell wall and tried to retreat from the burning in his eyes. But there was nowhere to go.

He reached out again, blindly, and fumbled for the apostle's hands until he found what he sought. The key. He took it and held it close to his chest.

"Why?" Longinus sobbed. "Why do you punish me so?"

But both God and the apostle had grown deaf.

CHAPTER XVII

Deep Run, Maryland
Three Days After Event

By her best guess, it had taken Eve half a day in the darkness to find the box of ChemLight glowsticks. She had felt blindly through dozens of stacks of cardboard boxes, tediously peeling back the tape on each and removing the packing. When at last she found what she sought, she at first thought it was plastic packages of condiments. But then she opened one and snapped the stick, and a red light glowed in her hands like she was holding an anglerfish.

It was like finding treasure.

Using that light, she read the label on the box. Twelve hours. There were twelve glowsticks inside, now eleven, with a burn time of twelve hours each. If she burned one a day, she'd have twelve days of light.

She searched for more boxes of glowsticks, but this was the only one.

Twelve days? Really?

As she turned and scanned the rest of the bunker with the light, looking over the half-opened boxes scattered everywhere, she realized her father had invested his stock in flashlights, and batteries, and a giant generator. Not glowsticks. And why would he do any different?

Under the red light, she again checked all the flashlights, changed the batteries, checked again. No luck.

She explored, panning the red light around, revealing more of her new home. It was mostly a single giant room, roughly twelve feet wide by sixty feet long. There were shelves along the walls, and a desk in one corner, and a bunk bed, and a gun cabinet stocked with rifles and ammo. A small accordion door that led to a little bathroom, and there was a small kitchenette, and in another side room were pallets of food in boxes and cans.

She was always thirsty after the change, so her first priority, now that she had light, was water. She lifted the handle on the bathroom sink and was rewarded with a low-pressure trickle. She slurped the water with her hands, grateful that something down here still worked.

In the red glow, she looked at her new face in the little bathroom mirror. After her first awakening, her once-curly hair had turned straight and black, but now it seemed lighter. Her cheeks were more chiseled, and her skin was dryer and tighter to the bone, though that might be because she'd starved some during her sleep.

She sorted through the boxes of MREs and stacks of canned goods. The MREs seemed complicated, so she dined ravenously instead on canned fruit, little Vienna sausages, and crackers.

When she was finished, she tried the generator. She wasn't surprised when it remained cold and dead. An air filtration system led to the surface, and she could only hope it didn't need a working generator to do its job—and that wherever it surfaced was hidden, so that no one on the outside could clog it and choke her out.

There were plenty of supplies. In addition to the stockpiles of canned goods and MREs and bags of beans and rice, there was toilet paper, board games, DVDs, and books. Some of the books her father had obviously bought just for her, because he apparently still thought she was into reading about sexy vampires.

On a shelf near the desk, she found the operational instructions. They covered the generator, the composting toilet, and the air system, among other things. She went back to the generator, instruction manual in hand, and followed all the troubleshooting advice, but she got no closer to reviving it.

Apparently she should have started her explorations at the desk, because when she finally examined it, she found a stack of folders at its center, and on top of the stack was an envelope with a sticky note. In her father's handwriting, it read, *EVE: READ THIS FIRST.*

Her hands shaking, she opened the envelope and read a long, typed letter:

My Dearest Daughter,

This is my attempt at a better late than never explanation as to why you're in this bunker. It is also an attempt to explain what led to all this in the first place.

But first things first.

READ ALL OPERATIONAL MANUALS on the daily maintenance of this bunker. You have enough food for three years, and I have bro-

ken down your caloric needs over the course of each month for that time period. I have also marked and highlighted all of your daily responsibilities on the equipment. By following these instructions, the bunker will easily support you for that length of time.

In the desk are green folders containing my notes and the CIA case files explaining everything I know about the man responsible for both your resurrection and for what has happened outside. His name is Josef Belac.

When I first saw the miracle of your resurrection, I was born again in the ways of Christ. I have debated many times whether what I saw was some kind of trick or delusion, but I believe it was not. It was Josef Belac who brought you back. He is a man who cannot die, and that makes him very dangerous to us.

When you came back to me, I pledged my loyalty to Belac and his organization. I didn't have much of a choice. Belac is older than the CIA, older than America, older than all of the governments on Earth. He has wealth and resources that have been hidden for thousands of years. He is a walking ghost, a man whose face and DNA and fingerprints constantly change, and he has dozens of followers who have the same ability. If I did not follow him and his Way, they would have gotten to us both.

I don't know exactly what's going to happen when Belac's plan is fulfilled. As I told you, Belac found a sponge containing the full DNA *of Christ, and he has used that to impregnate women in order to resurrect Jesus so that He can rise and cleanse the Earth. His organization believed that they were following the will of God, and that if they brought back Christ, order would be restored and we would all be saved. But for that to happen, his followers believed that the world as we know it would end.*

I have seen the pregnant women with my own eyes, and although I am at the mercy of Belac and follow his instructions to protect you, I am working to stop them. To learn how these pregnant women will end the world.

If it happens, though—if I don't stop them— and if you're reading this without me... I'm sorry. But there is still a chance.

In addition to my files on Belac, his organization, and his purpose, you will also find files documenting the next part of what I believe is supposed to happen.

It is not Belac's plan.

It is God's.

And that part involves us.

Or, if you are reading this, it involves you.

You will see that we found the pages of a gospel beneath the portrait that we found in Syria. The first page of this gospel is what led Belac to the desert and to the sponge containing Christ's DNA.

But the second page of the gospel I have kept hidden from him—I hope—and that page has led me to believe God has given us a way to save us from ourselves.

When you are done reading this, you will have a choice to make. As I said, you have everything you need in this bunker to survive. A working generator. Water kept in a ten-thousand-gallon underground tank. At some point, however, you will have to go outside. And if the second part of the gospel is not fulfilled, I'm afraid the world will be lost forever.

If I were there with you, I would do this myself. Now, you will have to make the choice.

Eve... Sara... I am sorry. My daughter. My baby. I'm sorry for my failures. I tried to be the best father I could be, but I know I often came up short as a man. Know that no matter what, I will always love you. Know that everything I did was always for you.

If I am without you, then I pray it is because I now stand before God, and He shall judge me.

But I fear your judgment more.

No matter where I am, you will always be my little girl.

Love Always,

Daddy

Eve lowered the letter. She read it again, her palms leaving sweat stains on the paper. She stopped, wiped some of the moisture from her eyes, then hit a few key parts of the letter over again.

The man who wrote this note was *not* the same one who hours earlier had tried to kill her outside. Was any of this man left at all?

She wanted to fold the letter neatly back into the envelope, but her hands were shaking and she couldn't get it to stuff correctly. So instead she laid the letter on the desk. She wanted to cry. She wanted to throw up. *This* was her protection? A dark, cold bunker that her father was now telling her she was going to have to leave?

She moved to the bunk, lay down, and brought her legs up to her chest like a teenage girl mourning a lost boyfriend. But what she mourned was the world. She mourned the love she wasn't going to find. The wedding she would never have. The children she would never hold. It had all been stolen.

And her father.

She wanted to hug her daddy one last time. Tell him she was sorry for the hurtful things she'd said to him. Tell him that she loved him too.

The tears came then, an ugly sobbing, and as the red glowstick eventually faded out, she fell asleep to the sound of a dead man still up above, banging, banging on her door.

* * *

When she woke in the darkness, God knows how many hours later, she had to fumble again in the dark for the glowsticks. This time she put a spare in her pocket, so she didn't have to repeat this step the next time she fell asleep. She returned to the desk and looked at the other contents. Beneath the first envelope was a second, this one a larger manila envelope, and the sticky note attached to it read *WHEN YOU'RE READY TO GO OUTSIDE.*

She opened it and pulled out the contents. Stamped in red ink across the first page was the word *CONFIDENTIAL.* And below that:

Recovered GOSPEL OF MARY-PAGES 1 & 2

CHAPTER XVIII

Rachaiya, Lebanon
Eleven Days After Event

It was still dark, and John Sunday had no idea how long he'd been asleep when he heard screaming.

He jumped up and checked the bed. Kat and the boy were both there, thank God, just waking to the shouting, and the dog was already headed to the door and barking.

Sunday ran into the hall and followed the shouts to the front door. The priest was standing guard there, and the junkie girl was screaming at him to open the door and let her go outside.

"What's going on?" Sunday shouted.

The girl turned, eyes wide. Sunday recognized that wild look. *Withdrawal.*

"My grandmother!" she cried. "She's gone!"

Sunday looked to the priest, who nodded. "I'm sorry. I fell asleep. I woke up and the front door was open. She's not here."

"Jesus Christ," said Sunday.

"We need to go out there!" shrieked the girl. "We need to find her!"

"That is absolutely the one thing we are *not* going to do," Sunday said.

"Then let *me* go! Let me out to find her! Please!"

Sunday's mind was racing. Why would she go outside? No sane person would go outside.

Then it hit him.

"We've been compromised," he said. "She's gone to tell them where we are."

"What?" shirked the girl. "Are you *crazy*? She's just sick, that's all."

"What do you mean, sick?" the priest asked, suddenly looking concerned.

The girl calmed, but only a bit. "She has... what do you say when you're old and your mind isn't right?"

"Dementia?" the priest offered.

"Yes, dementia. She sees things. Hears things. Forgets things. She's just an old lady. She needs our help." She turned to Sunday. "Please."

Sunday shook his head. "No."

"You can't stop me!"

"You want to leave, be my guest. But you're on your own."

A voice sounded behind him. Kat. "We all need to go," she said. "I had a dream. They're coming. We have to go."

"Where?" the priest asked.

The junkie pointed at Kat. "There's a hospital. For you. Maybe fifteen kilometers away. We passed it on the way."

"Hospitals are in cities," Sunday said. "Where there are too many of those *things* around."

"This one backs up to farmland. I can get you there. Please," she begged, "I can't leave her. She's all I have left."

Sunday looked back at Kat, round and vulnerable. He could hear her voice in his head, even though she wasn't speaking. She was telling him it was the right thing to do. To go find this lost old woman, because given the circumstances, he might well be running out of opportunities to do good things in his life, and his final steps needed to count for something.

"Pack up," he said. "We're leaving."

Ten minutes later they had loaded up the horse with the bags of supplies, and slowly, carefully, Kat was placed in the saddle. But Sunday would not be going with her. The snow had lessened during the night, and he had been able to find the old woman's footprints. They didn't lead in the same direction as the hospital.

They would have to split up.

He looked up at Kat on the horse. "I'll find you," he said.

"I know."

Kat, the priest, the junkie, the child, and the dog set off in one direction, and Sunday set off in another. Every bone in his body was crying out, asking him what the hell he was doing. In his old life, he would have just let this old woman die out here. She wasn't his mission. His mission was Kat. And if something were to happen to him, the odds of her survival decreased significantly.

But something was whispering to him, telling him he couldn't leave this old lady wandering the snow by herself.

He pushed forward, following the shallow depressions of her mostly filled footprints, wondering if he wasn't tracking her so much as she was luring him forward.

He decided that the reason he was out here must be the coma dreams, the terrible things he'd seen there, and the fear that those dreams would come true. That these *things* would feast on their bodies for all eternity. But perhaps if he showed he was worthy of redemption, if for once in his life he did the "good" thing... well, perhaps it would amount to something.

Maybe.

It was a rationalization, he knew. He was taking an action based on a gut feeling and trying to explain it to himself afterward. Because the truth was, he had seen plenty of "good" people who were dead, scattered, slaughtered. Including children. What sin could they possibly have committed that was so grave as to warrant their fates?

The footprints led him past trees that swayed in the cold. At least the crickets had fallen silent. There was no sound except for his boots penetrating snow.

Only twenty or thirty minutes passed before the footprints ended and he found the old woman curled up in a sad little ball beneath a dead oak. He stepped slowly, warily toward her, recalling the trap laid by the men who had sabotaged him in the dark grocery store. Those men had baited him, and she might be doing the same. These things were smart.

He nudged her with his boot. Her body was powdered with a light frosting of snow, and for a moment he thought she'd frozen to death out here. But then she moved, slowly rolling over and looking up into the barrel of his gun.

Her eyes went wide with terror. "I'm... I'm lost," she said.

Sunday stared down at her. Was she? Or had she found exactly what she was looking for?

CHAPTER XIX

Tel Aviv, Israel
Day of Event

There were six in the team headed topside, Jonah among them. He had volunteered for this. They all had. Brave, or stupid. But Jonah knew what he was volunteering for; he had seen what was up there waiting for them, and the other men had not. Each man was outfitted with Kevlar, an M4 with extra mags, and a Glock 17. Two carried Benelli M4 shotguns loaded with double-aught to scatter a crowd. Jonah, however, carried a Dan-Inject dart gun loaded with 315 milligrams of ketamine, to subdue and apprehend.

He would have preferred the shotgun.

He saw Ayelet watching as he and the rest of the men started for the stairs. Bringing up the rear, he gave her a slight parting smile, a working smile. He wanted to say something to her. No—not something. He wanted to tell her everything. Tell her that he wanted to take care of her. That he, too, was broken inside. That he'd lost his wife and child in a restaurant bombing in Jerusalem. That his heart ached, and all he wanted to do was save something in this world. Something broken like him.

Instead, he said nothing. Just the smile.

As he ascended the stairs, he wondered if he was reaching out to Ayelet because she was a fragment of hope. That when the world falls apart, you seek to find someone, anyone, to get close to, so you can hide beneath the rocks together as the stars fall.

The lead man spun the wheel to open the door, and the sounds of the unlocking latches echoed down the stairs. The men passed through, and the door was sealed behind them. They formed a semicircle, each panning the surface with their weapons.

Jonah was instantly struck by two things.

One, it was dark. The sky had turned completely black, and a fog had filled the street, so there was no light up here on the surface, not a single star visible in the heavens to light their way.

And two, it was cold. As he stepped forward, his boots immediately sank into snow. Snow in Tel Aviv... that was something he'd never seen. And this was real snow, not a light frosting, but half a foot deep. As the team moved forward a few steps, falling flakes fluttered against their skin.

Jonah immediately lowered his night-vision goggles, almost a reflex—only to discover that the gear didn't work. It had worked down below during the equipment check thirty minutes earlier, but now, nothing. Whatever was frying everything electronic was still active. He lifted the NVGs back up and over his helmet.

The point man pulled a flare from his pouch and snapped it. The flame formed a green umbrella around them as they stepped into the night.

A cry, more like a howl, sounded somewhere in the distance. Somewhere out there in the shadows and fog of the buildings, as if the city around them realized there was fresh meat here, and that now it would be sought.

The men stayed in a tight semicircle and didn't stray far from the bunker. The plan was simple. Stay close to the bunker. Lure whatever they could to them. Don't lose sight of the door.

They heard sounds close by, just beyond the light of the flare. A cold crackling of footsteps in snow. Not one but many, crossing the ice to come for them.

One of the soldiers fetched another flare from his own pouch. His hands were shaking from either cold or fear as he lit it, extending their circle of light. And there, just barely on the edge of shadow, Jonah could see something moving. And he could hear it too, dragging the snow, like a lobster tail scratching across ice.

The soldier extended the flare to peer farther, and as he did, that something latched onto his arm and yanked him into the darkness. The flare dropped and buried itself in the snow, and the soldier was gone into the depths of black beyond the remnants of green light.

The scream that followed sank Jonah's bowels. It was not the cry of a wounded man on a battlefield or in a hospital. It was a scream of sheer terror. A cry choked by a heart's inability to keep up with its lungs. The scream of a man who had seen a horror beyond all things he'd ever known.

A slamming sound, over and over, and the screaming stopped.

The men tightened their group, each weapon trained on the darkness and what they could not see within it.

And then in the light of the burning green flares, the other men suddenly fell to their knees. All except for Jonah.

"What are you doing?" Jonah shouted. "Get up!"

The soldiers convulsed and seized around him, weeping and crying and screaming and begging. Then they each bowed, over and over, slamming their faces into the snow, right down through it and into the asphalt below. Each head came up again, still screaming and weeping, before slamming once more into the ground.

"Stop! Stop it! Get up!" Jonah shouted.

He heard the chirping of crickets now, loud and closing in. Then he saw it. In front of him. A giant pit in the mouth of a mountain. A hole in the earth. And from it poured a black plume, and from the swirling plume, the energy of a thousand dark suns.

He raised the dart gun to his shoulder, aimed down at one of his fellow soldiers, and fired into the man's neck. The dart stuck like a prong, and when the soldier rose up to grab him, Jonah fired again, the dose probably too much, but he didn't care. The soldier collapsed into the snow.

Jonah grabbed him by the collar and dragged him hurriedly back toward the bunker door. Creatures in the darkness around him bayed and howled. The chirping of crickets was deafening.

As he banged on the bunker door, the remaining flare dimmed in kicked-over snow, and he was alone.

In that moment, he saw things.

The creatures around him were human, or pieces and parts of humans, merged together into grotesque shapes. They scrabbled through the snow toward him and when the door behind him opened Jonah practically fell back through it, dragging the soldier behind him. The man who had opened the door slammed it shut and spun the wheel.

Jonah lay on the ground and struggled to catch his breath. All his mind could do was repeat over and over the same conclusion.

We're all going to die.

CHAPTER XX

Messina, Italy
October, 1347

As Father Vicario unloaded the wagon beneath a full moon, beneath the shadow of the church, he felt a strange rumble in his gut, like his insides were being sliced open. A moment later, he waddled over to the ditch off the street, raised his wool cloak, and shat profusely.

A passing monk paused and shook his head. Father Vicario could only nod back with one eye closed as the excrement and groans rolled out of him. He held the key in his hand, but he had to place it down in the mud so he could better grip his robe, and as he continued to defecate, the stream of shit ran over the key.

When at least he was finished, he lowered his robe, collected and wiped the key on the cloth, and stood. He didn't know what had come over him, but he felt overwhelming relief that it had passed.

He resumed unloading the wagon. The duke's treasures would help pay for the completion of the church dome in Avignon, and that would put the priest himself in the pope's good graces. It was God's will, he thought, that he would find such loot.

A few minutes later, his stomach groaned again, and his hands turned to damp mops. A weakness washed over him, and instead of unloading the rest of the cart, he surrendered, retreating to his room and collapsing on the bed. He was going to put the key on the shelf next to his head, but before he could, he fell asleep, the key clutched in his hand.

The next morning the priest's neck was so swollen it felt like he had choked on two eggs, and he wept tears of blood, obscuring his vision. He rolled in the bed, blind and gasping for air, spurting phlegm and blood, alone with the knowledge that he was dying. As he seized, he heard the key fall off the straw bed and hit the stone floor with a heavy clank.

It was then that, in a fever dream, Father Vicario, though blinded by blood, saw a man standing at the foot of his bed.

A man he knew.

The man moved closer, standing over him, and touched the priest's forehead. His touch was warm, and he kneeled and whispered in the priest's ear.

The priest knew then what he was to do.

The next time he awoke, the illness within him had been cured.

But he would have to flee, and stay hidden, because as he looked at the key that he once more clutched in his hand, he knew that he was now a disciple.

And there would be more.

CHAPTER XXI

Tel Aviv, Israel
Four Days After Event

Corporal Mendel Horowitz was scared, but he was trying very hard not to show it. He'd heard the knocking while making his rounds. The bunker—the pit, as it was known—was a serpentine maze, and he had been tasked with making sure everyone had been accounted for.

The knock was faint at first. No more than a soft, sporadic tapping. But gradually it had increased in volume, and they had followed it here. Now it was like a loose shutter slapping in a storm.

Horowitz looked over at Private Abel Moyer, the lanky soldier who was on patrol with him. By the look of his pale-white face, the need for a shit-cork was mutual.

This was not an exterior door they were assessing. This door led to a hallway and then up to the giant concrete building that had been built over the pit. Perhaps the person on the other side had been in the building above when the bunker went into lockdown. Perhaps. Or perhaps there had been a breach somewhere and there was some kind of who-knew-what on the other side of this door. Horowitz had heard the stories. Stories about what the men had seen up there.

But then the knocking changed its rhythm. Though if it hadn't been for Moyer, the corporal would have been unaware what that rhythm meant.

"I think they're saying something," Moyer said.

Moyer had been in a Modi'in Boy Scout troop in Jerusalem. That was probably how he was able to recognize that the knock was tapping out Morse code.

"H-E-L-P," Moyer spelled aloud, listening intently. "I-M-K-E-I-R-A." He looked at the corporal. "Help. I'm Keira."

So—this wasn't a crazy thing on the other side of the door. It was a woman, rational enough to use a code to communicate.

Moyer kept listening to the tap-tapping, no longer saying the letters aloud, but his eyes widening at what he heard. Finally Horowitz could stand the mystery no longer.

"What's she saying?"

"She works upstairs," Moyer said. "She got stuck in the hallway." He paused. "And she's pregnant. I think we should open the door."

Horowitz hesitated. What if Moyer was wrong? What if the person on the other side was lying?

He had to steady his hand before he pulled the key off his belt. He didn't want the private to see him shaking; he was the senior officer, after all. He slid the key into place, turned the latch, and opened the door. And there she stood. A short girl, who indeed was quite round in the middle.

"About time," she said in Hebrew. "I have to pee."

They escorted her into the corridor and locked the door behind her, and Corporal Mendel Horowitz felt like a hero.

CHAPTER XXII

Langley, Virginia
Five Days Before Event

Lincoln Pierce had spent three months collecting a database of over six thousand keys, all from the first century, from various collections around the world. He had scoured museum records from the Cloisters at the Met, to the Getty Museum, to the University of Pennsylvania Museum of Archaeology, to the Smithsonian's National Museum of American History. Then he went overseas, where the collections got even bigger.

There were the British Museum and the Louvre, the National Archaeological Museum in Naples and a massive private collection in Velbert, Germany. There were door keys, chest keys, prison keys. There were keys with lions and horses and even phallic heads. There were ring keys, small enough to fit on your finger, long keys, rotary keys, folding keys... He had learned more about keys from the first century than he'd ever thought possible. More than he'd ever wanted. When he slept, he even dreamt about keys.

And yet he still had no idea how many more keys could be in the hands of private collectors and hobbyists. For the most part, these things weren't regarded as artifacts or national treasures, just collectibles, so governments didn't have restrictions on importing or exporting them. Some collectors filled out paperwork, put their name on an import license, followed the bureaucracy, but some had not. And on top of that, there were a ton of fakes. Hell, he could buy "Roman keys" on eBay.

What Ferguson was asking for was insane. What was Lincoln supposed to do? Just hand him a list of every single known key from the first century? What good was that?

Yet Lincoln knew he needed to please "Master" Tom, because the white man held power over him. So he sat at his desk, stacked with volumes of documents and books on ancient locking mechanisms, and he started over.

He looked over the list of keys, at the stacks of color photos with dates, makes, and materials. Bronze, and iron, and keys with ivory handles. And histories of each key, and region where it was found, and who was the owner, before it switched hands again to a new owner.

Okay. Stop. What are you looking for again? Some kind of key to heaven? Seriously?

Regroup. If there was a real *key of Christ, what would it look like? Would it be shiny? Have glitter?*

No, it'd be more like the cup in Indiana Jones. Plain. Ordinary. "That's the cup of a carpenter. You've chosen wisely."

He chuckled at the thought and flipped back through his notes on the gospels. He had pulled every instance of the phrases "key," "Keys of the Kingdom," and "Key of David."

But his mind wandered. He'd been at this too long. Gone too deep. Keys. Keys everywhere. And they always reminded him, strangely, of one thing.

His father.

Lincoln's daddy used to keep a big loop of silver keys on his thick black belt. Everything else he wore was white. White T-shirt, white pants, though not truly white—as the janitor the white was always stained with spots of dirt, or grease, or paint, as if to say "Look out, rich kids, this here's a dirty man."

Yeah, he'd had the keys to the entire school, but it didn't matter much. He and Lincoln were still locked out.

Lincoln remembered them driving together every morning out of the Richmond ghetto in his dad's old beat-up pickup, PVC pipe on the roof rack jostling around up there like plastic spears. He would always remember those conversations. His father was a smart man.

"Lincoln," his father said to him one morning. "They ain't ever gonna accept you. But you can beat 'em. Beat 'em at their game."

"Sailing?"

"You wanna do golf instead?"

"No. I don't want to do either. I just want to read."

"Son, these white folks think we're just here to suck off them. And that, when they're not lookin', we're gonna take what they got. You need to show 'em you just as good as they are, sometimes even better. Grades are a good thing. A noble thing. And you got your momma's brains. But if you want their respect, you gotta beat 'em at the game."

Lincoln shook his head and looked out the window. Damn white-boy preppy school. Didn't have a basketball team, because everyone knew old Webster High and all the other inner-city schools would beat them so bad they'd run out of numbers on the scoreboard. So what'd they do? Create their own damn sports teams, sports they knew only white boys would do. Golf and sailing.

"You ever see any black men sailin'?" Lincoln asked.

"Sure," his dad said with a smile. "Blackbeard."

Lincoln rolled his eyes. "He wasn't black."

His dad just laughed.

But dammit if his dad didn't prove to be right. Something about being out on that water changed Lincoln. When he was out there, sailing, he felt like he was in control. His black skin was made darker with that white sail as his background, but he could tack and move as fast as the wind. And he was *free*.

He racked up a few trophies too. Sailor of the Year. Invited to the US Youth Sailing Championship. Even helped win the Rose Cup.

All that because his daddy worked as the janitor— and that gave Lincoln a chance to go to that preppy private school. That, plus they had to meet a quota.

Lincoln was going places. He really was.

Up until the day he lost his faith in God.

And he remembered that day too.

* * *

Everybody took turns after Monday, Wednesday, and Friday mass to stay late and help Father Zula clean up the chalices and the communion plates and flip all the prayer kneelers back upright. When it was Lincoln's turn, and he was finished, he headed over to the church rectory to tell Father Zula he was done.

It was hot outside, and when the priest opened the door, his big round glasses seemed to stick to the sweat on his face. He held a glass of lemonade.

"Come on in, Lincoln," he said, handing Lincoln the glass. "I want to show you something."

Lincoln hesitated. "I really should be getting to class, Father."

"Just a few minutes."

Lincoln stepped into the house, which smelled of stale wine and old wood. Father Zula disappeared into another room. Lincoln sipped the lemonade, but it was much too sweet, and he dumped some of it in a potted plant.

When Father Zula returned, he was carrying a picture frame, which he handed to Lincoln. In it was a diploma from Dartmouth.

"You're a smart boy, Lincoln," said Father Zula. "With your grades and what you've done with sailing, I can help you with a recommendation to Dartmouth. It'll get you far."

"That would be great, Father."

"Can you imagine that, son? You'd be the first person in your family to go to an Ivy League school."

"First person to go to college."

"Oh, well, that *would* be something. Drink your lemonade, son." Father Zula waited for Lincoln to take a sip before he continued. "Can you imagine your momma's face, out there in the audience?"

Lincoln could picture it. His mom and dad in the audience, clapping their fool heads and fool hands off. He was so preoccupied with the image, he didn't realize that Father Zula was standing so close.

"Is it true?" Father Zula asked.

"Is what true?"

"That the black ones are bigger?"

Lincoln suddenly realized that the priest had pressed himself up against his backside and was reaching around and rubbing the front of Lincoln's pants.

"What the hell?" Lincoln shouted, and he threw his head backwards, slamming it into the priest's nose. The Dartmouth diploma and the glass of lemonade both fell on the floor and shattered.

He turned. Father Zula was wiping blood from his nose, and his big round glasses were broken.

"Look what you did, nigger."

The word hit Lincoln more than the assault. *Nigger*? Him? This priest, this man of God, just called him that? None of the rich white boys ever even dared use that word.

The priest settled and took a breath. "Well," he said, wiping more blood on the sleeve of his black robe. "Look at this. You just assaulted a member of the faculty. You've got two choices, boy. I'm going to lift my robe, and you can suck on what I give you, or, before I call the principal, you can take a moment and look at that diploma on the floor. Because that's the closest you're ever going to get to it."

Lincoln felt sweat pouring down the sides of his face. He was jacked, and pumped, but he was also scared. Because everything he'd worked for, everything his dad had worked for, was about to disappear.

For a moment, he contemplated doing it. Contemplated what it would mean to be under that man's robe. And he hated that moment so, so much.

Instead he pushed his way past the priest, and ran out of the house, and ran past the church, all the way to the dirty little garage at the far, far end of the school. He wept there in his father's arms in that garage that smelled like lawn clippings, gasoline, and axle grease.

His dad was able to get some of it out of him, and it was enough.

"Wait here," he said as he picked up a hammer.

"Dad, no," Lincoln begged.

His father looked down at the hammer in his hands. He paused, put it back down in his metal toolbox, and then turned and walked away.

Lincoln didn't see what happened next, but he knew. He knew his father marched over to Father Zula's house, banged on the door, and then beat the ever-living shit out of that so-called holy man.

The police eventually came. Father Zula claimed that he was attacked because he had observed Lincoln cheating on an algebra exam. According to the priest, when he brought this to Lincoln's attention, Lincoln punched him in the nose then ran to his father, who, enraged by the accusation, came over and also assaulted him. Father Zula's account of the situation was backed up by his swollen eyes, broken nose, and busted lip.

The police arrested Lincoln's dad, and Lincoln remembered thinking then it was all over. His academic career, his future, his dad's job, his dad's freedom.

But things had a funny way of working out.

It was May, and summer had come early in Richmond, and while the priest was making his statement, one of the cops on the scene at the priest's house apparently decided to help himself to a glass of lemonade. He soon grew woozy and passed out—and it didn't take much detective work to determine the lemonade was spiked with something.

And that was how the case against Father Frederick Zula began. When detectives searched his house, they found more. Much more. Supposedly, and Lincoln only heard this through rumor, there were jars of semen kept in his kitchen cupboards. Other jars had pubic hair. And there was a mountain of boy's underwear, dry and crunchy, under the bed and in a suitcase in the closet. Whose these various specimens belonged to was a mystery.

Lincoln didn't know for sure if any of this was true. Rumors around school swirled fast and heavy after the priest's arrest. But in time, other boys came forward. Turned out Father Zula had tried this with other children. At other schools, too. He'd been in Poland, where fourteen boys, now men, said they'd been abused. He'd been transferred to Paris. Then Boston. Then Palm Beach. Then Richmond. And everywhere he went, over the course of thirty years, his behavior continued. All told, he racked up seventy-two claims of sexual assault. And those were just the boys, now men, who came forward.

Years later, Lincoln would learn that Zula told the Church he blamed the Great Accuser, Satan, and begged forgiveness. A cosmic cop-out if Lincoln had ever heard one.

It took two weeks, but Lincoln's father was released from police custody. He wasn't allowed back at the school, because despite Father Zula's crimes, Lincoln's dad *had* assaulted a man, and parents expressed concerns that he was violent.

Lincoln, however, given the circumstances—and perhaps to prevent a lawsuit—was invited to stay.

He got into Dartmouth after all. Thanks to his grades and sailing.

And all it cost him was his faith.

It wasn't until later that it would cost him his father.

* * *

Lincoln was older. A man. He was wearing nice clothes, and he had brought home a pretty girl. No, not pretty—Carol Connors was *beautiful*. And white. And Lincoln couldn't believe she would be with a man like him.

He wanted her to meet his father. No—he wanted his father to meet *her*. He wanted his dad to see what his boy had become: a successful man with a beautiful girl on his arm.

But that was a bad idea.

When he brought her home, Dad had been in the midst of fixing a lawnmower. And as he picked himself up off that dirty garage floor, and offered up his hand for her to shake, first he had to wipe the grease off his fingers.

Carol Connors looked at him like he was a leper.

Lincoln was so embarrassed. Embarrassed that his father was wearing those dirty white clothes. Embarrassed that his father was... his father.

No, embarrassed wasn't a strong enough word. He was *ashamed*.

Because his father was ever only going to be a janitor.

They got into a fight that night. Lincoln screamed that his father would never amount to anything. And then he stormed out of the house.

Carol Connors never spoke to him again.

And Lincoln never again spoke to his father.

* * *

Lincoln sat in his office in Langley, surrounded by his research and his memories. Over the last few months he'd been thinking a lot about the relationship he'd lost with his father and the faith he'd left behind. It had become almost an obsession, occupying as much of his mind as his search for this ridiculous key.

He knew the two things were connected. Searching for the key meant reading through scripture. Not in the way he'd once read it, of course. He wasn't seeking divine truth. He was merely a historian, an archeologist looking for random words that might hint at the location of a lost key. But in so doing, he couldn't help but also absorb the other meanings in the text. And he was struck by one message in particular.

Forgiveness.

I'm sorry, Dad.

He sighed and looked down at his yellow notepad. He'd copied down the passage pulled from the second page of the gospel found on the mummy portrait that Kat Devier had been working on.

> *"I have trusted you with the key to my resurrection as I have trusted the Keys of the Kingdom of Heaven, the Key of David, to the first and last disciples, and when held by one pure in the Holy Spirit, only then can you unbind the Gate to God."*

Okay, Lincoln thought. *Keys of the Kingdom of Heaven.* He pulled up Christ's reference to that in the Book of Matthew, when he gave the Keys of the Kingdom of Heaven to Peter, which eventually became the catalyst for him being named the first pope.

> *"I will give you the keys of the kingdom of heaven; whatever you bind on earth will be bound in heaven, and whatever you loose on earth will be loosed in heaven."*

Not much there to work from. He moved on to the two passages in the Bible referencing the Key of David. He'd flagged both with Post-its.

The first was from Isaiah, and began, "In that day I will summon my servant, Eliakim son of Hilkiah…"— but though that one went on some more, Lincoln had researched both Eliakim and Hilkiah, and their paths had led him nowhere.

The second had a much more promising connection. This one was from Revelations.

"To the angel of the church in Philadelphia: These are the words of him who is holy and true, who holds the key of David. What he opens no one can shut, and what he shuts no one can open. I know your deeds. See, I have placed before you an open door that no one can shut. I know that you have little strength, yet you have kept my word and have not denied my name. I will make those who are of the synagogue of Satan, who claim to be Jews though they are not, but are liars—I will make them come and fall down at your feet and acknowledge that I have loved you. Since you have kept my command to endure patiently, I will also keep you from the hour of trial that is going to come on the whole world to test the inhabitants of the earth."

It was that "synagogue of Satan" reference that drove Lincoln to focus more on this passage. One of the verses on the mummy portrait also included that phrase:

And when held by one pure in the Holy Spirit, only then can you unbind the Gate to God.

Without it, the Synagogue of Satan shall destroy me, and us all.

There had to be some connection.

Lincoln read the passage from Revelations aloud. "To the angel of the church in Philadelphia..." He knew the church in Philadelphia was among the seven early Christian churches. And he knew that the ancient town of Philadelphia, near the Aegean Sea, had now come to be known as Alasehir, in modern Turkey.

Is there a key there? There's a strong Roman Catholic presence.

But that too led him nowhere. He pulled up everything he could, but if there had ever been a key there, there was no record of it, and the ancient church itself had long ago been consumed by time. All that was left were a few pillars and crumbling, pillaged sarcophagi. *If* this key even existed, and *if* it had ever been there... by now it would have been removed, and it could have been taken anywhere in the world. Maybe it was sitting in a secret Vatican vault. Maybe it had been sold as a trinket to a tourist. Maybe it was buried in the desert.

I'd have better luck looking in the real Philly.

He leaned back in his chair at his little desk in that office with no window.

No. Could it be? Philadelphia?

Pennsylvania?

He pulled up the list of keys kept at the museum at the University of Pennsylvania. There were dozens of Roman keys in their collection. None of them stood out. But he picked up the phone and called the museum.

"Good afternoon," he said. "My name is Lincoln Pierce. I'm with the Central Intelligence Agency.

Yes. For real. I'd like to speak to the curator of the Mediterranean section. Yes."

There was a pause, and then he was transferred. After a few moments listening to a recorded message advertising an upcoming exhibit on "Magic in the Ancient World," a woman picked up.

"Good afternoon. My name is Lincoln Pierce. Yes, ma'am. I am really with the Central Intelligence Agency. I'd like to talk to you about the keys in your Mediterranean exhibit. Dr. Vicario's collection."

CHAPTER XXIII

Near Kamad El Laouz, Lebanon
Eleven Days After Event

John Sunday guided the little old lady to her feet. She was small, baggy beneath her cloak, saggy within her skin, and he handled her with the same wariness he would an insurgent, unsure if she was hiding something that would blow him up. Her eyes were distant as he pushed her forward through the snow, in the direction of his own past footprints. They walked in silence, Sunday watching her the whole way, searching for some sign she might be like the ones he'd seen at the grocery, but he saw only a scared, disoriented old woman guided by a man with a gun.

When they got back to the house and finished retracing Sunday's own steps, they started following the steps of the others, which was easier to do. The old woman was slow, and Sunday started to despair that they would ever catch up to the caravan, but eventually they came into sight. They'd been going slowly, too— perhaps waiting for him, or perhaps simply too tired and weak to go any faster. The junkie girl in particular looked terrible, sick with withdrawal, as she embraced her grandmother.

They hiked another full day, or thereabouts; "days" were no longer a relevant metric in the eternal gray darkness. They stopped when they needed to, but Sunday urged them onwards, the sounds of crickets always in his ears.

At the edge of a forest on a hill, the town came into view. Sunday used the binoculars and looked past the wheat fields, their green nub stalks trapped in ice and snow, and the silhouette of civilization beyond. At this distance, he couldn't tell if there were things milling there.

The junkie girl nudged him and pointed to the right of their position, about a quarter mile out. A building stood at the edge of the crops.

"There," she whispered.

It was no big-city hospital. Only three stories, maybe with a few dozen beds inside. This was rural care, in a small farm town, surrounded by fields of low wheat that crackled and clinked in the cold wind.

Sunday felt uneasy at the thought of crossing so much open ground to get to the building. It bothered him that they hadn't seen anything. No sign of any creatures. Not when he retrieved the grandmother, not when they moved over dark miles and frozen forest to the hospital. Was it luck they hadn't been spotted? Or were they being *allowed* to move, only to be fed into something yet to come?

But they had no choice. Kat was approaching her due date, from what he could tell, and he didn't want her C-section to turn into an emergency. He couldn't deal with a breech or fetal distress. The C-section, complicated as it was, seemed far easier by comparison. At least he'd be able to see what he was doing.

He scanned the cold cropland once more, then turned to the posse that had formed in his wake.

"All right," he said, mostly to himself. He stepped over to the horse, where Kat was hanging on limply, half being held up by the boy behind her. Her face was pale and drawn, her eyes sunken and yellowed with jaundice. "We're going need to move faster now. There's a quarter mile of open ground here. Lots of time to pick us off. If we get surrounded, it's done. Stay behind me, but if it goes down, you ride on. *Fast*. You hear me?"

She nodded faintly. But Sunday knew he was talking more to the boy, since he was the one who held the reins. When the boy nodded too, Sunday pulled out the Winchester and held it up to him.

"You know how to use this?"

The boy nodded and took the rifle, eyes wide as the child he was. Sunday worried the boy would skip the aim and just pull the trigger to hear it go pop.

Sunday then surveyed the others. The priest was checking his own rifle. He loaded a round, then closed his eyes and whispered something under his breath. A prayer, no doubt. The priest was old, and fat, a bear of a man, but he had made it this far. He could move if he needed to, and he knew well how to handle a weapon.

The junkie and the grandma, on the other hand, were slow. As they huddled together, hand in hand, Sunday wondered if their slowness would be what saved the rest of the pack. The thought was cold, and he hoped God wouldn't judge him for making use of the very system He had devised to feed the things of His creation that were hungry.

Satisfied, Sunday stepped from the cold forest and raised his rifle, the weapon one with his body, and gestured for the others to follow.

They darted low as voles, the ice beneath their feet a traitor, crackling a call that there was movement here and it should be noted. They crunched and slipped, and a quarter way across, Sunday turned and saw the others tight in tow, the horse trotting along smooth at his side, and hope trickled a warmth through the cold that they would—

There was movement from the edge of the field, no more than a hundred yards out, following them in a bank of low fog. Sunday squinted. It was a naked, bearded man, but his arms were bone-thin and his fingers abnormally long.

No.

The old man opened his mouth, and from all around him came the sound of a thousand crickets, and more shadows filled the fog.

"*Move!*" Sunday shouted, and they broke into a run as a group of screaming humans, and spider-humans, their femur bone-tips carved to six points to hold their weight and carry them fast across the frost, emerged from the fog. There were at least a dozen of them, and Sunday knew the hope dream was over, and they would be swallowed whole, and the baby inside Kat would be claimed.

He fired as they ran, the shots a hot carbine whip through the cold, and the rounds hit their marks, but the creatures did not slow. The priest and the boy on the horse also opened fire, with no greater success, and the creatures closed the gap, their legs skating smooth over the ice.

The grandmother tripped and fell. Sunday was ready to let her go to feed the beasts, as he had planned, but instead he thought better of his own judgment. He stopped and held ground, firing more rounds, as he helped her to her feet.

Kat and the boy were ahead now on the horse, and a spider-human was closing in on them. Sunday ran and fired, trying to cut it down, but it soared through the air and tackled the horse, and Kat and the boy were thrown to the ground.

Oh God.

Sunday fired again and again, trying to steal the creature's momentum as it clambered over the horse, puncturing the poor beast's flank with bone claws, moving toward its true prey.

Kat.

She lay face down in the snow, her body still. Next to her the boy was on his hands and knees, scrambling for the lost rifle, and he found it and spun the Winchester and steadied it into his small shoulder, and fired. He cocked and fired again. Cocked and fired. As the creature came closer, the boy's face was chiseled into a mute scream.

As Sunday closed the gap, the creature coming at them hissed with a dozen mouths, the mouths of the condemned, their faces merged and melted together. Every face screamed as the child fired, peppering their pale flesh with thirty-thirty.

Sunday, too, fired at the beast until the mag ran dry, then he popped and clicked fresh, the method muscle memory, and fired again until the creature toppled. Racing past the boy, he scooped Kat off the ground, the snow red with her blood, lifted her onto his shoulders, and fired at the other creatures closing in. There were still more now, racing over the snow, different from the spiders, these with four limbs that went up high and arched down, their bodies lower to the ground, and at either end of the torso was a man's head, so it could see in both directions.

"Move!" Sunday shouted to the boy. The others were up ahead, even the grandmother, as they had not slowed to fight, though the priest backpedaled, providing covering fire.

Sunday ran, the extra weight of Kat on his shoulders now sliding his boots in the snow, and he tumbled to one knee, and behind him he could hear them closing. The hospital was still a hundred yards out, the length of a football field, and he rose and ran some more, his breath fast and cold and catching in white fog in his wake. The boy had sprinted forward, leaving Sunday alone in the rear, and he realized he and she would now be the sacrifice made for the rest of the herd to survive. In a moment it would be over, and he wondered if he would truly die or if he would be owned by these things, forever part of their flesh, possessed by the dark shadow they had not seen.

Fifty yards. The priests' gunshots had ceased, as they all now simply ran toward doors they didn't even know would open. The fat priest, the boy, the junkie, and the old lady, with the dog racing well ahead of them all.

Sunday sprinted full-out, his heart a clanking blood rattle in his chest, and even with Kat on his shoulders he caught up to the others. He found the strength to run even harder, passing the old woman and the junkie, the woman he carried the only thing that mattered, and he would hold her high until the creatures had hacked away every last inch of him to get to her.

Crossing into a parking lot filled with dead cars, he slid behind one and turned and reclaimed the rifle to his shoulder with a single arm. He fired off more bursts as one of the spiders closed in behind the grandmother. The four-legged things, hell wolves, raced across the snow field, their entry late, but their speed much faster.

Then it dawned on Sunday.

Legs.

He fired lower, chewing up the spider-human's bent knee joint on its right side, spewing bone and sin-ew into the night. The creature toppled forward and slid in the snow, its joint shattered. It lurched and tried to lift, but toppled again on broken bone.

Sunday looked over to the priest, who had also tak-en cover behind an abandoned vehicle. Sweat poured down his pale face and he looked close to a heart at-tack, but he had resumed the rifle.

"Legs!" Sunday shouted.

The priest nodded and fired, and another of the spi-ders toppled, sliding across the snow.

The junkie and the grandmother passed this make-shift line of defense, and in unspoken agreement Sunday and the priest left their posts and raced with them to the building. They were at the back, which featured only a single metal door. The girl yanked at it, but it was locked.

"Try the front!" Sunday yelled.

The junkie grabbed her grandmother by the hand and dragged her toward the corner, but before they'd gone a few steps a rattling sounded from inside, a shake of chains, and the back door opened.

A dark-skinned bearded man stood inside. "Come!"

The junkie and the grandmother ran inside and the boy and the dog followed. Sunday and the priest retreated, firing the whole way, as the creatures crossed into the parking lot.

The bearded man slammed the door closed as soon as they were inside. The creatures banged against the metal from the other side with their bone appendages, but the man was almost casual as he rewrapped the chain, as if merely closing up shop for the day. He was dirty and shaggy and looked near homeless. His face was dried and cracked as if he'd spent a life on the streets, and his skin was darkened by grime and sun spots, but he wore silver rings on all his fingers.

He turned to them and smiled. "Well," he said, his voice deep and grainy. "That was fun."

CHAPTER XXIV

Old City, Philadelphia
July, 1968

Daniel Vicario had his first vision on the day he found out his father was dying. It was the same day he received the dream box.

He was twenty-three years old and in medical school when he got the call. Up until that point, life had been relatively predictable. He went to high school, played basketball, went off to Boston College, and was prepared to go into the family business: pediatric medicine.

His father didn't explain why he needed to come home, only that it was urgent. Daniel was knee-deep in his residency and hadn't been home in months, but he dropped everything and made the drive. Because this was his father, after all.

He'd worked hard to follow in his father's footsteps, because he loved his father. Not a lot of college-aged guys could say that about their dads. His father had a calm wisdom, a gentle understanding of all things, and a way of making even Daniel's failures feel okay. When a very young Daniel dropped a jug of milk all over his mother's cherished living room rug, his dad was ready with a towel to mop it up. When a teenaged Daniel mistakenly put diesel gas in the family car—a mistake that cost hundreds to fix—his father was there to help with a smile. There were no harsh words, no harmful hands. Only a father who was always there in his son's times of need.

It was funny how much those little moments shaped Daniel's view of his father. Not the time they went to the Grand Canyon, or down to Florida. Not the "big moments" that were supposed to be etched into his mind. It was his failures, and his father's reactions to those failures, that had made the greatest impact. Instead of being angry, or disappointed, his father had cared for him even more. That was what made Daniel want to be like his dad. That was what sent him to medical school.

But when he returned home that afternoon after the morning phone call, he was shocked at the man he saw. For the first time in Daniel's life, his father looked old. Tired. *Weak.*

"Hey," Dad said as he pulled him in for a hug. "I missed you."

"I missed you too," Daniel said.

They went into the kitchen, made some small talk, and caught up a little bit, and Daniel wondered what was so urgent as to bring him all the way home on a moment's notice.

Finally his father rose from his seat and opened the door to the basement. "I need to show you something," he said.

They walked down the stairs, Dad flicked the switch, and the tungsten sizzled to life. And Daniel was washed in a memory. Of model glue, and little model airplanes, and sawdust, and wooden bird nests, and the things they had built together down here among his father's prized collection of keys.

Daniel looked around the little room that had occupied so much of his father's time. At the rows of little wooden drawers that always reminded Daniel of the card catalog stacks at the public library.

The key collection had always been a strange hobby. Daniel had never understood the appeal. His mother certainly never got it, and perhaps that was part of why she'd moved back to Maine after Daniel left for school. But Daniel figured some dads played golf, some spent hours building model railroads, some left the family for a too-young blonde. And his own father? He collected ancient keys. If it made the old man happy, that was good enough for Daniel.

His father gestured for him to sit on a stool, then pulled up another stool across from him. "Daniel," he said. "There's something I need you to do."

"Sure, Dad. Whatever you need."

His father stood with a groan, walked over to his workbench, and slid over an old wooden toolbox. Daniel had grown up with those tools. In fact, the only time his father had ever really been cross with him was when he messed with those tools. "Don't touch my tools, Daniel!" Dad had said. "They can hurt you."

His father pulled a key from his pocket, slid it into the lock—he had kept his precious tools locked ever since Daniel's unfortunate intrusion into its inner sanctum—and turned the key with a little click. He opened the box, and pulled out another box, a wooden one about the size of a cigar case. Lifting it out as carefully as if it were a newborn, he sat again on his stool, setting the box gently on his lap. A worn wooden cross was burned into the wood.

"The box has a lead lining, to keep it from getting out," his dad said. He seemed almost to be talking to himself. "But it doesn't matter. Things always find a way to get out."

He opened the little box and very carefully pulled out an old key. Three thick prongs on one end, a half circle on the other end. It was coated in a fine layer of light green, giving it a hue like the Statue of Liberty.

"It's another key," Daniel said. *He called me all the way home to see another key? I just drove five hours.*

"Not another, Daniel. *The* key."

"Oh yeah? To what?"

"To God."

What? Daniel was speechless. Was the old man losing it?

"This key has been in our family for seven hundred years, Daniel. Passed down from father to son. Your grandfather, his father, his father before him. For as long as we have been here, this key is our reason for being."

Daniel looked dubiously at the key. Just another old key in a room full of old keys.

His father continued. "Back in the 1300s, one of your ancestors, a priest, came across this while tending to a dying man in Italy. He realized that what he'd found was very, very special. Here. Hold it." He extended the key forward on two open palms.

Daniel reached out and took the key. "Yeah. It's nice," he said. He tried to sound appreciative, while inside he was wondering if he needed to get his dad to a doctor, or if the old man was just so lonely he was looking for any excuse to spend time with his son. Perhaps Daniel had been away too long.

"Here," his dad said. "I want you to hold my hand."

What? Daniel hadn't held his father's hand since he was seven.

"Come on." His father smiled.

Holding the key in one hand, Daniel slowly held out the other. His father took it and squeezed. Daniel could feel his father's brittle bones within his grip.

"Dad is here. Say that."

"What?"

"Say what I just said."

"Dad is here," Daniel said.

"Good. Remember that now."

Then his father took the key from him, raised it in the air next to his head like he was selling it at an auction, and slammed it down hard against the metal corner of the workbench.

Daniel's ears rang and his eyes felt like they were shaking in their jelly. Colors swirled around him.

"Dad?"

"I'm here. Dad is here," he said, squeezing Daniel's hand again.

The center of the room opened like the petals of a flower, and colors and light fell into it, as if gravity had suddenly decided to prove itself once and for all in their basement.

As Daniel looked on, shocked, a bright light filled his eyes. Within the light he saw a man whose face was melting, changing constantly. Then a woman who did the same. He saw a gravestone, an open grave before it. The gravestone bore his father's name, but from within the pit he heard a wail. He peered into the darkness of the hole, and there, swaddled, was a baby lying on the muddy earth. He heard crickets, and then insects crawled over the baby until it was devoured by the swarm. The insects then burst forth from the pit with great force, and the swarm covered Daniel and crawled over him, and filled his screaming mouth.

Daniel was suddenly back in the basement, and a sudden burst of bright white light almost sent him falling backwards off the stool, but his father caught him.

"Dad? *Dad! I can't see!*" Daniel rubbed at his eyes.

"It's okay, son. It's okay. It will pass. Your eyes have been flash-burned."

"Oh my God! Oh my God! I can't see! What was that? What was it?"

His father pulled him into his arms and held him as Daniel wept tears from blind eyes. When his father spoke, it was a whisper in Daniel's ear.

"That was the vision of the Lord. And what you saw is what will soon take place."

CHAPTER XXV

Near Kamad El Laouz, Lebanon
Eleven Days After Event

Sunday lowered Kat from his shoulders and propped her against the wall.

"You all right?" he asked.

She nodded, but even as she did she clutched her belly, turned her head, and threw up all over the floor.

Sunday quickly turned to the bearded man. "Are you a doctor?"

"No," the man said, looking down at her puke. "The janitor."

"She needs a bed."

"This way."

The janitor led them up the stairs to the third floor and a locked metal door. He pulled a set of keys from his hip, jangled them in his hands, found the one he needed, and unlocked the door. They walked down a dark empty hall of the hospital, the floors splattered with dried blood.

"Is there anyone else here?" asked the priest as they passed an empty room.

"Just me. That door is the only way in, and I keep it locked. Elevators don't work, and there's only the one stairwell. Here," he said, stopping in front of an open doorway and gesturing to the room within. "Good as any."

Sunday led Kat into the room and helped her onto the bed. The dog followed and hopped up on a chair next to her before anyone else could claim it. Sunday stepped cautiously toward the window, which overlooked the parking lot. The creatures were still down there, flailing about in the darkness, banging against the door, trying to get in.

The janitor opened a cabinet, pulled out a gray blanket, and draped it over Kat. Sunday came back to her side, and she reached out to touch his hand. Her eyes were framed in dark circles.

"When you do it," she said. "Just you. No one else." Her voice drifted, her grip on his hand already fading. "Okay?"

"Okay."

Her eyes closed, and he stepped into the hall and gestured for the boy. The child came forward, rifle in hand.

"Watch her," Sunday said.

The boy went into the room, sat on the floor at the foot of the bed, and rested the Winchester on his lap. He looked like he was close to crying, but wouldn't. Perhaps he felt like the gun made him a man. And men with guns don't cry.

"How is she?" the priest asked Sunday.

Sunday didn't answer. He turned to the janitor. "Are there drugs on this floor? Sedatives?"

"That's all on the first floor, locked up."

"You have a key?"

"No."

Sunday turned to the girl and pulled the little wrapped baggie from his pocket. She looked at it with hungry eyes.

"Is it clean?" he asked.

She nodded. "I cut it myself."

He studied her, gauging if he could trust her. It didn't matter if he did; the blood clock in the other room was ticking. "Find clean syringes," he said to the others. "Bottled water. Lighter. Needle and thread. Lots of sponges and towels."

The junkie looked at him with eyes sunk and dark. "You know how to do it?"

He nodded.

"I can help," she said.

"No."

Down the hall the grandmother paced back and forth in front of a window. Now and then she would pause and tap the glass, as if trying to get something's attention in the parking lot below.

* * *

Twenty minutes later, Sunday assessed the stockpile he and the others had collected. They'd found plastic sealed scalpels, and needle and thread, and packets of alcohol wipes. In a security guard's drawer, they'd found a handful of yellow ChemLights, and he gave some to the priest and took the rest for himself so he could operate.

Kat was clammy and sweating on the bed, and in the tinted chemical light, her skin was mannequin white. Her round belly lifted and sank with straining breaths.

They all stood around the bed, the dog curled in the chair, and the priest lowered his head.

"Lord, we beg you to visit this dwelling, and to drive away from it all the enemy's wiles. Let your holy angels be appointed here to keep her and her offspring in peace, and let your blessing forever rest upon her. Save them, almighty God, and grant them your everlasting light; through Christ our Lord. Amen."

"Amen," Kat whispered weakly, the obligatory response of the trained, but this time Sunday suspected she meant it, because it might be her final prayer.

The others departed, but the boy lingered. She smiled at him, and he smiled back before leaving.

Sunday stepped into the hall and spoke to the priest. "Guard the door," he said. The priest nodded, and Sunday went back inside and closed the door, leaving him alone with his patient. Alone except for the dog.

"Can you lock it?" Kat asked.

"There's no lock." He took a wooden chair from a corner and scooted it up and under the door handle.

"Better?" he asked.

"Not really."

He nodded, but his options were limited, so he just checked the rifle again in the corner before looking down at her. She was too thin for a pregnant woman. Her cheeks had lost much of their weight, and she had dwindled the reserves of fat that had been designed to sustain her and the baby.

"Don't kill me," she said, her voice weak, a slight smile beneath the words.

"Yeah," he said as he checked again that he'd laid everything out that he would need, and that he'd be able to reach it quickly. His checklist was ticking off in his mind, and when he was satisfied with the position of the tools and the sponges and thread, he picked up the small baggie of heroin. He went to work prepping it, cooking the junk in a metal spoon. He didn't know how pure it was, he had to trust some junkie he didn't know, and he was worried he'd kill her as soon as he slid in the needle. But he readied what he thought was enough to put her out, yet not enough to kill her and the baby. Hopefully.

He tied off her arm and saw a ripe vein. He cleaned the spot with an alcohol wipe and readied the needle. Before he inserted it, he looked to her to say something, but he didn't know what.

She nodded. "I know."

He slipped the needle through her skin. He pulled back a bit on the plunger, checked if blood entered the barrel, and registered the hit. A moment later her body quivered and her eyes rolled back in her head and he knew she tasted it, and he felt guilty for tainting her, and perhaps the baby, with forbidden fruit that had been rotten all along.

When she was out, he lifted her gown and went to work wiping away the dried blood from between her legs. She was unshaven, so he used a razor to clean where he would have to make the incision.

He looked up at her. With the electricity gone, there was no equipment to tell him her pulse, no machine to alert him that she was crashing, so he watched her chest to ensure that her breathing was slow and regular as her belly moved up and down. Outside he could hear the wind howling, churning and alive, calling for him like the abyss of the ocean, or the cold of space, to come and be with it.

He prepped the blade and readied the incision. He'd practiced this in his mind dozens of times. Slicing through the skin, then cutting through the muscle enough so he could pull out the head. If the baby was breech, he'd have to try and right it from within her, and he would be fishing and feeling inside her in ways that he knew would make her sore, if she were ever to wake at all.

He positioned the scalpel over her skin and held it there a moment. He was scared; the blade quivered in his hand. He'd had some remedial medical training in Delta, but that was on grown men who'd been shot or injured in an explosion. He couldn't have fucked them up any more than they'd already been fucked. But here, if he were to screw up, he'd kill her. It would be all on him.

He looked to the dog, who merely rested his head on the chair and looked up with brown eyes as if to say, just get on with it.

Fuck it.

He took the scalpel and gently began to slice her open.

* * *

In the hallway, Father Simon, the boy, the janitor, the girl, and the grandmother waited. The grandmother continued her pacing, back and forth, back and forth. The janitor used an old greasy pocketknife to clean out some gunk from under his fingernails. The girl had curled up in the corner and was using her elbows to dig into her gut, which obviously ached from withdrawal.

Father Simon watched them all, wondering how this unlikely group had come to be together in this wretched place here at the end of all things.

"What happens when she has the baby?" the girl asked him. "Will that change things?"

"I don't know," he said.

"Change what?" asked the janitor as he continued to pick his nails.

"The baby is special," answered the priest, sure of himself, as he nodded toward the hospital room door. "Formed from the seed of Jesus Christ Himself. If there's any chance we have of stopping what's outside, it's in that room."

The janitor chuckled. "Well then, send the baby out to deal with those things."

"I don't get it," said the girl. "Why doesn't the devil come up here himself, just appear, and kill us all?"

The janitor found something black and plump beneath one of his nails and cast it aside. "Why didn't the devil use his power to kill Christ the first time? Push Him off the cliff instead of tempting Him in the desert? Or show up at the manger? Kill him then?"

"Because Christ was protected by God," Simon answered.

"Not so much in the end though, huh? No, because the devil *allows* the Christ, because Christ was also a man, and therefore part of him. What is the devil but the animal within? If he removes it, he destroys himself. The devil doesn't want to kill Jesus. The devil *is* Jesus."

Simon scoffed and looked the janitor up and down. The man's trousers were caked in dry mud, his hair wild and dirty. "Jesus overcame the devil, overpowered the serpent," the priest said. "Showed us how to cast the devil aside. And he shows us the path of righteousness."

"The path *I* see crawls with monsters."

"Not all are bad."

"It's in their blood. The serpent filled Eve. He was her fruit, and her descendants filled with it too. And because of it, we are more *his* children," the janitor said, pointing down, "than His," he said, pointing up.

"You sure seem to know a lot for a janitor," said the priest.

The man smiled, the insult noted. "You learn a lot from people's messes."

Father Simon adjusted his rifle, if only to remind the janitor that he held it. Something about this man was making him nervous.

"Relax, holy man. It wasn't the devil that killed Christ," the janitor said. "It was people. People like you. And you'll do it again."

"Why would we do that?" asked the girl.

"For the same reason the priest holds the gun. To survive, one must kill."

"That's right," said Father Simon. "I have killed. I killed those things out there, and during the war, I killed men. And right now, I'm wondering which you are."

The janitor smiled. A sly little curl of the lips as he closed his knife. "I'm the one here with you now. The one who let you in."

The man stood and dusted himself off—although the priest couldn't see why, as the dried mud would never come off—and walked over to the grandmother, who continued to pace and tap on the window. He leaned in and whispered something in her ear. And whatever he said, it hit home, because she turned sharply and looked him in the eyes. With a nod of understanding, she sat down in an orange chair as if waiting for a bus.

The janitor whistled as he moved farther down the corridor, the song known to them all. When he reached the last verse, he filled it in with lyrics.

"Row, row, row your boat, gently down the stream. Merrily, merrily, merrily, life is but a scream."

And it was obvious to the priest, then, that this man... was no man.

CHAPTER XXVI

Deep Run, Maryland
Six Days After Event

Eve McAllister had read through all her father's notes and the analysts' reports, and now she was left with a hard truth. That this cold, dark bunker, prepped so meticulously for her, would soon fail. She was a little mouse in a box, buried in the snow, with a dead man who occasionally tapped against the outside door to remind her that her clock was ticking, that the darkness would come for her one way or the other.

She was running out of light. Every time she snapped a glowstick, she used up just a little more of the precious light she had left. She'd tried to get on a twelve-hour sleep/wake cycle, to be in sync with the twelve-hour usage time for each stick, but she found herself waking and lying in the darkness for what felt like hours.

It was also cold. Freezing. There was a heating system, but without the generator, it was useless. She wore lots of layers, waddling around like the Michelin man, filling the bunker with the ghostly contrails of her own breath.

Now she sat in the swivel chair at the desk, a half-eaten can of tuna fish beside her, re-reading some notes from her father and a CIA analyst named Lincoln Pierce. Since her bunker stay included homework, she'd dedicated herself to it, learning everything her father had left her about the "Gospel of Mary" and how that had led the world to its current state. How it had taken a CIA team to Jordan, in search of the body of Jesus Christ, where they were attacked and killed. She learned about what was found there, and about Josef Belac's plan to impregnate women with the DNA of Christ.

And she learned that there was a second page of that gospel.

If the first page had contained Christ's instructions, then the second listed His safety warnings:

"The Savior spoke then in sadness of what was to come next. 'A great darkness shall be loosed upon the Earth that will hollow the hearts of men and wear them as its flesh. Men will wander a new wilderness, hunted by beasts they once called kin. And as in the time of Herod, they shall hunt me.

'I have trusted you with the key to my resurrection as I have trusted the Keys of the Kingdom of Heaven, the Key of David, to the first and last disciples, and when held by one pure in the Holy Spirit, only then can you unbind the Gate to God.

'Without it, the Synagogue of Satan shall destroy me, and us all.'

When done, the Savior..."

Eve finally understood why her father had feared the end of the world was inevitable. Why he'd started prepping. He'd seen a man bring his daughter back from the dead. What does that do to one's belief about what's possible? When a man seems to have the power of a god?

Her father had done all this, had prepared this bunker for them, for her, had taken seriously the possibility that this man Belac, who could defy death and bring back his dead daughter, could also truly conjure the Christ and the end of days.

She put the pages she was reading back into the folder and set it on the desk. Enough homework for now.

But really, what else was there to do? Most of the board games in the bunker were for two players or more, so she was stuck with Solitaire. She wondered how many games of Solitaire she could play down here, stacking cards under a fading red chemical light, before she was absorbed into the darkness forever.

She adjusted the blanket around her shoulders, picked up her can of tuna fish, the little plastic spoon a mockery of civilized cutlery, and swallowed a fishy scoop. There was no life for her here. Not like her father had planned. And not for long. Soon, she was going to have to try to make it on her own on the outside.

She wondered if her father's instructions on how to retrieve the Keys of the Kingdom were legit… or he had been trying to fight something that had already won.

CHAPTER XXVII

Old City, Philadelphia
Four Days Before Event

Lincoln Pierce parked in front of the white twin house in what was, for America, a very old neighborhood. It had been built in the 1770s, and ever since, it had been in the same family's name. Lincoln stepped up the narrow walkway, past the bordered hedge of gardenias, and knocked on the door.

There was no answer.

Lincoln waited, then knocked again.

"Coming," called a weak voice from within.

There was some fumbling, perhaps a struggle with the lock, and then the door opened, and there sat a bone-thin man in a wheelchair. He had large watery eyes, wispy strands of gray hair against an overly large forehead, and skin the color of old parchment. He smelled of Vicks VapoRub.

"Dr. Vicario?" Lincoln said.

"Yes."

"I'm Lincoln Pierce. Dr. Graham at Penn told you I was coming?"

"Yes, yes. Please come in."

Dr. Vicario turned the wheelchair around and spoke as he wheeled away. "Close the door, will you?"

The house was old. Wooden floors, white paneled walls. The old man led Lincoln to a door beneath the stairs and tapped on it. "You can go down through here," he said. "I have to take the chair lift."

He slid open another door—a black metal bi-fold door—revealing a small compartment. He turned the chair and rolled in backwards, closed the gate, and pushed a button. With a low whine, the elevator descended.

Lincoln opened the first door, which led to a narrow stairwell down to the basement. Arriving at the bottom before the old man did, he waited patiently in a room stacked floor to ceiling with little wooden box drawers.

The elevator landed, the gate opened, and Dr. Vicario rolled out.

"Well, this it," he said.

"Curious thing to collect," said Lincoln as he looked around.

"Yes. Hardly exhibition ready. I suppose I should have at least pulled some of my best pieces. Put them on display for you."

"How many keys do you have?"

"Seven hundred seventy-eight."

"Wow." Lincoln moved toward a little wooden drawer he'd chosen at random. It was marked with the number 242 stenciled on a placard. He gestured with his finger, asking if he could open it.

Vicario nodded. "Be my guest."

Lincoln slid the drawer open to reveal a bronze key with a smooth coat of green upon it. It ended in almost a heart shape with a circle tip. "Very nice," he said.

"That's a rotary key, bimetallic, with the iron still intact."

Lincoln nodded and smiled. Three months earlier he would have had no idea what that meant. But now, he appreciated what the doctor had said and the primitive craftsmanship of what he held in his hands. "Dr. Graham says you're the museum's expert on keys. That you even wrote the descriptions for the handbook on their exhibit on ancient keys and locks."

"Well, yes. It made sense. Most of the exhibit was my collection."

"How did you get all these? It must have cost you a fortune."

"Not really. Keys kind of slip through the cracks. No restrictions on importing or exporting. I do have records of provenance though, if you need to see them."

"I'm not here for that."

"Why don't you tell me why you are here?"

"I'm looking for a particular key."

"Oh? Which one?" the doctor said. He spun his chair again, this time already bound for something.

Lincoln leaned against a dinged metal workbench with a lamp, where he imagined the doctor got his little keys shipped to him and then opened the little brown packages as giddy as a child on Christmas morning.

"Doc, are you a religious man?"

Dr. Vicario nodded, but he didn't really seem to be paying attention to the question.

"Would you say you're a man of God?" Lincoln continued.

"Yes, I would."

"Good. Because I need someone with that kind of mind. Someone who can help me track down keys that might have been in Christ's possession."

Lincoln gauged the doctor's reaction. All he got were those wide-gray eyes looking up at him. So he continued.

"Keys of the Kingdom. Key of David. Are you familiar with those phrases in the Bible?"

"I am."

"Good. I'm looking for some kind of key that could represent that. Some key that looks religious, perhaps. Symbolic of the early Christian church. Have you ever seen a key that might fit that description?"

The little doctor shifted back and forth in his wheelchair as if he were loading the answer.

"May I ask why the CIA is interested in something like that?" he said at last. "Seems such an unimportant focus these days, wouldn't you say? Given all the terrible things going on out there."

"I agree, Doc." Then Lincoln lied. "But we've come across some references to the key in some communications involving the terrorist group Al Taresh. So we're trying to track down why that group would be interested in such a key."

The doctor nodded and slowly rolled over to the workbench. Lincoln scooted out of his way. On the floor next to the bench was a toolbox. The doctor leaned down and lifted it, groaning as he did, and for a second it looked like the box would win—but then he managed to set the toolbox on his lap. He fished in his pocket for a set of keys. They jangled as he slid one into the lock and opened the toolbox.

"There *is* a key, Mr. Pierce, one most special to me, that fits your description."

Lincoln perked up. "That's great!" All he needed was something "close enough," "religious enough," so he could take a picture and send it on to Ferguson and then maybe he'd be free of keys once and for all. Because really, how would Ferguson know if there was any merit to a key or not? He wouldn't even know what century it came from. And frankly, Lincoln was ready for his goddamn promotion now.

The doctor pulled a little wooden box from the toolbox, returned the toolbox to the floor, and cradled the smaller box in his lap.

"I call this my dream box."

Slowly, carefully, he opened the little wooden box and took out a key, which he held in his palm. It appeared heavier, thicker than the ones Lincoln had studied. But there wasn't anything... special about it. No cross, or ichthys, or Chi Rho. No monograms. It was just a key. Three prongs on one end, a half circle on the other. It was coated in a fine layer of copper hydroxycarbonate, a greenish patina that gave it a hue like an old penny.

Lincoln was disappointed. He doubted this key would be enough to convince Master Tom.

"This key was my first," said Dr. Vicario. "Given to me by my father. His father before him, and so on. Funny thing about this key: it's a first-century design, but it is most certainly not first century."

"What do you mean?"

"Years ago, I took it to a friend of mine at the physics lab at Penn for radiocarbon dating. Just to see," he explained. "The results were inconclusive."

"Inconclusive?" asked Lincoln. *Then why tell me?*

"Yes. The date was beyond fifty thousand years. Past the point of being useful."

"Doctor..." Lincoln began. "Forgive me, but that's impossible. It's metal, yes? We weren't making metal fifty thousand years ago."

"No, we weren't. When those results came back, my friend was concerned there was something wrong with the mass spectrometer. But he tested several other objects, all with known dates, and the machine was accurate. Then he re-tested this key. Same results."

Lincoln looked down at the key again. He'd seen so many keys over the last few months that he had—reluctantly—grown to appreciate their artistry. The hand-carved head of a hound. The bent-hook simplicity of an iron latch lifter. Even the beauty of a ring key with small carved hands grasping each other on the surface, symbolizing the unity of the household. They all reflected the eye of the one who crafted them.

But this key had none of those features. It was just a plain, greenish key.

Indiana Jones came to mind again. *That's the cup of a carpenter.*

"Doctor Vicario, if we can't even ascertain its age, what makes you think this key has any association with the early Christian church?"

"It's not the key itself that makes me believe that. Though it does have some very interesting features.

Take the green hue for instance. It isn't patina. Put the key in vinegar, and it doesn't come off. It's a chemical added to the metal. It's been colored to make it *look* old."

"They weren't mixing chemicals in the first century."

"That's right. And the metal is an alloy. The closest thing we have to this now is something called a high-entropy metal alloy. If we were ever able to build a nuclear fusion reactor, that's the metal we would use to build the inner structure."

"Doctor... come on."

Dr. Vicario smiled. "I'm just telling you what my friend at the lab said when I brought him the key. He said this is a key made from a process we only discovered a few years ago. Before that, this kind of metal, this combination of elements, could only be formed in the hearts of dying stars."

Lincoln leaned back against the workbench and sized up the man in the wheelchair. "Doc, look... I'm not here to buy it. You can save the sideshow stories. Just tell me why you think this key is associated with early Christians."

"I can do better than that. I can show you." The little doctor rolled over to a desk stacked with papers. As he scooted his mouse back and forth and jarred the computer on his desk back to life, he explained. "After the radiocarbon testing failed, my friend wanted to move to an ultrasound test, to determine the strength of the metal. Look for imperfections. We videotaped it. Ah, here it is."

He clicked on a file named *Key Test 3-7*, and a video began to play. Lincoln moved closer to the monitor and hovered over the doctor's shoulder.

The lab in the video looked more like the back of a welding shop. This was where they tested hard science, not beakers and test tubes. Dr. Vicario was there, along with an older man with a gray mustache and dark-rimmed glasses. His scientist friend, apparently. The scientist set the key on a red velvet pad, then sat in front of it and pulled over a piece of equipment that looked like an ohmmeter an electrician might use to test which wire is hot. Dr. Vicario stood behind him, watching him work. Whenever this video was taken, he wasn't yet in a wheelchair.

The scientist placed what looked like a stethoscope on top of the key, like he was about to listen to its heartbeat. He turned a knob on the device, and the video flickered.

Lincoln watched as the key on the velvet pad began to vibrate like a tuning fork, with increasing intensity, until it glowed. First red, then white. There was a bright flash, and the colors of the video fluctuated and rippled, then another flash, and the video flickered again, all the colors shifting to shades of red. The two men in the video froze in place, then slowly faded from sight as if they'd never really been there at all.

Lincoln looked to Dr. Vicario. "What is this? What happened?"

"Keep watching," he said.

Lincoln watched the video of the red-tinted, empty lab. After a few moments, there was another flash of blinding white light, so bright he had to squint at the computer screen. Color returned to the video, and the two scientists were there again, right where they had been to begin with.

Except that Dr. Vicario's scientist friend was now slumped back in his chair, his mouth and eyes wide open, unmoving.

Dr. Vicario opened his eyes, looked down at his friend, and then nudged him. The older man didn't move. The doctor nodded and whispered something in his friend's ear, then reached forward and closed his open eyes.

Sparing one more glance at the key, now sitting quietly on its velvet pad, he walked over to the camera, and the video ended.

Lincoln looked down at the doctor in his wheel-chair. "What the hell was that?"

The doctor smiled. "Certainly not that. Jerome's heart was bad. It was his time. For some, the vision can be too much." He smiled again. This one was almost malicious. "Would you like to see it?"

Lincoln was suddenly unsettled by the crippled doctor in the wheelchair with the curious key collection in his basement.

"I can show you," the doctor said.

"Show me what?" Lincoln asked, distantly realizing he was slowly backing away from this little old man.

The doctor picked up the key with his thin bony hand. "This is not a Roman key. It's not Hebrew. Or Greek. Or Egyptian. Or Babylonian. This key is not human. It was made by something... more. And Lincoln

Pierce, it has shown me *you*... long before you ever knocked on my door."

"What are you talking about?"

"I have seen your envy, Lincoln. Seen you plotting inside your heart. You have been selfish."

"What?"

"Take my hand."

Lincoln froze. "Doctor—"

"Take it," he said, extending his bony fingers.

"Are you crazy?"

The doctor smiled once more. "No." And with that he banged the key hard against the metal workbench. The key vibrated in his hand, and as Lincoln watched, it felt like his pupils were shaking in their skull beds, quivering like an astronaut on return entry.

That was when Lincoln said the most profound words he'd ever say.

"I can see it."

CHAPTER XXVIII

Near Kamad El Laouz, Lebanon
Eleven Days After Event

John Sunday sliced the skin away easily enough. Beneath it was a layer of fat, chunky as curd. Then he went to work on the muscle, striated and marbled with more yellowy fat, and he tugged gently to separate the dark red cords. She groaned slightly, and he worried the tugging would rouse her. Her chest moved up and down, and he worried about the dose and that she'd seize or convulse on the table or wake halfway through and stare down at her open gut. The dog snored lightly in the corner, and he tried to make its breathing the slow metronome to his nervous heart.

As he cut, he had still more concerns. Like nicking her bladder in his race to get to the uterus tucked behind. If he did that, he'd have to stitch it up as well. Or God forbid if he didn't *know* he'd nicked it, he'd stitch her back up and a week later she'd be dead from infection.

The medical book he had read had told him that given modern incision size, the surgeon wouldn't see much and would have to feel their way around. But

Sunday couldn't rely on feel; the risk was too great, his fingers unfamiliar. So he made a longer incision to see what he was doing.

He was pretty sure he saw her bladder resting there like a glossy, red pearl. Pretty sure because the book only had diagrams and drawings, not real photographs. But when he saw her uterus, he was sure. It was a darker pink, like overly ripe fruit, right where it was supposed to be.

He replayed in his mind the cut he'd need to make. A smile-shaped slice, or U-incision. Though he'd practiced this mentally, he wasn't sure exactly where to start the points and exactly how big to make the cut. He gauged it would be roughly the size of the baby's head, so he decided the cut should be roughly bigger than the size of his own fist. He hesitated a second, then made the incision, a smile marked upon her by him, as if he were carving his initials into her tree.

He slowly saw dark wet brown within, and he gasped when he realized it was the baby's head. It moved a bit, saying it was here and ready. He reached in gently, and at the same time pushed down upon her belly, a hard, milking push.

"Come on," he said.

He pushed some more, gentle yet firm, and the baby squeezed through the opening and he caught it like a fleshy ball and it was curled and small and slightly blue and fetal in his hands.

Sunday quickly clamped the cord at two points. Then he grabbed the scissors from the tray near the bed and moved to cut the umbilical. Through the metal of the scissors, he felt the strength of the cord, the pulse of flow from mother to child, and when he snipped it, a part of him felt sad that he had, because that is a link that can never be returned.

He placed the baby on a padded cart, wiped away the vernix, and used a bulb to suction out the mouth and nostrils. The infant took a breath, the first of the air of the new world, and cried. And John Sunday looked down, and was surprised, because...

Because the child was beautiful.

* * *

Father Simon heard the wind howling outside, and the unseen things scrambling about, and he wondered when they would find a way into the hospital and kill them all. The janitor had disappeared, and the priest wondered about him too—when he would return, and with whom.

Then he heard it. A baby's cry from within the room. And Simon smiled, and looked to the girl, and despite the obvious pain in her gut, she echoed his grin.

* * *

The old woman in the plastic orange chair turned her head as well. The sound of the baby had rattled something loose, and she saw a light in her mind, and she remembered who she was, and she was here again in the world she had lost.

She tried to speak, to call out to her granddaughter, because she just wanted to hold her and feel her, but then it came back over her. The shroud.

Movement caught her eye, scurrying in a shadowed corner. She rose to her feet and walked toward it, searching, and there it was, on the floor, a little baby crawling down the hall. Its little face was hidden in the shadows, but she heard it crying and she wanted to pick it up and comfort it.

She followed the baby farther than she realized, and when she looked back down the hall, toward her granddaughter and the priest and the boy, it was as if she looked down an impossibly long tunnel. She called for them to come and see, but the words could not escape her mouth and all that she heard was silence.

It was then she realized she was back on the shore, and her mind was one with it again. She was afraid, because she knew it had claimed her, and she was theirs again.

She watched the baby crawl into a hospital room. Room 333. She did not want to go inside. She did not want to see any more. She knew that what lurked on the other side of that door was darkness itself.

But it didn't matter what she thought. Because she was not the one making the decisions.

* * *

Sami looked away from the priest's smile and toward her grandmother to see her reaction to the infant's cry. But her grandmother was gone.

Sami stood suddenly, despite the pain in her belly.

"Grandma?" she called into the darkness.

There was no reply.

The priest searched as well, then reached into his pocket and snapped one of the glowsticks, painting the hallway in yellow shadows. With the light, Sami could see the corridor was empty and her grandmother was gone.

"Grandma!" she shouted again. The boy, too, rose to his feet, and picked up the gun, and was ready.

The priest looked to the boy. "Stay here," he said. "Guard the door."

The boy nodded.

* * *

Father Simon adjusted his rifle and moved slowly down the hall, the yellow light illuminating the corridor but casting shadows that looked like distorted people. And they were dancing.

He moved to the door closest to the chair where the old woman had been sitting. The placard on the door read *Room 333*. He reached out slowly and turned the knob.

Nothing but an empty bed.

He was thorough, clearing the room with the rifle before stepping back into the hall and moving on.

The next door, Room 335, was also closed. He opened it. And saw what he would never have expected to see.

The church. And not any church. The Church of the Holiest Savior in Warsaw. This was where he had been sent after the Lebanese Civil War, after he'd quit being a soldier, after he'd studied at the Holy Spirit University of Kaslik, after seminary school. It was where he was sent to become a priest, to become a man of God, to repent for his sins from the war, and to preach the word. And it was cold, and hard, and somehow beautiful, like most of Cold War Europe.

As he stepped forward, his mind shifted, and he was walking down the marble aisle, his shoes tapping out an echo in the empty church, the chandeliers above producing a low, hallowed glow. He was closing for the night, checking the pews to make sure no one had left anything behind, and then he went to the back of the church to get the last box of old hymnals to take to the basement.

As he descended the narrow back stairs and navigated the dim corridor, he heard it.

A little whimper.

At first he thought a kitten had somehow gotten down here, and he wondered how that could be, and so he searched for it in hopes he could rescue it. He traced the sound to a door, and he opened the door to a room lit by a single hanging bulb, dim to the point of uselessness, and when his eyes adjusted to the lower light, he saw that the whimper had not come from a kitten, but from a boy. A naked boy, no more than fourteen, gagged and tied with leather straps to a bed. The sheets were bloody, and on the table next to the bed was a crucifix, and it too was bloody.

He moved to the child to unbind him, and as he started to loosen the straps he heard a man at the door.

"Leave him!"

Simon was frightened by the sudden voice. He turned, and in the dim light, he could barely make out who was at the door. But he knew this man.

"Father Zula?" said Simon. "What is this?"

"What does it look like?"

Simon looked down at the child. There were dark circles under his eyes, his skin was pasty white, his ribs protruded from his little chest.

"I don't know."

"That boy is possessed, Deacon. Unhand his straps. His parents have brought him to me, to clear the devil from him."

Simon looked down again. *This boy?*

"How is this child possessed, Father?"

"How?" Father Zula stepped into the low-lit room. He stepped past the priest as if he weren't really there, and stopped close to the boy, judging him as he spoke. "His parents tell me he has become aroused around other boys in the locker room. He masturbates to pictures of men from the weekly sales catalog."

"And this, this is the devil's work?" asked Simon.

"What would you call it?" Zula asked. He seemed perturbed by this questioning of his judgment. In the dim light, shadows filled in the craters of his pockmarked face. "This is not pretty work," he said, "but it must be done. To save this poor filthy wretch. Now leave us."

Simon stood, unmoving.

"I said *leave!*" And this time Father Zula's voice seemed impossibly deep. He shoved Simon out into the hall and slammed the door behind him.

Simon stood there. He opened his mouth to say something, but he could not speak. From his throat came a gag and a choked whine, but no words.

On the other side of the door he heard Zula speaking to the boy, followed by the muffled sound of the child sobbing and pleading beneath his gag. And as Simon raised his fist to bang on the door, he was back in the hospital and it was dark again.

He stood in an empty room. Room 335. He knew then that something had just crawled inside his mind—burrowed in deep to show him the sin from which he could not hide. Even his flight to become a man of God could not cover the secret he had kept. Because no word or testament could ever acquit a heart that shields the light so darkness can be born.

Then he heard it. A voice. One that cleared all his thoughts and spoke without words, but that showed him what he must do to wipe the slate clean. And then he would be rejected from this place and perhaps collected by another.

Perhaps.

* * *

Sami and the boy stared down the hallway for what felt like a very long time. The boy looked like he wanted to call out to the priest, but as always, he said nothing. Sami did shout though, and then her body doubled over in pain and she felt the sudden need to vomit, although she'd eaten so little she wasn't sure if anything would come up.

She wanted to run down the dark hall and find her grandmother and turn the lights on, and have it all be back to normal.

"Something's wrong," she said to the boy. "Something's here. With us. It's splitting us up. We have to stay together, okay?"

The boy's eyes were wide, and he looked panicked. Perhaps he felt it too. That there was something else with them, and it needed no weapon or gun, because it held its sway with particles and time, and all the forces of the universe that men adhere to fell under its command.

Sami debated whether she should take the gun from the boy, but the boy had proven his worth with it, and she'd never shot one before.

"Do you have another light?" she asked.

The boy shook his head.

She banged on the door of the room where the one-eyed man and the pregnant woman were. "Open the door!" she cried. "There's something out here!"

She banged louder, but the door did not open.

"Do you hear me?! *Open the door!*"

* * *

A few moments after she'd given birth, and with the baby crying on the cart next to him, Sunday moved back to her. He grabbed hold of the umbilical that hung from the slit he'd made in her belly, and gave it a gentle tug, pulling it like a fishing line, until the placenta fell out of her and he used a small metal bowl to catch it. He used sponges to sop up the blood, tossing the used ones onto the floor, but she continued bleeding. He worried he had done something wrong, because she just kept on bleeding.

He began to panic, because he was running out of sponges. He raised the light closer to the opening and searched for the source of the bleeding. He was amazed that he saw it there, a small tear in a vein near the uterus. He hadn't sliced it, he didn't think, but it was there nonetheless, the vein thick and red, a ruptured pipe inside her.

From outside the door, he heard what he thought was a voice. He hesitated, listening harder, wondering if he needed to grab the rifle instead of the needle and thread.

The dog woke and raised its head.

"Everything okay?" Sunday shouted toward the hall.

There was no response, and he started for the rifle. But then the priest spoke from outside the door.

"Yeah," the priest said. "It's okay. Keep going."

Sunday settled back over her and clamped one end of the vein again to stem the bleeding, then grabbed the needle and thread. He was worried he wouldn't be able to stitch such a small thing; he had only been planning on the big stitches for the big openings, not this single throbbing little vein that continued to fill her with blood. But he went to work, suturing, threading around it as she pulsed. The ChemLight threw him off by casting strange shadows, as did working with only one good eye. The pooling blood filled the hole, and his fingers were fat and clumsy.

Eventually he tied the thread around a hook and brought the hook around the vein, and then made a basic square knot, and pulled it tight to tie off the vein. He did it again, for extra measure. And then the moment of truth. He released the clamp on the vein, to see if it would continue to dump blood.

It held.

And in his mind, he said, *Thank God.*

* * *

Sami and the child banged upon the door, but there was no answer. The boy was looking to her the way her little brother had once looked to her: for direction and compass. She wasn't capable of providing either.

She felt the surge in her gut again, and this time she turned and ran and vomited violently in the darkness of the hall. The boy started toward her, but she waved him back that it was okay, and she closed her eyes a moment to regain herself, and when she opened them again, he was gone.

She searched the hallway for him, but the little mute boy was not there.

And she knew.

She had not been an educated woman. She had grown up on the streets, and her knowledge of math and science had not gone past the fifth grade. But that was more education than some. She had some lessons about the stars, and how some of the universe worked, and with that knowledge she had tried to dismiss the magic of her people, who often used card reading and superstition and fortune-telling to make their money and to explain that which cannot be, even to the educated.

Now, however, here alone... she thought her education had been wrong and her people had been right. There *was* magic, and it was real, despite what her books had told her in elementary school. It existed, and man simply didn't know it yet, because his books were too young.

She moved down the hall, into a darkness that draped over her, searching for anyone who could hear her.

* * *

The boy was worried when he saw the older girl vomiting. He wanted to help, for she had been kind to him, and he moved toward her.

She waved him back. He understood that too. He turned away to give her dignity.

As he did, he saw someone walking down the hallway toward him. The figure radiated a yellow hue, and the boy thought it was the priest returning with the light stick.

It was not the priest.

The boy could only see the hand holding the light, but the knuckles and fingers were cracked and chapped with streaks of mud. That hand was wrong, and the shadow attached to it, though he could not see it, was worse. Far worse.

The boy turned to warn the girl, but she was gone. Her puke was still there on the floor, but she had vanished.

He turned back to face the creeping light. He so wanted a voice, to tell this thing to get back. To go away! But the only sound that came from his lips was a stern exhale, a panicked gasp. He searched beyond the yellow orb of light. He should have been able to see something there, something attached to that hand, but there was nothing. Only that unnatural darkness. Ominous. Wrong.

He felt a warm trickle of urine down his leg as the light moved closer. He realized then that some light was bad and he wanted to run, run away from it, but fear held him there, and he resigned himself to this collector and hoped that somewhere deep within it would understand his fear, and therefore take pity, and not hurt him too badly.

Turning his head, not wanting to see the shadow that approached, he realized someone was standing beside him.

His mother.

Her body was clean and free of marks, and she said his name, and he heard it clear in his head, even though her lips had not moved. She reached out, her wrists free of harm, and stroked his cheek.

And then behind him the light grew brighter, and he turned, and the collector that was nothing but shadow was holding the boy's little brother. The booties of his monkey pajamas were caked in mud, and the boy wondered if any of this was real.

His mother spoke to him again in his mind. She told him what he must do to free them from their suffering. And then she reached out to him and gathered him in her arms. He could not resist her, because she was as she had been, and her smell and the softness of her skin felt like home.

She clutched him tightly. Too tight. He tried to pull away from her, but he could not.

She spoke in his mind with a voice that was not hers. It was dark. And it owned him.

Whatever held him was not his mother, though he so wished it was. And he knew that for it to be so, and for their pain to end, he must do as the voice said.

* * *

Sami stopped at a door and stepped inside. On the bed lay her grandmother. The old woman was rolled on her side, her back to her granddaughter.

"Grandma?" Sami called.

She moved around the bed and saw them. Her grandmother hunched over, her old, shriveled tit hanging out, and a suckling infant in her arms. But the baby was wrong. It was pale, and its face was stretched and its mouth born into a twisted scream. It was one of the things from outside, but small, merged together, its little bone fingers kneading at her grandmother.

"Grandma?"

Her grandmother looked up at her and smiled.

"Shhhh," she said.

The whispers came then, all around Sami in the darkness. They were talking about her. About her sins. About who she was and what she'd done. Sami turned to leave, but there was no door. She fell to her knees and wept, tears she could not hold back.

Her grandmother stood, gently carried the baby over to the hospital bassinet, and lowered the baby into it. Then she stepped toward her granddaughter, exposed, her top still down, and kneeled.

Sami shrank back from her.

"Shhhh," her grandmother said. "It's okay, Sami." She reached out and stroked her granddaughter's hair, and though Sami pulled away, she felt the ice-cold hand on the side of her face.

In the bassinet, the baby made a strange gargling sound.

"Sami," said the grandmother. "Get the baby."

Sami looked at her grandmother and shook her head.

"Sami…" The old woman's voice was firm. "Bring me the baby."

"No!" Sami wept and curled into a ball.

Her grandmother hovered over her, threatening. *"Bring me the baby!"*

Sami closed her eyes and screamed for it all to go away.

The voice that came next was only in her mind, and Sami understood that they held her grandmother, and that there would be no escape for any of them.

And then she was back in the hallway and the soft yellow hue of a glowstick came drifting down the hall, and she knew not if this was dream or reality, or if there was any longer a difference between the two. And from the darkness the priest emerged, and at his side was her grandmother, and beside her was the boy, as if he had just suddenly appeared, because she could have sworn he was not there a second ago.

"Grandma?"

Her grandmother nodded, but she looked frightened, as if unsure of where she was, or perhaps who she was.

They came together as a group, and she wondered if each had taken a journey through the darkness alone.

A cry sounded from the hospital room where the one-eyed man and the pregnant woman still sheltered. The baby. It cried for reasons she could not know, but she felt that, perhaps, the infant wept for all of them.

CHAPTER XXIX

Tel Aviv, Israel
Day of Event

The soldier who had been shot topside with two tranquilizer darts in the neck was named Alexander Kaminski. He was twenty-six years old, had a wife and a newborn daughter, and was a first lieutenant well on his way to captain. He was career military. He had lost his teenage sister at the hands of a Palestinian with a pipe bomb at a bus stop six years earlier in Herzliya, and that was a motivation that could not be taught.

As Dr. Geller watched over him though, it was obvious that most of who Alexander Kaminski was, or had been, was no more.

The sedatives had begun to wear off, and Alexander's eyes fluttered. Dr. Geller eyed the leather restraints to make sure the patient was indeed bound to the gurney, then looked to the two armed soldiers who were in the room for his protection.

No one knew what Alexander would do when he woke.

What he did... was scream. And not a sudden short burst triggered by a nightmare. This was long and sustained, the scream of a man in sheer terror. And it scared Dr. Geller and the two soldiers too, because none of them had ever heard a man scream like that.

Geller moved closer to the man strapped to the table, the soldiers following, hesitantly. "Lieutenant," the doctor said, trying to be calm. "Lieutenant!" he said again, louder, to pierce the screaming. "Kaminski!"

Alexander's eyes rolled back down from the recesses of his skull, and his pupils dilated in the light. His scream finally, mercifully, ended in a sobbing wail of incomprehensible pleading, a slurred mixture of words.

"You're safe," the doctor said.

Of course, Geller had no idea if that was true. He was a doctor of internal medicine; he had no expertise here. No more knowledge than anyone else in this room. Or in this bunker. His dabblings in physics and cosmology, and his faith as a Jew, were probably more relevant than his medical training, and even they could provide him no answers.

Another minute, and Alexander inhaled sharply and desperately, as if he'd just surfaced from underwater. And for the first time he spoke in words that could be understood.

"Please!" he cried. "Please don't let them get me!"

"Shhhh," said the doctor. "It's all right. No one is here. It's just us."

"Noooo, it's not." Alexander wept, the snot and tears blending until his entire face was damp.

"Lieutenant. Alexander. What happened? What's happening outside?"

The man sobbed some more and made a kind of low, mumbling whine. "Please get them out. It hurts so much." He squirmed against the restraints like he was being skinned. His body was rigid and white, his fingers curled so tightly the doctor wondered if he was going to go into cardiac arrest.

"Who? Who is in you?"

"Forgive me. I'm so sorry," he said through gritted teeth.

"Alexander, who's here? Where did they come from?"

"The. Cave."

"What cave? Where?"

"Banias…"

The lieutenant stopped, his eyes going even wider than before. He seemed to see something in the room beyond the doctor's shoulder. Dr. Geller turned to look, but saw nothing. Then Alexander opened his mouth to scream once more, but all that came out was a strained rasp. Within his restraints he convulsed and seized, the veins in his neck concrete, and a stench filled the room as he soiled himself.

Geller grabbed a syringe from a tray, readied it, and plunged the needle into his patient's arm. After a moment, Alexander Kaminski's convulsions slowed, and he collapsed back onto the bed.

Dr. Geller could only hope the sedative had momentarily freed the man from the horrors he was experiencing… rather than sending him deeper into the terrifying hallucination that now claimed his mind.

CHAPTER XXX

Philadelphia, Pennsylvania
Three Days Before Event

"Who's there?" Lincoln called from his hospital bed.

"It's Tom Ferguson."

Lincoln Pierce couldn't see his visitor; his eyes were covered in thick white gauze bandages. But he could hear him moving toward the bed.

"Did you find him?" Lincoln asked.

"No. But we will. How far can a guy in a wheel-chair get? We cleared everything from the basement. The tech guys are going over the keys. So far, it's just keys."

"Did you see the video on the computer?"

"I did." There was a pause, and Lincoln half wondered if Ferguson was smelling the flowers that had been sent by his mother. "I'm curious," Ferguson continued. "What did you see? When he showed you the key?"

"It's in the report."

"Yes, I read it. There was a bright white light. Anything else?"

Lincoln shifted in the bed. "Isn't that enough? I mean, that in itself doesn't make any sense."

"Well, given your report and what happened to you, I had concerns about a possible WMD. I had them check the house, and they found radiation."

"What?"

"Don't worry, it wasn't a lot. The team suspects it's due to a slow trickle that built up over decades—that whatever was down there had a nuclear component. It's the only way to explain how you have retinal burn from a blast of thermal energy in a man's basement."

Ferguson had taken a seat near the bed. Lincoln turned away from him, hiding his bandaged face.

"I think there's more to this than what was in your report," Ferguson said, leaning in closer. "It's not a weapon, is it? This is something else. And you saw it."

Lincoln didn't answer.

"I want you to know that *I* have seen things too," Ferguson said, his voice low and quiet. "Things I can't explain. Things that just don't make sense. I could try to rationalize such things in some… scientific way. But I've chosen to accept them as something more."

Lincoln rolled back to face Ferguson, though he could see nothing either way. "As what?"

"A miracle."

Lincoln scoffed. "What miracle? I'm blind!"

"What happened in the basement, Lincoln? What did you see?"

"A hallucination. Some kind of shock to my system from goddamn radiation."

"Okay. What did you hallucinate?"

Lincoln leaned his head back against the pillow. Master Tom was going to get his answer one way or the other. "All right. I saw a woman. Her face was melting. Changing from one face to another, like she was made of wax. And I saw a man. His face changed too. Over and over again. And then I saw me sitting in a hospital room, just like I am now, with bandages over my eyes. I heard thunder in the sky and then a loud chirping like crickets, and people screaming. I watched myself take off the bandages and I looked to the door and saw people running down the hallway, and something horrible was chasing them. A beast, but made of human flesh.

"Then I stood, or I watched myself stand, and I went to the curtains and opened them, and the world was burning and the skies were filled with black. And I knew..." Lincoln paused. "I knew that what I saw was real, and the passage from the gospel was true. That the synagogue of Satan had come."

There was a long silence. Ferguson didn't move, and all Lincoln could hear was the beeping of machines.

"You can see why I didn't put any of that in my report," he added at last.

"Is that it?" Ferguson asked.

"No."

"Tell me."

Lincoln took a deep breath. "I heard a voice. Come and see." He turned his face toward the window, though he couldn't see it. "That's what it said. 'Come and see.' And that's when I was struck blind."

CHAPTER XXXI

Near Kamad El Laouz, Lebanon
Eleven Days After Event

Father Simon was waiting with the others in the dark hall of the hospital when the door at the end of the corridor opened. The light from the glowstick in his hand didn't illuminate that far, but the whistling, that same stupid song again, told him who it was that approached. The janitor had returned.

And he wasn't alone. From beyond the whistling came the sound of crickets... and the clicking of bone feet on the linoleum floor.

"Get behind me," the priest said to the others.

Father Simon held the light up high, and the edges of the yellow hue revealed what was coming. Beasts that once were human but were now sewn or stitched together, with awkward limbs and legs, like spiders or crabs, and many faces and eyes.

Father Simon gripped his rifle, but hesitated on the trigger. In truth, he had hoped that God would come. That God would save them. That these things of hell couldn't be here without there being some counterpart. He knew this baby in the next room was special. Knew it because his dreams had told him so. And thus he had hoped, had hoped and prayed, that perhaps there would be some kind of miracle here, right here on this hospital floor.

There was none.

So instead of shouting a prayer or raising a cross, the priest put his faith in his gun, because its truth was known, and he pulled the trigger, and in the light of the gunfire and the yellow glowstick, he could see the twisted beasts crawling across the floor, the janitor in the lead, his whistle tender and fine.

"Get back!" Father Simon shouted to the others, and they retreated behind him.

He fired again and again, but he barely slowed their advance. Thirty feet. Twenty. There were too many. A sea of creatures crawling over one another.

The girl banged on the door of the hospital room where the infant now cried softly. She threw her shoulder against it, but couldn't get it to open.

"Open the door!" she shouted. "They're here! *Please!*"

The boy stepped up next to Father Simon, and he too fired into the twisted mass. Then the priest ran out of ammo, and the boy was their last defense. But the Winchester was too slow, and the boy's shots too ineffective. The creatures continued to scrabble over the floor, coming closer, always closer.

The priest closed his eyes, because all he could do now was ready himself for death. He asked God for forgiveness. And he asked for the forgiveness of sins for all of them here, here and everywhere.

And even as he prayed, he wondered if this God who was so willing to leave them to such a demise, took joy in his pleas.

* * *

John Sunday threw open the door, rifle to shoulder, and fired like a cold machine, clipping the closest beast in the legs.

"Go!" he shouted to the priest and the others, although they hadn't waited for his instructions and were already moving into the hospital room.

He kept firing even as he retreated after them. Then he slammed the door shut and slid the chair back up under the door handle. It was a feeble lock on a door that didn't have one, and he knew from the size and numbers of what he'd seen in the hall that it wouldn't hold, that soon those things would be in the room with them.

He handed the rifle to the priest and moved back to Kat, her gut still partially open.

Something slammed against the door, and then again, and the chair started to scoot. The dog barked and the priest threw his ample weight against the door as Sunday returned to sewing up his patient.

"We have to get out of here!" the junkie cried. "Just bring her!"

Sunday was almost done. He'd stitched the inner muscle and now was suturing her skin closed. He moved as fast as he dared, focusing on the stitch and not what banged on the door.

The banging stopped, and there was a silent pause. Then, from the hall, a voice.

"John? It's me. Remember? The man from the cave. I know, I know. I've... changed. So, John, listen. We're going to get our hands on that whore."

Sunday ignored the words, and kept stitching until she was as sealed as good as he could get her. He wiped the blood, to make sure there was no leaking, then turned to the window. A third-floor window. It was the only way out.

"We're going to rip her back open and claim her, John. Everything you've done for her, it's for nothing. Or you can give us the baby, and we'll just call it a day."

Sunday opened the window and looked out into the darkness. Snowflakes fluttered around him and into the room. There was a large bank of snow built up against the base of the building—that might help. But Kat was in no condition to move. He'd have to bind her somehow, make a sling and lower her. And he'd have to get the baby down as well.

The banging resumed, and the priest strained as he tried to hold them back.

Sunday looked to the boy. It would have to be him. He could hold the baby, and Sunday could lower them both down together.

He beckoned the boy forward, then lifted the swaddled baby from the bassinet, wrapped the child in a towel, and tied the ends of the towel around the boy's back, so the baby was tucked in front of the boy. The baby gazed up at the boy with wide eyes.

Sunday then pulled a cord out of the wall and used his knife to slice the other end right where it connected to some machine. It was only about seven feet of cord, not enough to get the boy all the way down, but it would lessen the drop.

He pushed the chair to the window, dislodging the dog, then lifted the boy onto it and looped the cord around the boy's wrists, threading it up and through his palms so he could clutch it. He helped the boy out the window, and looking around, saw nothing. Moments later the boy was dangling in the air, the baby attached to him as Sunday lowered him down.

"You have to drop the rest of the way," Sunday said. "Bend your knees as you land."

The boy looked down. He was still uncomfortably high.

"Hurry," Sunday said from the window. "And protect the baby."

The boy unthreaded the cord from his wrists, wriggled free, and let go.

He landed in the snowdrift with a soft squish and was buried for a second before emerging as if from a foam pool. He quickly checked the baby.

Sunday watched with his heart in his throat. Had the baby been hurt?

The boy looked up, raised one hand above his head, and gave the thumbs-up.

With a sigh of relief, Sunday turned to the junkie girl. "You're next."

The girl dropped down smoothly, followed by the grandmother, who was frightened by the drop but clearly more frightened by the things trying to break through the door. She hobbled as she emerged from the snow, and Sunday wondered if she was seriously hurt, but there was nothing for it to keep going.

He saw that the boy was pushing more snow into the pile after each landing, and the junkie was helping as well. They would need all the snow they could get, because Kat was next, the drugs still thick inside her, and she was dead weight, unable to control her own landing.

Looping a blanket under her armpits, Sunday lowered her out the window, forgoing the cord. When she was as low as she could go, he dropped her some fifteen feet into the mounded snow below. The boy and the junkie dragged her out of the snowdrift. He couldn't tell if she was injured. They probably wouldn't know until she awoke. If she awoke.

Sunday picked up the dog, the second time he'd cradled it in such a way, and he wondered if the dog would be as willing to be collected a third time after it had been tossed out a third-story window. He dropped it down, and the dog flailed in terror as it fell, then hopped quickly from the snowbank and looked back up at Sunday as if to say *What the hell was that?*

Finally, Sunday turned to the priest. The man still had his giant bulk pressed up against the door, his face white, sweat streaming down his cheeks. It was a miracle the man had held up against the pressing beasts for this long. Or perhaps it was his obesity that was the miracle—a thinner, healthier man would likely have given way by now. If God had a hand in any of this, it was in making this man so fat.

And that was all the divine help they were going to get.

"Let's go," Sunday said.

"No," said the priest through gritted teeth. "You go."

As if in answer, or protest, the door began to pull off its hinges, the wood of the frame cracking.

"It's over! Go!" Sunday shouted, grabbing the priest and shoving him toward the window.

As Sunday took the rifle, the priest clumsily climbed onto the chair, teetering on the sill, hesitating, the drop too high.

Sunday ran at him and pushed him out the window.

The door pushed away from the frame about an inch, the hinges about to come loose, and there in the crack was the janitor surrounded by a swarm of creatures.

"John," the janitor said calmly. "You can't escape this. You belong to us, remember?"

Sunday slid the rifle through the opening in the door and fired. "Fuck you," he said.

But the creatures had swarmed around the janitor to absorb the bullet.

A second later, the door finally breaking free behind him, Sunday dropped from the window and landed in the snowdrift below. The priest already had Kat on his shoulders in a fireman's carry, and the boy still cradled the baby, and the junkie helped her grandmother as they all fled into the night, not knowing where they were going or what was coming after them.

CHAPTER XXXII

Deep Run, Maryland
Twelve Days After Event

Everything changed when Eve McAllister had the dream.

Until then, she had debated staying. True, she was a prisoner to a hole and was running out of light, there was no denying that, but at least she was safe. She could learn to live in darkness, couldn't she? She would have to. Because it was better than the alternative.

And the reason her father had given her for leaving, for risking her life out there, didn't even make any sense.

In his notes, he had indicated that a Dr. Daniel Vicario, a collector of keys in Philadelphia, might have the Keys to the Kingdom referred to in the second page of the gospel. A CIA analyst named Lincoln Pierce had gone to visit this doctor, only to wind up blind and in the hospital and relating to her father a vision he'd had about the end of the world. His vision included a woman whose face was always changing.

Is that supposed to be me?

Daniel Vicario had disappeared then, somehow evading an all-out manhunt. And then the end of the world came, and... well, plans changed.

Am I really considering doing this? For some key?

Eve assessed the gun cabinet. She'd been around guns her whole life. Her father, ever the marine, had made sure she felt comfortable around them. She'd fired her first twelve-gauge at the age of ten when he took her skeet shooting. From time to time they hit the range, and whenever pressures mounted in their lives, it helped them both release the tension.

A magic key? Really?

She assessed her stockpiles of food, and what would be the lightest to carry, and pulled out a big hiking backpack just in case.

She tried to convince herself that the idea of a mystical key—a key to heaven, of all things—could be a completely rational proposition. Because, really, was it any less rational than the dead things that crawled around outside? Or the fact that she had died and yet lived again?

In short, nothing made sense anymore. She was living in a world that provided glimpses of something far more powerful than she had ever imagined. And that made her feel very, very small.

So the debate went in her head, back and forth, until she got tired of thinking and went to sleep, and had the dream.

It started with an old man lying in a bed. She was sitting next to him. In his hand he held a key.

And then before her, a bright white light... and a sign.

It was not a sign from God.

It was from the Department of Transportation.

US 1 North. Philadelphia Next Right.

When she woke, she thought she'd conjured the contents of the dream. That her subconscious had created it.

The next night, she had the same dream.

On the wall near the desk was a map of the US, and she measured out the distance with her thumb and forefinger. From here to Philadelphia was roughly seventy miles. If she averaged two miles an hour, that was thirty-five hours of hiking. With sleep, she could be there in about three days.

She had no idea what she was supposed to do when she got there. She didn't know where this Daniel Vicario's house was. Where Vicario himself was. If he had the key with him. Philadelphia was a big city. To just walk there with no plan... it was beyond foolish.

But what scared her most was what she was going to face when she set foot outside the bunker. The dead man at her door had stopped knocking two days earlier. Had he given up? Or was he just resigned now to waiting quietly?

And if her father and the dead driver were any indication of what was going on up there on the surface, there would be more like them out there. Which meant she'd have to stick largely to the woods and hope for the best. And if all went well she'd arrive at Philadelphia, a city of more than a million people, now a million dead people, all of whom would probably chase after her like those things outside.

Why am I even considering this?

And yet she was. In fact she'd already decided.

She looked at the empty backpack and contemplated what she needed. Only the lighter food, so she packed the dreaded MREs and some vacuum-sealed dried fruits and nuts and beans. She popped a .45 into a holster on her thigh, put another .45 in a secondary holster for good measure, and strapped a shotgun on her back. She packed three boxes of hundred-round hollow-point ammo and followed it with four boxes of twenty-five-round shotgun shells. Then she moved to the meat and potatoes: the M4. She packed ten mags, hesitated, and stuffed in ten more.

She tucked a Bastinelli hunting knife into the sheath on her body armor. Beneath that was her camelback, which held a hundred ounces of water. She plopped on her brain bucket and would have brought the night-vision goggles too, but when she'd found them on her second day in the bunker she'd discovered that, like everything else that required electricity or a battery, they didn't work.

As she packed it all, she wondered if these would be the last items she ever owned. Lentils and shotgun shells.

Before she slung the backpack over her shoulder, she looked around one last time. Everything her father had built for her had been for naught. She'd lasted ten days.

She snapped the glowstick she had duct-taped to the end of the M4 and climbed the stairs to the bunker door. She pressed her ear against the ice-cold metal, listening to see if he was still out there, waiting. Perhaps he'd brought others. Perhaps when she spun the metal and opened this door, a vast army of dead things would pour down upon her like the flood upon Noah.

She took a deep breath and turned the wheel. It squeaked, loudly, announcing to anyone on the other side that she was coming out.

When it clicked, she pulled open the door, quickly tilting the rifle back into her hands and scanning the darkness.

There was no one there.

She stepped outside, grabbed by an even deeper cold, frigid fingers that clung to her. As she moved across the snow, between the two snowbanks that led up to the door, her feet let out a little *crunch, crunch* to let them know she was here now, she was moving.

Her hands shook, from both cold and fear. Mostly fear. She'd only ever trained on skeets and paper targets, not things that moved and ducked and dodged and chased. Things that once were, and still could be, people.

She reached the end of the snowbanks and peered around the corner to the open ground outside. And there they were. Not one. Not two. But a dozen now. They were abnormally tall, and they had clearly been waiting for her, still candles on a white-iced cake, and she raised the shotgun as they leapt across the snow like spiders, their bodies stretchy and sinewy as if they'd been pieced together with extra bones, and she fired, again and again, the rifle choking out puffs into the cold.

Still they kept coming.

CHAPTER XXXIII

Near Kamad El Laouz, Lebanon
Eleven Days After Event

They ran through the night, Sunday fairly certain they were being chased, but it was too dark to see by what or how many. The road outside the hospital turned and split, and Sunday led them off the snow-covered path that led toward the city and along another that threaded the fields. The clicking of crickets was loud in his ears, and Sunday wondered if the creatures used the sound to see, like bats, and if the sound reverberated around their bodies making them visible to these things while being blind themselves.

The boy slipped in the snow, but caught himself with his knee, so he didn't fall on top of the baby. He was staying strong, pushing himself beyond his limits; they all were. The old woman, the junkie going through withdrawal, the fat priest bearing not only his own weight but the weight of a grown woman. But they wouldn't last long out here. Not like this. They were behind enemy lines, and without the sun, Sunday wasn't even sure what direction they were going in, or if they were headed smack into something he couldn't see.

They ran solid for about a mile before Sunday took Kat from the priest and draped her over his own shoulders, gripping her with his left so he could still shoot with his right. They continued to run, but the old woman was moving ever more slowly, and even the dog was tiring, so Sunday at last called for a rest behind a low berm, and he lowered Kat to the ground and scanned the darkness desperately for some sign. Some hope.

There was only the infernal gray.

He knelt next to Kat. She was breathing, and his fingers on her wound felt no blood. It meant little, but it was as much as he could ask for at the moment.

"We have to keep moving," he whispered to the others, rubbing his hands and warming them with his breath.

"Where?" panted the priest next to him. "There's nowhere. We die here, we die there, it doesn't matter."

Sunday had expected their eventual resignation. It was easier to give up, roll over, let the things come and consume them. And frankly, Sunday was inclined to agree. He was tired. Tired of running. Tired of being hunted.

But if he gave up, Kat would die.

Next to him, the boy reached down to touch the smaller fingers of the baby. The baby gripped the tip of the boy's finger and held it there as if to say, *You have me, and I have you.* A reflex, Sunday thought. Just a baby's need to cling to a food source.

But perhaps it was more.

He scanned once more, not even sure where the horizon was, because that implied light and there was so little. He closed his lone eye and considered a prayer again, but frankly he couldn't bring himself to do it. At this point, if there was a God, He'd turned His back on them all, and while Sunday had come closer to finding Him now more than ever, he wondered if the journey would end with him at the castle door, knocking for a king uninterested in the whims of the peasant.

He started to get up, to pick any direction except for the one from which they had just come, and he heard it. Low. Faint, just beyond the chirping of the crickets.

The sound of water.

He crossed the field, drawn to the sound, and nearly fell when he came upon a sudden sharp drop that led down to a thin river. Snowbanks frosted the sides, but the dark muddy water rolled freely along through the forming ice that tried to choke it. And from downstream... was that the sound of water lapping against a hull?

He followed the shore for a hundred yards until he saw it. Tied to a post was a small boat, probably used to cross the river without having to seek a bridge.

He heard footsteps behind him. The priest had followed.

"Where does this go?" Sunday asked.

"South," he said. "Into a lake and dam."

"How far?"

"Ten, maybe eleven kilometers."

Sunday nodded, considering the price of the land, the weight of the water.

"The boat?" the priest asked.

"The boat," Sunday answered.

* * *

The rowboat wobbled as they climbed aboard. It could fit six, but the priest skewed the math. Sunday lowered Kat into the vessel, leaned her head gently against the side, then untied the boat from the post. He pushed the vessel from shore and climbed aboard, barely aware of the ice water soaking his boots and pants. Picking up the lone oar, he pushed off, and in moments they were drifting through the dark, headed south, the current their navigator. Sunday wondered again if they had been let go, or if they were being fed toward something.

He positioned Kat's head more comfortably, checked her pulse and then her eyes in the eternal dusk. Her pupils were rolled back, but she was breathing and still. He pulled back part of her dress to assess her stitches. He saw no fresh blood, no leakage. Maybe he'd done all right and his seam was stable.

As the boat rocked, the water cradling the wood, he reached down to her face and touched her cheek, for the first time in a long time, brushing her hair away from slightly parted lips. He looked upon her then as he once had, and he felt like the boy must have when the baby gripped his finger.

The boat contained an empty Styrofoam cooler, a small tackle box, and a life jacket. Sunday laid the life jacket upon the boat bench and then gestured to the boy, who laid the baby on the makeshift bed. Sunday unwrapped the baby's blankets and went about cleaning the infant's skin as best he could with a rag he found among the hooks and lures in the tackle box. The priest watched without speaking, but Sunday knew what he was thinking.

Sunday rewrapped the baby, not knowing the proper procedure, just wrapping the blanket like he was folding a tent, and handed the baby back to the boy. The boy's eyes widened with pride and, perhaps, joy that he would continue to be the one tasked with the infant's care.

* * *

As the boy took the baby from the one-eyed man, it reminded him again of the times he had held his baby brother. This baby made him miss that feeling. Of his brother. And of his mother. With their memory in his arms, he missed them again, and he felt the hollow.

He wasn't sure if he could do as his mother had asked him in the dark hospital hallway, because as he gazed upon the infant's soft face, he wanted to protect this child at all costs, because although the rifle had aged the boy, the baby was making the man.

* * *

The priest spoke of the river.

"This is the Litani," he whispered. "The Canaanites named it after the serpent, since it snakes through the valley."

"Great," said the junkie.

Sunday barely heard them; he was looking downriver at a sight he knew only he could see. The little boy in the hooded blue winter coat. The one who had haunted him before. He stood near the shore, then began to wade toward them as if he too would join their journey.

Why is he here? What does he want?

He moved deeper into the water, his face shaded by his hood, then swam toward the boat. Sunday held out the oar to him, and at that moment the hood fell away and he saw that most of the boy's face was gone, a pit of crawling maggots.

Sunday froze, and others within the waters grabbed hold of the oar, tugging on it, the muddy river crawling with bodies, hundreds of them, pale and fleshy like bloated fish. They clambered over the edges of the boat, and the others on board screamed and cried, and the boat started to tip...

Sunday woke, the boat rocking gently back and forth beneath him. He had fallen asleep on the bottom of the boat between the benches, and sitting above him, looking down at him, was Kat.

She leaned down and touched his arm.

"It's okay," she said. "You're safe."

* * *

The river had opened up some, and there was now a good fifty feet of water on either side of them. Kat knew John was at the back, searching the shoreline. Always on the ridge, watching.

Kat had taken the baby from the boy. She was sore, and her stomach felt like it had been twisted in two, but she had to hold him. She'd used the towel that had been the baby's papoose to cover them both like an umbrella, and beneath it, in the darkness of their cocoon, she looked at the child. Sweet soft cheeks, skin that smelled new and clean. She found herself nestling against his head to smell his scent.

She knew what she must do, so she revealed her breast, though it was a challenge to handle the dress and the towel and the baby. She didn't know if he would take it, but her milk was ready, and he latched to her readily and sucked so that she could feel the tug, and from within her there was another pull, and she looked upon the baby as her own.

Her son.

Not inserted. Not made and placed within. This baby was given to her, yes, but for a reason. *She* had survived to carry it to term, *she* had brought it into this world past the point of both their intended lifespans, and now she wondered if she held the child that would end this dark charade.

When the baby finished, his little eyes rolled back and his head lolled with an open-mouthed satisfaction that resembled a drunken smile. Kat let out a little giggle. She fixed her dress and rolled down the towel and covered the baby again as he snoozed in her arms.

She looked back at John. He smiled at her, and she back at him.

"He's beautiful," she said.

"Yes. She is."

Kat looked at him again. "What?"

Sunday smiled. Kat looked around at the others in the boat.

Kat quickly unfurled some of the blankets and pulled down the baby's swaddling to check for herself.

She looked back up and grinned.

Sure enough.

She was.

CHAPTER XXXIV

Tel Aviv, Israel
Four Days After Event

The room of senior officers and the deputy prime minister had regrouped in the war room. Jonah sat with Ayelet in the corner, studying the men at the table—in particular the five Sayeret Matkal soldiers, all in Kevlar, who sat together at one side. Jonah knew only one of them—Deputy Commander Yonatan Berg. They'd served together seven years ago. Berg was a good man, the kind of leader who wouldn't send you to do something he wouldn't do himself.

Jonah knew something had been planned here, or was in the process of being planned. He didn't know what, but the items at the center of the table told him he didn't like it.

The first item was a dark-green backpack with two thick straps. It was round in the back, like it was carrying a pony keg. The second item was a stack of dark-gray raincoats. Together, they gave a pretty clear indication that this plan, whatever it was, required going back up to the surface again.

Which was not the first thing on Jonah's to-do list.

He wondered how much the others really understood about what was happening up top. Of course he'd given a full report after the last disastrous mission to the surface, so they knew the facts, but... did they get it? Did they understand the background? The why?

Or were they just pushing forward with another suicide mission?

Ayelet had filled him in on the Christian apocalyptic cult that Mossad had been following. She'd told him about Silas Egin, and the man with scars named Josef Belac who they all called the Father, and the pregnant nuns. She told him about the American, John Sunday, who, despite his injuries, was dead set on tracking the cult to Banias to rescue a woman.

"Banias," she said to him, "is the key."

None of this explained anything as far as Jonah was concerned. And he wasn't even sure he believed it to begin with. Jesus babies bringing all this about?

He just didn't know.

After what he'd seen up top, he didn't know anything anymore.

* * *

Ayelet tried to find a comfortable sitting position, but no matter how she sat, the stitches made themselves known. She wondered if she would ever be comfortable again.

She looked around the room at the men with guns on their hips, men who had been trained to kill. She could tell they were afraid. Their faces were pale, their gestures frantic and stiff. What was happening was something that no one could control, and for men, that was always their greatest fear.

The deputy prime minister cleared his throat to bring the room to attention.

"Gentlemen," he began. "Before I turn it over to the deputy commander, I've asked Dr. Geller to summarize his findings. Doctor, can you explain what you think we're up against?"

"Thank you, Deputy Prime Minister." The doctor stood. "The first question is the nature of the event. It was most certainly some kind of electromagnetic pulse, but that still leaves us with two important possibilities. The first is that this pulse was a singular event. It might have been the result of a nuclear explosion in the upper atmosphere, or even a solar flare, and it simply fried everything in its wake. However, we tracked no nuclear launches prior to the event, and a solar flare is highly unlikely. In addition, seismic data is inconsistent with this hypothesis."

He held up a piece of paper. "This is data from the earthquake recording site at Neve Ativ. Just before the power went out, it indicates that something big occurred in the ground near here. We wouldn't have gotten this kind of ground reading from a nuclear blast or a solar event, so we're discounting that possibility. Besides which, even if it was for some reason a singular event, there's nothing we can do about it now. It's just done.

"The second possibility is that this EMP is still emitting. That there's something acting effectively as an antenna, broadcasting a constant EMP signal. Although it's far from clear how this might be accomplished, by process of elimination, and given the effects we're seeing, I deem it to be the most likely. The question then is, where is this transmission coming from? And that's where our subject has proven useful."

Ayelet noted how the man brought down from above, the man Jonah had shot in the neck with a dart gun, a former lieutenant and trusted ally, had been reduced to nothing more than "the subject."

The doctor pointed to a map on the wall. "The man's ravings are at times hard to decipher. But he has repeatedly mentioned Banias—here, to the south of Mount Hermon—and has referred to it as 'the source.' If there is an EMP transmitter, I believe this is where it may be found."

Ayelet looked at Jonah. *See?* She'd been right about that one.

"Thank you, Dr. Geller," said the deputy prime minister. "Based on these conclusions, we've developed a plan. I'll state up front that I wish it were a better one. But it is the best we can manage under the circumstances." He turned to a middle-aged man with cropped gray hair. "Commander?"

The commander rose, and the doctor took a seat.

"The mission," said the commander, speaking directly to the soldiers arrayed on one side of the room, "is reconnaissance. What the doctor has just summarized is, at this time, speculation. You will travel to Banias and determine if there is any truth to it. Unfortunately, there will be no way for you to communicate with us, so if you determine that the site is somehow transmitting, you will immediately proceed to the next phase of the mission. Demolition."

He pulled the green backpack toward him and unzipped the Velcro to reveal a metal device. "This is a five-megaton nuclear bomb. It uses no electricity. You simply lift this metal bar, the atoms on two opposite sides collide, and the explosion is triggered. There is no countdown clock. Whoever lifts this, isn't coming back."

Jonah raised his hand. "Sir, the men who went up with me, they were affected by the pulse within a minute of leaving the pit. These guys go outside, and whatever is out there, it'll get in their heads."

The commander pointed to the stack of gray suits. "That's why we have these. Faraday suits. Linemen use them when working on high-voltage wires. They're infused with metal that directs the electricity away. There's no voltage limit, so theoretically, they'll prevent any EMP from entering your body. Of course, we won't know for sure they work until we go topside."

He looked once more at his men. "Look, I wish I could tell you this wasn't a suicide run. But the truth is, we're desperate. With the number of people down here, food will run out in forty-five days. Water in sixty. At some point, someone is going to have to go to the surface."

"And even if the suits aren't entirely effective," Dr. Geller said with some enthusiasm, "there's good news. When we first brought Lieutenant Kaminski down, he was uncontrollable. But within the confines of the EMP shield, we were eventually able to bring him some of the way back. We broke the signal. With more time, we might have had an even better outcome."

"More time?" asked Ayelet.

"He died. Heart attack."

The commander grabbed one of the suits off the table. "Look, this will either be on our terms, or theirs. That's why I'm going with you."

"I'm going too," Jonah said suddenly.

Ayelet had known that was coming. She started to protest. "Jonah—"

But just then the lights went out and the war room went dark.

CHAPTER XXXV

Philadelphia, Pennsylvania
Day of Event

Lincoln woke to screaming. He still couldn't see, and he was terrified that whatever was causing those screams was hovering over him now.

It's happening!

The voice shouted in his mind like a drill sergeant. He flailed and fumbled, and in an instant he was on his feet. He raced for the door of his hospital room, slammed into a chair, then re-routed and found the door handle.

He opened the door but hesitated to step into the hallway. Out there was more crashing and banging and screaming. People were running past him, and a woman was crying somewhere down the hall, and others were begging.

He wondered if there was some kind of gunman in the hospital and he'd slept through the shots and was now entering the scene mid-rampage.

Then there was a kind of slicing sound, like a whip through the air, and the crying woman stopped. He took a step forward and felt something warm and wet under his foot, and he wondered if he had stepped in urine or blood.

He quickly backed into the room and closed the door, feeling for a lock. There wasn't one. He ran to the bed, slamming his toe into the chair again, went around and crouched behind it. Feeling the bed frame, he realized it was more a gurney than a bed, and he couldn't hide underneath it. But he heard the whisper in his mind again:

Stay.

He did, and waited, and listened to the sounds in the hallway. There was more screaming and running. Gradually it faded, and a few minutes later, he heard nothing more. All was silent.

He leaned back against the wall and felt the sun on his face. He let it warm him, savoring its feel, and then it faded. The room turned slightly colder, just a degree or so, but on his face he could tell the shade had come. It had come quickly—a storm cloud must have moved in fast. He adjusted the bandages on his face and tried to peek out with a blind eye, but all he saw were smears of light and black.

Lincoln waited where he was for a very long time—hours, he imagined—before he dared to get up and check the door again. He was grateful the hinges were quiet. As he stepped out, he made a giant step over where he thought he'd stepped in a puddle earlier. Instead he stepped in it again, slipped, and fell on his rear.

The liquid had cooled, and it was becoming viscous, and he realized it had to be blood. And his lower half was now covered in it.

He didn't know where he was going. He didn't know if he should even bother getting there. He didn't know if he was alone or being watched.

But he rose to his feet and kept moving, slowly, pushing one foot out as a feeler, then the next, until he bumped a toe against a body.

Lincoln reached down and felt at it. The body came to a sudden end where its lower back should have been. He felt more, but only grabbed air, and then went farther and felt something cold, and soft, and squishy, and he realized that somehow this body had been torn in half.

He screamed and backed away, and pulled his hands from the person's insides, and wondered what could have done this, what could have split a person in two.

Lincoln found his way back to his room and tucked himself back into his little corner. He couldn't venture out there blind. He could walk smack dab into whatever had done... that. Hell, it could be sitting on the bed above his head right now and he wouldn't know it. His heart was pounding in his skull, and up the back of his neck, and behind his ears, and he wondered if he was going to have a stroke and just save the thing the trouble.

He slowed his breath, and closed his blind eyes, and tried to go back to the open ocean. He imagined the wind, the sail flapping on the mast, the hull hitting the water.

Then he remembered something else as a whisper in the back of his mind. Like someone leaning into his ear, or a feather on the wind. He heard the words.

He had not uttered them in a long time. Not in his heart. Not out loud.

But he did now. And he spoke along with the whisper to make sure the words were heard.

"Our Father, who art in heaven, hallowed be thy name..."

He finished the prayer. And the whisper in his mind hung on a passage, like a song stuck in his head.

"Forgive us our trespasses."

He repeated it several times, until he switched it up to "Forgive me my trespasses."

He fell asleep sometime after that, the prayer and the permission still looping in his brain.

CHAPTER XXXVI

Near Qaraoun, Lebanon
Twelve Days After Event

After some hours of drifting in the dark, they neared the lake, where an orange hue glowed like a low candle on the far bank. The dog growled, and Sunday realized it was a fire, a large and long one, hidden by a berm along the shore.

"Maybe there are survivors," whispered the junkie. "Like us."

But as they came closer that idea faded. They heard screaming, and wailing into the night, thousands of voices and sobs that floated into the heavens along with the smoke.

Sunday steered the boat into the open waters of the lake, aiming for the opposite shore, away from the fire and the screams. But the hull of the boat struck something, and then again, and again, nearly stopping their progress. He looked over the side of the boat, but in the darkness he couldn't tell what they were running into. He pushed at something with his oar, found it solid, and shoved off. They bumped again, and this time the boat came to a complete stop.

"There's something in the water," he said.

The priest reached into his pocket for a glowstick.

"No, no light," Sunday said.

He peered down into the darkness, waiting for the fire behind the berm to leap high enough to illuminate the surface of the lake. And when it did, he saw. A giant swath of ice had choked nearly the whole of the lake.

"Ice," the priest said. "The lake is frozen."

The junkie, who had been leaning over the side, suddenly jumped back. "They're people!"

Sunday leaned down over the edge, his face close to the water. The nearest ice chunk was twisted and gnarled in a strange way, and part of it looked like a frozen hand. Only then did he realize that a dead, frozen face was staring back at him.

The fire burned brighter, and his eyes were adjusting, and he could now see that the rest of the lake, from this point forward, was frozen with thousands of bodies, all bound tightly together, each body locked to its kin.

And on the far shore, as the orange embers of the fire drifted skyward, a silhouette appeared. A sinewy creature taller than any man. He seemed to be scanning the lake.

"Down!" Sunday whispered.

They lowered into the bottom of the boat, quiet as the night, and Sunday watched the native and gauged the far shore. They were still several hundred yards out. But they had no choice. The boat would take them no further.

Carefully, he climbed over the edge of the boat and touched down on the frozen island of bodies. His boots sank a bit into the icy dead—they weren't entirely frozen, but more slush on top—but they did not rock or shift or crack beneath his feet. He was satisfied it would hold.

"Come on," he whispered.

The others climbed over the sides, and Sunday grabbed the Styrofoam cooler.

"Give her to me," he said to Kat.

She looked to him uncertainly, but handed him the baby. He wrapped the infant snug in the towel and set her in the bottom of the cooler. He closed the lid and clutched the black handle, and they walked along the islands of frozen dead.

* * *

The priest was worried. The ice might hold the others, but he weighed as much as any two of them combined, and the ice cracked a bit beneath his feet. And then it happened—one foot broke through, and he gasped as it hit the icy water, and though he pulled it back out without falling, his fear heightened. He did not want to die here, frozen among these bodies.

As he looked down into the hole he had made, he saw the bloated face of a fat dead man staring back up at him. Startled, he hurried on, cursing his weight as he went.

* * *

Kat fell too. She didn't crack the ice, but her foot found an opening, and tripped her up, and she fell to her hands and knees.

Directly beneath her gaze was a man's frozen face in the ice, looking up at her. His face was distorted, but she recognized him.

"Daddy?" she asked.

John pulled her to her feet. "That's not your father."

She looked down, unsure.

"Hey," John said. "We do this together. Remember?"

She pulled her gaze from the dead man.

* * *

They came to a spot where the ice turned completely to slush and then ended in cold dark water. They'd run out of ground and were still some fifty yards from the shore.

"We have to get in the water," Sunday said.

The others looked at him like he was crazy. And perhaps he was. But there was no other way forward, so he didn't even bother making his case. He simply slid into the water, the cold stabbing every inch of his skin, holding the cooler so it floated next to him.

He heard the others getting in also, gasps leaking from them as the cold water seized their skin. He checked to make sure Kat could manage, and he stayed at her side as they swam. Stray frozen bodies bumped against him in the dark water, and each time he wondered if one of them would clutch at him with cold blue fingers and drag him to the lake bottom.

But they made it to shore. And when Sunday flipped open the cooler lid and checked her, she was dry.

* * *

Steering wide of the fire, they passed through a forest of oak trees and came across the outskirts of a village. Nestled among a few houses on a hill was a small Catholic Church. Sunday scoped it hurriedly, but it was cold and his body was aching, and the others were faring no better, and he returned to them in the oaks and said it was safe without a close inspection.

Their first thought inside the church was to seek warmth. They found no blankets, but used the priest robes and altar cloths and mass linens to dry and wrap themselves. Sunday was wary of creating light, but he was worried about Kat and the baby succumbing to the cold, so he stacked prayer books in a pile, tore and crumpled their pages, and used his lighter to start a small fire in a gold baptismal bowl.

"The word," said the priest, "has always warmed my soul."

They pulled food from their packs, but also found jars of wheat hosts and bottles of grape wine, and the priest seemed to think it was communion, and so he said some brief words before he blessed them.

"Take this, all of you, and eat of it: for this is my body *which will be given up for you.* Take this, all of you, and drink from it: for this is *the chalice of* my blood, the blood of the new and eternal covenant, which will be poured out for you and for many for the forgiveness of sins. Do this in memory of me."

Now apparently in the mood, and with all of them regaining their warmth, the priest asked Kat if she wanted to baptize the baby.

"She will need a name," said the priest.

Kat looked to Sunday.

"Perhaps we should wait," he said.

"For what?"

"Until we make it."

Kat looked down at the baby, then nodded at the priest. "Her name is Mara."

Sunday nodded as well, because she had made it so. *Mara.* And as he looked around at the others, he realized that perhaps all of them should be given names, for as far as he was concerned, none of them had one. If he had been told, he had since forgotten. Even the dog was just the dog.

Kat wrapped the child in a white lace altar runner with the Greek letters for *Ihsous* on it, then she stood before the altar, beneath the dark of the stained-glass windows, in the light of the flickering fire, and the priest baptized Mara. Perhaps the water, or the words of this strange rite, would offer some protections.

And as Sunday looked on, at the woman, and at the baby in her arms, he wondered if it was the fire or the wine or something else that warmed him.

CHAPTER XXXVII

Deep Run, Maryland
Twelve Days After Event

Eve McCallister raced through the snowy woods, the creatures hopping behind her like giant crickets, bouncing off the trees and using their high-bent knees to hurl themselves through the air again. She wasn't accustomed enough to her new body to know for sure how well it worked, and as she ran she already felt her heart chugging, her lungs gasping for the cold air. The snow was growing deeper, and while that slowed her progress, it seemed to have no effect on the creatures, which were gaining.

If they caught up to her, she'd be dead. She'd killed two outside the bunker, but it had taken a dozen shots each, and the rest would have overrun her had she not turned and fled.

And yet the snow was simply too deep. She couldn't get her knees up high enough to clear it; it felt like the earth itself was dragging her down. So she turned, half-buried in snow, rifle in hand, and fired again, hoping a magic bullet would somehow save her.

She squeezed the trigger again, and it clicked empty, and she felt her heart drop.

She dropped the rifle and moved to the pistol on her hip. She clipped one of the creatures in midair, and it spiraled as it fell, but it righted itself on the ground and kept coming.

They were closing in on her from all sides. They moved through the trees, and cleared the shadows, and stepped forth, circling her.

It was over.

She looked down at the pistol in her hand. If she put the gun into her mouth and blew out her brains, she'd fall into the snow and she'd die. Temporarily. She'd wake in three days, these things would be gone, and she could move on.

But then she remembered her father. And the driver. They had been dead. And they had been consumed. There was no escape for them. Death was but a door for these things to step through.

Oh, God. Why didn't I just stay in the bunker?

She pulled the other .45 from her hip and fired both weapons, the smoke from the barrels hanging in a gunpowder fog, and though she hit some, it only made them more determined. They circled her fully, and though she did not want to look, she couldn't take her eyes off them. Each one was the mixed, merged bodies of multiple people, arms and legs awkwardly long, flesh covered in scars and eyes and faces.

And then one approached. Its head was extended on a long neck, but the face... the face was one she recognized.

It was her father.

He was no longer of his body, but that was his face all the same, mixed with others. He opened his mouth as if to speak, but no sound emerged. Perhaps the throat was no longer tied to anything that produced voice.

She knew then.

Knew she was about to be claimed.

Her heart sank, and she lowered the gun, and she was almost okay with it, because if she was to be taken, at least it would be someone she knew. Then at least she could be with him again. Perhaps, in some strange, awful way, this was a heaven too, because you could still be with those you had loved.

She closed her eyes and waited for them to attack. To do whatever it was they had done to each other. To rip her arms or legs from their sockets, to peel her skin.

Instead, she heard a gunshot.

CHAPTER XXXVIII

Bab Mareh, Lebanon
Twelve Days After Event

When they left the church, Sunday had no clear direction, no destination. He merely followed the road outside, and when that road came to an end, he kept going, moving over the fresh-fallen snow toward the mountains, eventually finding a path. No one questioned his leadership. No one asked where they were going. Perhaps it was all they could do to keep putting one foot in front of the other.

After some miles, they came to a sign. The priest scraped away the ice to read it.

"Niha," he said.

"What's that?"

The priest scanned the darkness. "It's an ancient fort, in the mountains. Ahead."

The path was clearer now, if narrower, and Sunday led them snaking up the side of the mountain, the cold whipping at them more, the snow blasting their faces as if to say *rise no more*. Sunday guided Kat, and the junkie aided her grandmother, and the boy and the dog stayed at the priest's side.

The "fort" was not one made by men. It was a carved-out slice of mountain beneath an overlook, a jagged rip in the earth, a cave in the side of a cliff.

"The Muslims and Crusaders held this place once," the priest said as they stepped inside. "Now it is ours to hold."

Sunday tried to assess the cave's depth, but in the darkness, he could see nothing. But they were sheltered from the winds that whipped the narrow path, so he posted guard at the entrance, and the others, exhausted, curled up as they could, and despite the cold of the stone, they were soon asleep. Sunday was alone once more, looking out at the dark clouds that swarmed the mountains.

Below, in the distance, he could see fires burning. And among the leaves of a scrub brush a few feet away, a blue butterfly was frozen to its branches, locked eternal, its wings stiff and cold, its retreat to the sky never realized.

In that quiet, he pondered what was to become of them. He wondered whether the child who now slept in her mother's arms was somehow a magician, or was simply a manifestation of their hope for something better within themselves. Perhaps the child would inevitably become just like them, and would grow to sin, as connected and locked to it as that butterfly on the branch. Perhaps the child was a story they told themselves, because there were no angels here. No wise men or guiding star.

If this child was somehow their deliverance, then it too had been cast far from sight… and for now the task of salvation fell to a one-eyed man who clutched a gun in the cold recesses of a dark cave.

* * *

The priest woke a few hours later to relieve Sunday, and himself.

"We are close," the priest said as he finished and took the gun. "Maybe fifteen, twenty kilometers."

"To what?"

"This fort was used to guard the road between the valley and Sidon, on the coast. There, perhaps we can find a boat. A bigger boat. But Sidon is also very big. Very crowded. To get to the shore unseen, will be very hard."

He patted Sunday on the shoulder. "Sleep, my friend. You will need your energy."

* * *

As Father Simon stood watch in the eternal night, he heard the muffled cries of children coming from the dark of the cave. And another voice telling them, *Shh, shh, it will be okay.*

He knew the voices were only there to taunt. He knew they were within him. He had been possessed somehow, at the hospital, and the creature that hunted him now was not out there in the darkness… it was in his head. Scurrying around, a whisper in his mind that he could not silence. He could hear the crickets too, chirping and chirping, but he understood them now as a series of voices, layered one over the other.

He knew then that no sermon or holy words were going to save him.

He rose to his feet and drifted into the cave, the snow falling outside, a soft patter that he thought was no longer a winter but falling pieces of the sky. He could feel them in his brain, the bugs chewing on his thoughts and memories, but it wasn't until he was standing over Kat and looking down at the baby on the blanket beside her that he knew the decision had already been made.

He was to feed one more child to the darkness.

He leaned down, picked up the baby, cradled her close to his chest. Should he walk with her into the night, back toward the lake of ice, and deliver her there upon the shore? Would the natives welcome him, revere him, because he had risen high now among their ranks? Or should he just throw her over the cliff and sit on the ledge and put the shotgun in his mouth?

He had come to realize that despite his best efforts, there was no door for him to heaven. The white collar around his neck was always a noose.

Seventy-two.

That was the number that churned in his mind.

The number of boys Father Zula had molested.

What number, Simon wondered, was the child he had seen tied to the bed that day? Was he the first? The twentieth? How many boys could Simon have saved from that frocked devil?

Zula was ultimately caught, arrested, and wound up taking his own life. But not before... seventy-two.

Simon wondered then if Father Zula was out there in the shadows too.

The soft begging cries from the back of the cave turned to whispers that washed his ears. They were telling him what to do.

He looked down at the child, still sleeping in his arms. She shifted, a slight stretch, and even in the cold he could smell the baby on her. The smell of new. He wondered whether he could actually do it, but the voices said he could. And he wanted to see her fly. See her fly out over the frozen trees, hang in the dark air for a split second, before she was pulled back down to earth. From this height, she would die quickly. It wouldn't hurt. She would just be... gone.

Father Simon stood near the mouth of the cave, ready to hurl the baby over the cliff, when he saw him standing there, rifle in hand, the dog at his side.

The boy.

The boy was watching. Protecting. Rifle raised.

The priest returned to Kat and placed the sleeping baby back on the blanket. Then he walked toward the boy as if no such horrible thought had ever been.

"She's safe. Go back to sleep." The priest gestured for the gun.

The boy squatted instead at the entrance to the cave. He leaned his head back against the cold rock wall, the dog still at his side, and kept his eyes on the priest, the rifle never leaving his hands.

CHAPTER XXXIX

Philadelphia, Pennsylvania
One Day After Event

"Lincoln?"

He started to stir.

"Lincoln?"

Lincoln came to, his mind clearing. Someone was in the room with him.

"Who's there?" he asked, searching the space in front of him with his hand.

"You're safe," the man said.

"Who are you?" Lincoln whispered. Whoever was talking to him, was close.

"It's Daniel."

"Daniel? Vicario?"

"Yes."

Lincoln pressed his back against the wall, the threat of the key returning in his mind. He waved his hand before him again, flailing at air, touching nothing.

"Lincoln," Daniel said again, drawing the name out like he was talking to a child. "I told you. You're safe."

"Where are you?"

"Right here."

And with the words, Lincoln could suddenly see Daniel in his mind. He sat in a wheelchair, across from him in the hospital room, a room that Lincoln had never seen before with his own eyes.

"Go ahead," Daniel said. "Reach out. Take my hand."

"Man, stop it."

"Lincoln, I want you to come to me. Come to us."

"Why would I do that?"

"Because the vision you saw has come true. Hasn't it?"

Lincoln paused. There was no denying it. He could feel its truth in his mind, and in his heart, even though he had seen none of it with his own eyes. "Yes."

"Yes, Lincoln. Because the key I showed you is special. And you know that too. And you, the child who turned from God, you have wondered now if you should turn back again. *And* because... because we both know that if you don't come, you'll die here."

"Where are you?" Lincoln whispered.

"At a church. In the city. Would you like to see it?"

"Yes."

"Then let me show you the way."

Lincoln's mind filled with the vision of a giant steeple against a dark sky, and beneath it a church, its interior all in white, a giant white organ in the loft, an arched glass window over the altar.

"A great fight lies ahead, Lincoln. Are you ready to follow the way of our Lord?"

"Yes."

"Then remove your bandages."

Lincoln unfurled the wraps from his eyes. The room around him was still dark, but he could make out the shadows, and he could see his hands as he waved them in front of his face.

"Do you see?" Daniel asked.

"Yes."

CHAPTER XL

Near the Fortress of Niha, Lebanon
Thirteen Days After Event

The caravan made its way down the opposite side of the mountain, along a narrow stone path, the snow rising only a few inches here before the wind swept it away again. The storm had grown in intensity, perhaps because they were higher now, though no closer to God.

Kat carried Mara close to her to shelter her from the winds. As she walked, she pondered the images of her father she'd been seeing. It could not be him—which meant the creatures must have somehow gotten inside her head and this was like an infection. She wondered if the others had it as well. Either way, the business of her father was not over, because her heart had been hollowed by his absence, and that had haunted her long before this dark winter had come.

John helped her along the narrow path, and several times she had to clutch his hand as she cradled the baby. But after five or six times of grabbing his extended hand, she realized she wasn't doing so because she needed his support, but because she felt comfort in knowing he was there.

* * *

The boy brought up the rear and kept turning his head to look back along the path from which they'd come. They were there, like lost children, hugging the cliff-side, as pale and dead as the snow. His mother, and his brother. Trailing. Following them. There if he needed them.

Like Mommy had always been.

* * *

Sunday led them through frozen vineyards, the grapes locked in ice, and to lower ground, where they came to the edge of a dark road piled with snow and dead cars. He crept forward cautiously with his weapon ready, joined by the priest and the boy. Sunday half expected creatures to leap from the vehicles at any moment.

The priest said the road led south to the tourist town of Jezzine. Sunday opted instead to turn west through the woods. He was uncomfortable around all these cars. Cars meant people. People were a threat. So they moved through cedars and pine until they came to another road, this one empty, and the priest wasn't sure but he thought it might lead them to Sidon on the coast, and even though there were no cars in sight they followed it from within the trees at its side.

When a small gas station appeared on the road, Sunday instructed the others to wait as he moved ahead to check the building. When he returned, the priest and boy both raised their guns at his approach.

"We're good," he said.

He led them into the black emptiness of the gas station store and bolted the door locks, although the doors were made of glass and would stop nothing that was dead set on coming in. They were sealed away from the wind, and Sunday figured this place would serve well as their tomb if the things outside found them and laid siege.

They dined on bags of chips and snacks and nuts and little cakes and pastries sealed in plastic. None of it was healthy, but they crunched it down with glee, and the priest joked that although man might not survive long on this earth, some of his food just might be eternal.

The junkie offered to take first watch, but Sunday was hesitant to give her the rifle.

"It's okay," she said.

He gauged her eyes, judged to see if she still heard the needle's hum.

"I can do this," she said.

He handed her the rifle.

By the priest's estimate, they'd made it ten or so kilometers from the icy cliffs, but he seemed to feel this was some grand sum, and he settled back, cookie crumbs on his table of a chest, and was asleep in a matter of minutes.

Sunday sat next to Kat, leaning against the freezer glass, and she fed Mara again beneath the cover of the blanket. When she was done, she found some diapers on a store shelf and laid the baby out on a red gas station vest and cleaned her.

"You want to help?" she asked him, although it seemed to be more a statement.

"Uh…"

"Sure you do," she said, handing him the diaper.

Though the diaper was small in his hand, it was large on her. He wrapped her in it, and it was loose and she was wiggly and it was full of gaps around her small legs. He held her up to look at his work, and she wiggled again, little legs kicking like a frog, and the diaper slid off her and she urinated down her leg as if renouncing his work.

He looked over at Kat, who smiled.

Sunday found a solution on one of the shelves, and by the time he handed Mara back to Kat, she'd been swaddled in diaper and duct tape, because Delta always finds a way.

Later they slept on the gas station floor, close to each other, closer than they had in years.

CHAPTER XLI

Tel Aviv, Israel
Four Days After Event

Keira was her name, but she was no longer Keira.

There was still enough of her inside, though, to miss who she was. Who she had been.

What she had said to the soldiers who had let her in had been true. She was pregnant. Seven months along. And she had worked in the building upstairs; she was a finance resource officer and spent much of her day going over audits for the Israel Defense Forces divisions. It was good work, if boring compared to other jobs here, and allowed her to parlay her accounting degree into something that contributed to the homeland. She believed that, in her own way, she was making a difference by working for the IDF. She'd even met her husband here, an accountant as well, and they were excited to have their first child.

Life, all in all, was good.

Until it wasn't.

She was in the bathroom when it happened. She had gone to make one of her many trips to urinate and was sitting on the toilet when she heard people screaming outside. She dismissed it as people joking around in the hall, and finished and flushed.

She opened the stall door and stepped out, and there, standing at the end of the row of sinks, was an older man in a suit.

Obviously he had the wrong bathroom.

"Sir, you're in the ladies' room," she said, moving toward one of the sinks.

He looked around the bathroom as if assessing. She expected him to apologize and move on. No harm done.

Instead he moved closer to her as she washed her hands. She didn't move at first, because her mind couldn't wrap around the idea that this man was a threat.

"Sir," she said in a scolding tone.

That was when he dragged her to the floor.

She tried to protect her belly, instinct, but he pinned her wrists to the floor, that dirty bathroom floor, and she struggled and screamed, squirming beneath his strength and weight, thinking the whole time about the baby.

Her mind raced. *What is he going to do? Rape me? Here in the bathroom? Get him off your belly, off the baby.*

"Help!" she screamed.

He pinned both wrists with a single arm and raised his free hand over her. His wrist flapped violently backwards with a sudden cracking sound, and his radius jutted through the skin of his forearm.

The end of the bone was hooked like the tip of a scorpion's tail.

He brought it down and jabbed it into her neck, and her veins felt warm as something pumped into her, coursed upward, past her ears and into her brain.

Her eyes opened wide. And she screamed there on the floor with the man in the suit on top of her because she saw. A place of suffering, and pain, of skinned creatures that wait in the darkness to devour the children who have turned from the light. Creatures that exist merely to execute His will. Alas, He held high His promise to them, until this destruction born of men, and their intent He would not stop.

And Keira bent. Succumbed. There on the bathroom floor, her will was no longer her own, her identity consumed by a thing that controlled. Who she had been fell into the pit, and she and the baby within her were both devoured, and she kneeled over and over again, bowing to the one.

* * *

Inside the bunker, Keira sought out the generator room. She unlocked the metal door and stepped into the narrow corridor as the diesel generators roared. She moved to the control panel, tore the metal face away, and then ripped out the cables.

The emergency lights kicked on, but the batteries were unstable, and they flickered and sputtered as she stepped out of the generator room and back down the hall. People ran past her, panicked, and she stabbed at them with her bone claw, piercing flesh and filling them with her fluid. Though the signal could not reach here, their seed would still grow.

There was enough of her left to bear witness to her deeds. She had just wanted to be a mother. A wife. And now she was killing people. She had not wanted to do this. To ever do these things. But the creature silenced the voice of her mind, and now she was only mute eyes watching what the master was doing.

She ascended the stairs, going back to the door through which she had originally entered. She spun the big wheel on the bunker door and opened it. On the other side of the corridor, in the flickering light, were a horde of twisting bodies. Some were melted and merged, forged of flesh fires; others were like her, their outward appearance unchanged, but their insides tainted with the blood of the garden serpent.

Keira knew she was going to do a lot more killing. And inside herself, she wept, because even when it was done, she would never be able to escape.

CHAPTER XLII

Near the Fortress of Niha, Lebanon
Thirteen Days After Event

As Sami sat on her makeshift stool of stacked soda boxes, watching the door, she felt it. An electric sensation that made her ears hum and her skin tingle. The crickets outside grew louder, and something that was somewhere beyond the glass was also now here in the room with her.

The windows had fogged from the warmth of their bodies in the small space. She used her sleeve to clear away the moisture, then looked through the streaks. She saw only cold darkness.

But that darkness was... full. To her left and right were ordinary shadowed silhouettes of trees and a distant street pole, but directly in front of the store, there was a solid wall of black.

The glass fogged again. And just before it did, she caught a glimpse of her grandmother standing outside. The girl gasped and wiped the glass once more, searching again, but there was no one out there, and when she turned, she saw her grandmother sleeping on the floor.

Still she felt an urge to go outside and see, to double-check, to be sure. But that was suicide. Instead she backed away from the glass, worried that whatever she had just seen was about to come through.

She jumped when she backed into someone. The pregnant woman. Though she was no longer pregnant.

"Is everything okay?" the woman asked.

Sami nodded, and she felt the sweat on her brow from fear and withdrawal. "Yes."

"I have to go to the bathroom," the woman whispered. "Can you watch her?" She gestured toward the blanket on the floor where the baby slept.

Sami couldn't believe she was being asked to do that. Look after the baby? Her?

The woman nodded. "I'll be right back." And she disappeared into the tiny back hallway and tinier bathroom.

Sami kneeled next to the baby's blanket. She wanted to reach out and touch the baby's little curled hand. But she didn't want to wake it, and she was afraid that somehow she might taint it. So she just sat there next to it, doing as she was asked, the one-eyed soldier sleeping close by.

There was a calm here. On this dirty gas station floor, next to this child. Sami could hear the infant's little breathing, a hesitant rhythm, her new lungs still learning the air. Again she wanted to touch the baby, but she couldn't bring herself to do it.

After a few minutes, when the woman had still not returned, Sami rose and pushed through the door into the little hall. Immediately she felt the cold on her face.

The back exit to the gas station stood wide open, and little flurries danced in the breeze.

Someone had come in. Or someone had gone out.

Sami flung open the bathroom door, not bothering to knock.

The bathroom was empty.

Fear dumped into her already queasy gut, and she darted back to the one-eyed man and shook him awake.

* * *

The bathroom was pitch black, but Kat fumbled her way to the toilet, lifted her dress, and urinated. When she wiped, she wanted to check that the bleeding had slowed, but she wasn't going to carry the used toilet paper out into the dimness of the hall. Instead she flushed, found the sink, and washed her hands in the gurgling water left in the pipes.

When she opened the bathroom door, he was standing in the shadows.

She gasped, the fear clenching her sore gut.

And then she focused, and saw that there was no one there. She had been tricked in the dimness by a stack of soda boxes with a mop leaning up against it. She breathed a sigh of relief.

"Kit Kat. You okay?"

She spun around, expecting to see him in the hallway behind her, but there were just shadows again.

She felt a vibration in the air, and a light flicked on beneath the door that led outside.

"No."

She heard the little voice in her head, but it was very weak, and she was going to turn and run, but the back door opened, and he peeked his head in.

"Are you all right?"

And her father stepped into the darkness and approached her outside of—she couldn't remember. And the shadow...

It was her bedroom. That's where she was. All along. In her bedroom, her nightlight in the corner casting the shadows, and he sat on the edge of her little bed and leaned over her. Over his little girl who had just screamed his name.

"Did you have a bad dream?"

"Yes," she sobbed, the covers held high around her neck in one hand, her baby doll clutched in the other.

"It's okay. You're safe," he said, his voice gentle and reassuring.

"He's here," she whispered, as if not to alert him that she knew.

"Who?"

"The shadow man. He's in the corner." She nodded with her head toward her little dollhouse.

Her father turned on the light next to her bed. And the shadows disappeared.

"See?" he said. "There's nothing there. It's just your mind playing tricks on you. Sometimes your brain sees things, and it doesn't know what they are, so it makes up a little story."

"I saw him, Daddy. The shadow was breathing."

"It's not real, Kit Kat. It's in your head." He smiled. "You know what helps me sleep?"

"What?"

"A big bowl of vanilla ice cream."

She hesitated. "Mommy will be mad."

"Our secret. Come on."

She slid out of bed in her little nightgown, and he waited for her by the door. Her doll was still lying on the bed.

"Do you want to bring your baby?" he asked.

"No, she can stay."

Then she took her father's hand, and together they walked out her bedroom door.

* * *

Sunday was up and to his feet before he even knew where he was or where he was going. The junkie was talking to him, pointing to the rear of the gas station, and his tired mind was trying to put the pieces together.

"She's gone," the junkie said again, frantic.

Sunday grabbed his rifle off the floor and moved to the hall. The rear door stood open.

By now the others were awake as well. He pointed at the priest. "Watch the baby."

And before the man could answer, Sunday was out the back door.

He pulled a flare and searched the snow for her footprints. He saw them, but not only hers. There had been someone else walking with her.

He decided to call her name because by now the flare would already have alerted them to his presence. "Kat!" he called.

The crickets were his only answer.

CHAPTER XLIII

Philadelphia, Pennsylvania
Two Days After Event

Lincoln had only been to Philadelphia one time before this. He'd come as a kid to see the Liberty Bell and run up the steps like Rocky. Yet somehow he could feel the pull of which way to go, as if he'd lived here his whole life.

The streets were unlike any he'd seen before. Cars were abandoned, empty, their doors hanging open, and there were trails of blood in the snow. He'd tried to start a few of the cars, along with one motorcycle, but none of them would turn over. The power was out, too—the streetlights, the businesses. Everything was empty and cold. If there was anyone left alive, they were hiding from him... or from someone else.

As he crossed the South Street Bridge, he was getting colder. At a Goodwill store, left unlocked, he sifted through the racks for a winter jacket and some work boots. He shouted to the owner that he was taking the stuff, though he knew there was no one there to hear; it just felt like the right thing to do. He zipped up the jacket, raised the collar around his neck, and grabbed a black cotton beanie that he slid down over his ears.

As he was about to leave, he heard shuffling from the changing rooms. He moved closer, bent down. Beneath the half door of one of the rooms, a pair of legs stood in the darkness.

There's someone alive!

"Hello?" he said.

From the changing room came a grunt. A kind of "hmmpf."

Lincoln moved closer to the dressing room door. "Do you need help?"

"Linnncoooollln?" The word was stretched out in a long drawl.

"Who? Who is that?"

The door to the dressing room opened, slowly, a creak in its hinges. And there stood his father wearing the white T-shirt and white pants he'd worn so often when cleaning the school.

Lincoln's gut dropped. He couldn't be here. Couldn't be...

"Dad?"

"Lincoln," his father said, a smile on his face.

"What are you doing here, Dad?"

He's here. And he's alive. No. No. My father died seven years ago. You went to the funeral, saw him in the casket, his big old working hands clasped over his big chest. And you sobbed, because there was no getting that time back.

Lincoln felt the tears on his cheeks.

"Dad, is that you?"

"Come here, son. Daniel sent me."

"He... he sent you?"

"That's right. Sent me to get you. Now come on. Give your old man a hug. I ain't seen ya in a dog year."

Lincoln moved slowly toward his dad, his brain a firecracker of electrical impulses.

Am I dead? Did I die back there? Is this a ghost?

Then he heard the whisper again in his head.

"It's a lie, Lincoln."

"Quiet!" his father shouted into the air, like he was screaming at flies buzzing around his head.

Lincoln warily eyed the man standing in front of him. In the blackness of the three-way mirror of the dressing room, he caught his father's reflection. And this was not his father. It was something being held up, supported from the mirror glass by some kind of fleshy tentacle that jutted forth into his father's spine. The tentacle emerged from the mirror itself as if stretching between worlds.

When Lincoln looked at his father once more, his face was a melted amalgam of flesh, of eyes, of other faces, all smeared and merged. Its arms unfurled, wide, accepting, and instead of hands it had bone hooks.

"Come home," it said, but it spoke with the voices of many.

Lincoln turned and ran, his new boots slipping on the cold tile floor. Behind him, the creature snapped free from its umbilical in the mirror, severing its tie to that unseen world, and hopped after him on backward-bent limbs. It soared over the racks and landed in front of Lincoln with a thud, blocking his escape.

Lincoln almost slid into it. He caught himself and righted, then fell back into a spinning rack of bargain shoes. He scurried away and kicked the rack in front of the creature to try and stop its approach. But the thing merely extended its abnormally long legs and stepped over the insignificant obstacle.

Lincoln's mind couldn't process fast enough. But he knew enough. He knew that he needed to run. Now.

He jumped to his feet and ran deeper into the store. He spotted a pair of double doors in the back and sprinted full speed for them. The creature leapt after him and he heard it, felt it, land inches from his back foot. Something slick, a tentacle arm, grabbed at his leg and he sprawled headfirst, crashing through the swinging doors.

He scrambled back to his feet and slid up the top latch lock on the right-side door. He did the same to the left, but as he slid the lock up, the creature on the other side slammed against it, pushing the door open a bit so that the latch he had erected was now preventing him from closing the door all the way. Putting all his weight into the door, he lowered the latch and tried to bring it back in line so he could lock it. The creature was so heavy. So strong.

"Please…"

He used his back leg like a kickstand and shoved, but it was like pushing against five men. He groaned and yelled, and looked up, keeping his eyes on the door/lock alignment.

Just another inch…

Come on!

He dug his boots into the concrete floor and pushed with everything he had, keeping his eye on that lock, until the creature stepped back to give another full lunge and Lincoln lined up the door with the lock and pushed up on the latch, driving it home.

He paused to make sure the door was going to hold, and it did, but as the creature slammed against it, both doors buckled at the bottom. The creature pushed a tentacled arm through, and its long, exposed bone fingers grabbed at him.

Lincoln looked frantically for an escape. He was in some kind of back warehouse area, and all he saw were high racks of shelves filled with old record players, old computer monitors, and old swivel chairs that had lost their swivel. He ran past a few aisles, searching for an exit door, but in the darkness, he couldn't see much. He picked an aisle and dragged his hand along the shelf as a guide, made it to the back, and ran into a wall. A dead end.

He heard the crack as the creature broke its way through the double doors.

Lincoln was out of time.

Now instead of looking for an exit, he looked for a place to hide. He grabbed a moving blanket off a bin, climbed up one of the racks, pushed aside a coffee maker, and laid flat on the shelf like he was repurposed goods. He pulled the blanket up over him and tried to catch his breath, to still himself, but his heart was chugging too damn fast.

Bone feet tapped along the floor. It was coming down the aisle. Coming for him.

Lincoln realized he'd made a fatal mistake. He should have just kept running. Now he was stuck. And it was out there, its *tap tap tap* getting closer.

Beneath the blanket, Lincoln closed his eyes and raced through a prayer in his mind.

Please, forgive me. I've been a selfish man. Please, God. Please.

The creature stopped, just a few feet away, and hovered there. Searching? Waiting? In Lincoln's mind, he could see it there, inches from the shelf, scanning the rack. He tried to hold his breath. Was it waiting to pull back the blanket? And then what?

Lincoln just hoped it wouldn't hurt too much.

He prayed that God would come. He knew he'd led a lifetime of denial, and he couldn't blame Him if He didn't show.

It's going to hurt.

Another sound came from elsewhere in the warehouse. A rolling door sliding open.

Then bursts of gunfire. Loud.

The creature let out a scream that sounded like a collective cry of many humans wailing all at once, then fled down the aisle.

The gunfire doubled, then tripled, and Lincoln could smell the powder drifting through the air.

The gunfire ceased, and a man shouted.

"Come out!"

Lincoln lay still a moment, contemplating. Whoever was out there, they knew he was in here. They had guns. He didn't. He stayed put, wondering if—

"Lincoln!"

They know my name?

He pulled back the blanket and saw a flickering red glow at the end of the aisle. He slid slowly, quietly off the shelf, raised his hands in the air, and headed toward the light.

He turned the corner, and near an open rolling door were three men clutching shotguns.

"You Lincoln?" asked a large Hispanic man holding a red flare like a torch.

Lincoln brought his hands over his eyes and squinted in the sudden brightness.

"Are you Lincoln?" the big man repeated.

"Yeah," he answered.

"Daniel sent us. You ready?"

"For what?"

CHAPTER XLIV

Tel Aviv, Israel
Four Days After Event

In the darkness of the war room, his eyes desperate for light, Jonah resorted to what he knew. He pulled his Jericho 941, the textured grip comforting even though he couldn't see it. The emergency lights kicked on after a second, though they were dim and sputtering.

From outside, somewhere down the hallway, came the sound of gunfire.

So—this wasn't an electrical problem. They were under attack.

Two soldiers, weapons drawn, moved to secure the door that led to the hall, while the others collected the deputy prime minister and moved him toward a rear exit. Commander Berg scooped the backpack nuke off the table and strapped it over his shoulders. He collected the gray uniforms in a black duffel and slung that over his shoulder as well.

"Safe room!" he shouted.

The handle on the main door jiggled violently. Someone was trying to get in. Then something slammed against the door. Something strong.

Jonah and the others weren't going to wait to see what it was.

They retreated out the room's back exit, Jonah bringing up the rear with Ayelet, who limped along as fast as she could. The exit led to a long corridor lit by dimming back-up lights, and as they hurried along, more gunfire and screaming echoed from throughout the bunker.

The safe room was at the end of the hall, around a corner. But the door was blocked by a single woman. A pregnant woman. And in the flickering of the emergency lights, her arms unfurled and bones extended from her flesh like she was spreading her wings.

Jonah had been trained to shoot, the reflex muscle memory, but there were too many men in the way, and all he could do was watch this thing unfold before him. It was a thing that shouldn't exist and yet was as much a part of this world as he ever was.

The men at the front fired, quick double-taps to the woman's skull, and her head recoiled, agitated, and the men fired more, the sound of the gunshots amplified in the narrow concrete corridor. Finally, the woman dropped.

They moved forward then, slowly, reloading.

As the men stepped past the woman's body, they looked down at her. She lay on her back, and from her open mouth came a final asthmatic exhale. One man paused, and as he did there was a rustling beneath her clothes, in her belly, and something dropped from between her open legs. Jonah heard it but sure as hell didn't want to see it. The man opened fire, shooting down upon her and the space between her legs, sending the thing scurrying away in the darkness.

"Move!" he shouted.

But at that moment the open gunshot wounds in the woman's chest and belly bubbled and boiled and smoked and her gut burst open, blasting fluids and rind across the nearest soldiers. Jonah and Ayelet were at a safe distance, but four men were covered in her liquid, in bile and blood, sac and stench.

One of them turned back, and Jonah could see the dark fluids around his eyes and mouth. And it seemed to come upon them quickly, and the men stopped and screamed like they were burning, and they dropped to their knees, shouting at something that no one else could see.

And Jonah knew it had come.

He held Ayelet back. "Wait," he said, pulling her back to the corner of the hall.

And as he did the four men raised their rifles and opened fire again, this time into their former friends and allies.

Jonah dragged Ayelet away, and Commander Berg, who stood nearest, ran with them as they raced back the way they'd just come.

"Where are we going?" Ayelet said.

"Up."

"What?"

Jonah guided her, limping, down another hall, this one leading to a stairwell. They climbed to the top and a lonely metal door.

"Commander," Jonah said. "The suits."

Berg unslung his duffel and passed out the gear, and a minute later they were emerging from the bunker and into darkness. Snow fell onto the mesh stainless steel fabric that cloaked them, and while Jonah hoped it would keep out the electrical signal, it did nothing to keep out the cold.

CHAPTER XLV

Near the Fortress of Niha, Lebanon
Thirteen Days After Event

The woman was gone, Sunday had gone after her, and the baby on the blanket on the gas station floor was crying. The boy was the first to soothe her. He rushed in, scooped her up, and bounced her gently back and forth in his arms as if he'd done all this before.

Perhaps he has, thought Father Simon. *Perhaps with his brother.*

The old woman had been leaning her head back against the freezer glass, but suddenly she shot it forward and spoke in a voice not her own. A soft, womanly voice.

"Hand me the baby," she said.

The boy looked up, his eyes wide, as if he recognized that voice. Father Simon knew that look. A look of trust.

"Come on," she said again, gesturing with a hand. "Be a good boy. Bring her to me. I need to feed her."

Simon pointed his rifle at the old woman. "Who are you?"

She spoke again, facing Father Simon, but this time she used a different voice. The voice of a man. "Bring me the baby."

Now it was the priest who recognized the voice. "Father Zula?"

"Go," she said. "Get the baby."

"No," said Father Simon. He pressed the rifle against his shoulder and prepared to fire.

The girl placed her hand on the end of his barrel, her eyes welling with tears. "Please," she said. "Let me do it."

Father Simon nodded but did not lower the rifle. The girl raised her own and pointed it at her grandmother.

The old woman smiled at her granddaughter and spoke again in her normal voice. "Sami," she said. "Fadia, and Khaled, and Ali and Hasnah are here. And Papa. Do you want to see them? Papa is outside."

"Grandma?" The tears now spilled from the girl's eyes, and she lowered her weapon.

The priest held his own steady.

"Shhh," her grandmother said. "Go. Look out the window. See."

A knock sounded on the glass doors. Then a voice from outside. "*Saaammmmmiiiii.*"

Sami? The girl's name?

"Make them stop!" the girl shouted. She raised the rifle again, and it seemed she was going to do it this time.

"Sami," said the grandmother. "Please. If you kill me, they take me. Forever." She sobbed. "Please help me."

The girl, crying, lowered the rifle.

With a sudden blast, the old woman's head exploded into a mist of splatter against the freezer door.

For a moment the priest could only look at his weapon in shock. But it was not he who had fired. It was the boy, the rifle still smoking in his hands, who had put down the baby long enough to kill.

* * *

Kat and her father were eating ice cream. It was cold outside, and snowing, but inside her little house it was warm.

Her father smiled at her. "See?" he said. "Isn't everything better?"

She smiled back, but as she did, she saw a man pass by the window. A man with a gun, carrying a yellow light.

"Daddy?" she said. "There's a man outside."

Her father turned to look.

That's not your father.

She heard the voice. In her head. Very far away. A little voice. A whisper.

That's not your father.

She looked at her father again, and when he turned back around, she saw that his face was all black. No, not black... just not *there*. It was as if he had not been formed yet by the cosmos. Like she stared into the emptiness of the universe itself.

This was not her father.

"Daddy?"

It was the void.

"Kit Kat," it said, but its voice was very, very deep.

* * *

Despite the flare in his hand, Sunday stood in front of a wall of utter darkness. All his light was absorbed by it, and he could not see into it.

She's in there.

He hesitated, the memories of the bunker in his mind, but he stepped into the darkness anyway.

She was kneeling in the snow. She had been eating it; it was all over her face. He picked her up and called her name, but her eyes were rolled back in her head.

"Kat!" he called again, shaking her.

Her eyes rolled back down, and she looked at him. "John? Where am I?"

* * *

Most of her grandmother's head was gone, yet Sami stared at what was left, focusing on what was still recognizable, what was still left of the woman she had loved, and who had loved and cared for her. She wondered if she had truly just sentenced her own grandmother to some eternal hell of possession and horror.

"Come on!" the priest called to her, but Sami ignored him, kneeling before her grandmother and clutching her dead hand.

"Grandma," she said.

Her grandmother's dead, broken mouth moved, and she spoke from a half-shattered face.

"It's all right, dear."

Sami tried to pull away, but the dead woman gripped her hand, and Sami screamed.

As her grandmother stood, her head still half-missing, the boy ran forward with his rifle, presumably to fire again, and this time Sami could not question his choice. But her grandmother lifted a bony hand, knocked the rifle away, grabbed the boy's arm, and held him high, his feet dangling above the ground. He wriggled, and slipped free of his parka, dropping to the floor, and at the same moment another gunshot sounded behind Sami—the priest—and her grandmother's arm shattered, and Sami was able to pull away.

She looked back in terror as her grandmother changed, the creature within her surfacing. It stretched and pulled from within her skin, and her jaw snapped loose, and long clawed fingers emerged from inside her mouth.

The priest continued to fire, and the boy grabbed the baby from the blanket, and in seconds all of them were out the back door and fleeing into the dark woods.

CHAPTER XLVI

Deep Run, Maryland
Twelve Days After Event

The shots came rapidly, one after the other, with so much fury and precision Eve had to check herself to make sure she hadn't taken a bullet. Some of the creatures fell in a bloody pile on the snow, while the others, including the one that contained her father, scurried off like startled sheep.

A shadow emerged from the tree line. His face was covered in a dark scarf and snow goggles, and he wore a hooded jacket. He clutched an M-16 and pointed it at Eve.

The pistols were still in her hands. She pointed them skyward indicating her give, because she was done fighting, then placed the weapons gently on the snow.

The man came toward her, the snow crunching beneath his boots, and gestured again with the rifle, and she followed his instructions and climbed out of her sunken snow pit.

"Thank you," she said.

He just stared. Then he turned to leave.

"Wait," she called. "Where are you going?"

He didn't stop, didn't pause, just walked across the snow and disappeared into the darkness, leaving her alone.

She grabbed her weapons, returning the pistols to their holsters and reloading the rifle with the flare on the end as she ran to catch up with him.

"Wait," she said again. "Don't you think it's better if we stick together?"

The man's pace quickened, and he didn't turn. But he didn't try to stop her either, so she followed behind, at a short distance. Two were better than one, she figured, and he was a better shot than she was, and truth was, she just didn't want to be alone anymore. She resented the idea she would need anyone, especially any man, but this was a different world from the one in which she had been proudly independent.

He left the trees and crossed a snowy field, walking straight for a farmhouse. He stepped up onto the porch as if he lived there, knocked the snow from his boots, and stepped inside.

He left the door open.

Eve hesitated. This man had just saved her life. But that didn't mean she could trust him.

She stepped up onto the porch, clutching the gun, but went no farther.

She watched through the open doorway as he leaned his gun against the wall, removed his scarf and goggles, and lowered the hood of his jacket. He opened a black wooden stove, stoked it, added another log. The embers kindled, and she could see his shadowed face.

He was a man, not a beast, dark hair, maybe mid-forties, with a week's worth of stubble on his chin.

He took down a mason jar from a shelf and poured some of its contents into a kettle on the stove. His back was to her then and she couldn't see what he was doing in the darkness, but after a minute or so he lit a candle, and in its flickering light she saw a smoking hot mug and a plate of cookies sitting on a table.

He took the seat at the other side of the table, away from the mug and cookies. "Cider?" he said, still not looking her way.

Eve wondered if this was bait. If he had some other weapon on him. Or if he'd drugged the drink. She kept her grip on her rifle and knocked the snow off her boots and stepped slowly inside. She left the door open despite the cold. Even so, it was much warmer in here.

She sat opposite him, the chair dragging on the wooden floor. In the candlelight she could see him better. His fingers were dirty, and his hands looked rough. His face held several scars, like he'd been in a knife fight.

She set the rifle in her lap and picked up the mug, wondering if it was drugged like the frat boy had done to her beer, but she was cold and she at least wanted to feel the heat of the mug in her palms. She cradled it in her hands and blew into it so she could feel the steam on her face.

The man stood and poured himself a mug. "I'm going to start a fire," he said. He moved toward another room. "Do me a favor and close the door."

She was alone then, again, always alone, and she watched as the snow fell outside in the dark. She rose to her feet, mug in one hand, rifle in the other, and closed the door. She considered locking it, because she didn't want anything to get in, but she was also worried about getting out, so she left it unlocked.

Then she followed the man into the other room.

He was kneeling with his back to her in front of a brick fireplace, feeding kindling into a small flame, and a minute later the fire took and the room filled with dancing orange light. He sat on a couch and sipped his mug and nodded toward the fire.

She approached it. It had been more than a week since she'd truly felt warm.

"What were you doing out there alone?" he asked, his voice low and gentle.

"I was in a bunker, but the generator didn't work. I had no lights, no heat."

"Engines don't work. Neither do batteries. Anything that runs on electricity or holds electricity. It's all dead."

She wanted to sip the cider, but she was still worried about it, so she placed it on the hearth and held up her rifle-free hand to warm it in front of the growing flames.

"Where are you going?" he asked.

"I don't know," she lied. "I just couldn't sit in the dark anymore."

He sipped his mug.

"Are you alone?" she asked, looking around the room. It was quaint. Country-style living with dark paneled wood and red checkered blankets.

"My wife is somewhere, out there. With those things."

"Do you know what they are?"

He sipped again, and in the firelight the steam looked orange as it circled his face.

"The damned."

"One had my father's face."

"Then he's part of them now."

She nodded, and a lump stuck in her throat. "Do you think he's suffering?"

He paused.

"Yes."

She nodded, and she picked up her mug again. This time she sipped it, because she didn't really care what happened after that.

Later that night he offered her the bed, while he would take the couch, but she refused. So he set her up on the cushions with some checkered blankets and he retired to the bedroom.

She lay there and watched the crackling fire. The flames danced and swayed to the crackling of the burning logs. She thought about what she was going to do. What her father had asked of her in the letter. She wondered if the key he had written about truly held some power. If it could somehow save him.

If she could even find it. And figure out what to do with it.

If it wasn't just some worthless Roman artifact.

Her eyes started to get heavy, but she was scared to fall asleep. She kept glancing to the closed bedroom door, wondering if he was going to come out and cut her into little pieces or rape her.

She thought then of the man with the eye patch. The one who had appeared out of the darkness that night and swooped in and saved her from the frat boys with that same intent. She wondered again who he was, and how he had known where she lived, because she had woken the next morning in her own bed. Safe and sound. She wanted to know who he was, and as her eyes started to close, he was the last thought on her mind.

* * *

He looked down at her as she lay sleeping on the couch, her mouth slightly parted, a slow, low breathing coming from her lips. She had changed since he'd last seen her.

She had his ability. His blood. Some of the blood of the Christ.

Child of dust.

Daughter of mine.

But she was purer of heart. What sins could she possibly have committed? None as vast as his own, for certain. She had to be the one. The one who could wield the key and open the gate.

But he'd kill her before she could.

CHAPTER XLVII

Lanciano, Italy
39 CE

Longinus rested against the handle of his hoe and wiped the sweat from his forehead. The ground here was thick, and the clay wasn't cooperating with his blade. Longinus certainly didn't have to be out here fighting it—there were more than a hundred slaves working next to him in the morning sun—but he enjoyed a productive day of sweat.

As he took a break to look out over the olive tree seedlings in the distance, flanked by acres of more mature orchards, a cloud of dust appeared on the road leading toward the villa. Longinus watched the plume kick along the road until its source came into focus. Riders. Two dozen Roman soldiers.

Did Rome have need of him again? Though he had retired to his father's land, as a centurion he was always subject to be called back.

Setting his tool aside, he headed back toward the villa.

The riders galloped hard into the courtyard just as Longinus stepped onto the veranda. The lead man, glistening in golden plate, removed his red-crested helmet. "Longinus!" It was Tiberius, Longinus's old optio. He approached with open arms. "It has been too long, my friend."

This...this seems...

The two men embraced.

"I see the land fights back," Tiberius said with a laugh, pointing to the dirt stains on Longinus's clothes.

Something feels off. Like I've done this before.

He brushed his dirty hands across the front of his tunic. "Yes," he said slowly. He'd given this answer before. "But in silence."

"I bring news. We must speak," Tiberius said.

Longinus's wife appeared in the entranceway. She wore a simple blue tunic, and her long black hair framed a tan, delicate face.

Longinus gestured to her. "You remember Licinia."

"*Salve,*" she said. "Welcome to our home."

"The years have been far kinder to you, I see," Tiberius said with a smile, taking her hand.

"And your charms have not dulled," she replied.

"No children scampering around?"

She's going to say something. Something about how we spend our time here.

"Not as yet. But we try. Often. An enjoyable way to pass the time." She smiled at her husband.

What's happening?

Tiberius cocked an eyebrow. "Indeed."

Longinus led Tiberius to the tablinum, which was rarely used. Longinus preferred to work the land rather than write letters like a pompous ass in his office.

"So how is the life of a Praetorian?" he asked as he sat behind his desk.

Sitting across from him. Seeing him in this room? I've had this conversation here before.

"A battlefield has less deceit." Tiberius took a seat and stroked the horsehair plume of his helmet. "Gaius Caligula has brought back the treason trials. He has gone mad with power."

"I'm a long way from the affairs of Rome."

"You are not far enough," Tiberius said as he ceased the grooming of his helmet.

"I have fulfilled my duties."

"You have." Tiberius paused, as if searching for words. Longinus studied his old friend's face, looking for a tell as to why he was here, but could read nothing.

Tiberius continued. "The trials are only a front. The coffers have run dry and he seeks to seize land from the wealthy." He looked up at his former superior. "Do you wish to continue this farce?"

"What?"

"Do you see what we have built for you?"

Longinus searched his optio's face for answers.

"This memory, this day, you know where it leads," said Tiberius. "You know what happens tonight."

Longinus leaned back, his mind searching for some answer. Then it was there and he remembered.

"Yes."

"Would you rather live that moment over and over, watching us take turns on top of her, slicing her open again and again, or does this time before serve you better?"

"I was pleased as it was before."

"Then we have need." He smirked. "Rome calls again."

"For what?"

"Tom Ferguson has come to us. He has knowledge of the location of the key. The key you once held in your possession."

"What good is that? It never worked for me."

"The key can only be used by those on the road to salvation. You have never been on such a path. Even when you preached the way, it was only a means to an end."

"What do you want?"

"Return. Find the one who can seek out the key."

"And then?"

"Destroy both, or the second gate shall be opened."

"If I refuse?"

"Do not forget where you are, centurion. Your heaven is in hell."

CHAPTER XLVIII

The boy ran with the others through the woods. They could hear it behind them. The old woman. What she had become. It was clicking and cracking and snapping the tree branches. The baby was crying as they ran through the night, but the boy was in no position to soothe her.

They took a stand near the edge of the trees, but the boy had left his rifle in the gas station, and after a few rounds the priest and the girl both clicked empty, and still the thing had not slowed.

They fled into an open field, and the priest shouted and pointed to a barn, and they sprinted inside. The priest shuttered the double doors behind them as quickly as he could, but said he didn't think it would hold long.

There was no back door.

The stench inside the barn was ripe, even in the frost. The place was filled with dead animals. Fallen sheep and lambs, their white fur matted with globs of ice, their mouths and little lips frozen open. Starved to death. A black goat was still alive, barely, their reflection upon its glossy mirrored eyes, and he moved his head with them as they passed, as if to make sure they saw him too, because he was hungry.

They tucked into shadows in the corner of a pen. The boy tried to quiet the baby. Since he could not speak to soothe her, he tried instead to stick his finger in her mouth for her to suck on, but she wanted none of that.

"Here," the girl said. She took the baby and soothed her with her whispers, and the boy remembered his mother doing such a thing for him on nights when he was scared of the things in the dark.

Quieting her didn't matter. The creature was already at the barn doors and slamming against them with such force the rafters shook. It took only a few blows before the doors broke and there were bone clicking steps on the hay-covered floor. It was in here with them now.

A low growl sounded, and the boy realized suddenly that the dog was not with them. It had taken an interest in sniffing around the barn at the dead things, and in their haste to hide they had not brought it into the shadows with them. The dog's growls turned to barks as the thing approached.

It came into view of their hiding spot. A tall, spider-like creature made of human flesh, on long legs made of bone. It possessed the faces of the damned on its head, and it towered over the barking dog, and the dog was going to die.

The boy wanted to race over to save it, because in their mutual silence, they had grown close. But all he could do was watch—and then not watch, squeezing his eyes shut because he did not want to see his friend die.

A dozen gunshots rang out in rapid fire.

The boy's eyes flew open, and the creature turned and scrabbled back out of the barn. There were more gunshots out there in the darkness, and then all was quiet.

A minute later, a voice called from the barn door. The one-eyed man.

"You all right?"

"Yeah," said the priest, and even though it was a one-syllable word, he could barely get it out.

* * *

Not all the animals were dead. Four horses had survived in one large pen at the back. They were gaunt, but in much better shape than the goat, and even greeted Sunday with a flap of lips as he approached. He saw that there had been another horse in the pen, a colt, but it had since starved and was rotten in the corner. It had been plucked and eaten at by the others, a notion he thought was rare in the hearts of horses.

He checked again on Kat and Mara, and they were as he had left them, cuddled in the corner. She had told him she could remember nothing that happened in the woods, and he had left it at that. But he knew he would no longer be sleeping now. He would have to stay by her side—even if it meant he tied himself to her.

There were some sacks of feed in one corner, and he hauled one over to the horses' pen. He slit the bag and filled their buckets, and they were so eager to eat they pushed him and one another aside to get to it. Then he pulled a tin of carrots from his pouch, opened it, and placed it in front of the dog, who looked up at him surely wondering why this man kept feeding him this awful stuff.

"Yeah, I know," Sunday said.

The boy had apparently lost his parka back at the gas station, but the priest had rummaged through some storage and come up with a puffy blue winter coat that was only a little too large for the boy. Sunday wondered if it too had belonged to a child, and if so, what had become of him. But when the boy put it on, Sunday did a double take.

Boy, blue jacket, hood. But not imagined this time. If it ever had been.

When the horses were fed and watered, he outfitted them with bridles and reins. The kind thing would be to let them loose, as they had done for the goat. But their own need was too great.

* * *

They found their way back to the gas station road and followed it, this time on horseback, again staying in the trees to either side. When they came near a town, Sunday went in alone with an empty duffel, and found a hunting supply store. It was loaded primarily with shotguns, Anakon semi-auto, but also Deryas with a vertical load giving them a ten-shot capacity. He grabbed what he needed, not just the weapons but spare magazines and chest rigs to tuck them into, and more spare guns and mags for the horses, and a backpack used to haul camping gear, which he rigged with carabiners and straps to make a baby harness for Kat to wear on her back. When he returned to the others, he geared them up and showed them all how to use the long guns, because they were different than the rifles, and how to load and reload.

They had horses, they had food, and they had weapons. For the first time since this all began, they were well equipped.

Maybe they stood a chance.

CHAPTER XLIX

Outside Tel Aviv, Israel
Four Days After Event

Ayelet couldn't believe she was still alive. They'd been on the move for only a few minutes, and yet she was surprised they'd survived even that long. She had fully expected to die the moment they surfaced, the creatures waiting to ambush them in the cold darkness. Instead the three of them—her, Jonah, and Commander Berg—had emerged from the bunker alone, closing the door on the screaming below, like sealing a submarine hatch on drowning men.

Now they were tucked inside a grocery store, to hide, to regroup, and to load the duffel with some food. They walked the dark aisles in their mesh metal suits, stepping over the dead, and she tried to push them from her mind by debating whether it would be better to go with canned goods, which were heavier, or with bread, which was lighter but less nutritious.

She turned the corner at the end of an aisle and practically walked into a dead child, a young boy, slumped in a grocery cart. His little fingers were cold and dead, his head tilted back, his mouth open. He wore blue zip sneakers, but they were stained blood red, and his feet dangled like stiff dead weights.

Ayelet felt the tears swell. She didn't want to cry and have the men see it, so she turned away toward a shelf of cookies, as if she were choosing between chocolate chip or oatmeal raisin.

What kind of god would do that? To a little boy?
Where is God now?
He doesn't care. Not about the boy. Not about us.
We're on our own.

Ayelet had so wanted a child of her own. She'd had a husband, but she wasn't ready yet, and by the time she was, he had left her. Because he knew what she did, how she slept with other men for the homeland, and he made her feel like a whore. Which she was. And so eventually he left, and she was alone, like always.

And then there was something else she desired. Something very, very different. She got the pills easily enough. She kept them on the nightstand next to the bed, even packed them on her trips, and every night she stared at them and wondered if tonight would be the night. It wasn't because her husband had left her. That wasn't why she contemplated suicide night after night. It was because she knew that if she ever did have a baby, then one day that child would ask her about her work, or even about what she used to do, and she, Ayelet, would lie to her child, not mention that she had slept with men, with many men, that she had let them do whatever they wanted to her because it was something she did for her country. She would know this lie in her heart, but she could never tell her child, because deep down she knew it was wrong.

Deep down, she knew that she was a whore.

Berg and Jonah emerged from another aisle, and Jonah hesitated. He must have seen the child in the cart, seen how Ayelet was staring away, put two and two together.

"We'll get the food," he whispered. "It's okay."

The men collected the food in the duffel, and they loaded up a cooler as well, and Ayelet said she felt strong enough to carry the cooler strapped over her shoulder. By the time the three of them walked to the front of the store, they were hauling forty cans of food, two can openers, ten loaves of bread, plenty of gauze and antibacterial cream and baby wipes, two Jericho 941s with twenty-four rounds total, and one five-kilo-ton nuclear bomb.

Berg picked up a map by the register and unfurled it across the conveyor. He measured with his fingers, confirming what he already knew. "One hundred sixty kilometers."

"I'll just slow you down," Ayelet said. "You could get there in a day or so without me."

Berg nodded in agreement, but Jonah wouldn't have it.

"You're coming," he said. "Either you walk or I carry you. But we're all going."

"Then let's go," said Berg, adjusting the straps on the backpack.

They stepped back into the snow, Ayelet hobbling, Jonah bringing up the rear to cover her. They moved slowly, because of Ayelet, Berg scanning back and forth. So far, the suits were working. None of them had felt the need to go crazy and kill anyone.

So far.

CHAPTER L

Sidon, Lebanon
Fourteen Days After Event

The city was on fire, a thousand embers in the night, houses and buildings puking inky black into the already dark sky. Tall buildings along the distant shore burned too, giant coal chimneys, beasts with a thousand simmering eyes.

From the outskirts, John Sunday used binoculars to scan the streets. In the light of the fires he saw more of the spider humans creeping along streets slick with blood and snow and entrails. One group of creatures had assembled a writhing stack of humans, some thirty feet high, piled like bloody plywood, and as Sunday watched they dragged one from the pile, a young man, still alive and screaming, and they ripped off his arms and legs as if he were a bone branch, and three of the creatures took his legs and arms and seared them to their own flesh. What was left of him on the ground continued to slither, for there was no death here, and now he was a pulpy trail of organs and broken bone and a head that could only scream and weep for mercy.

Sunday panned the binoculars. On the fronts of some of the buildings, men and women were spiked to the wall, their faces peeled to skull, their skin ripped from them in strips, and yet they too wiggled and squirmed. In some places they were nailed together so closely and thickly that the very buildings appeared to be alive, writhing red sails of flesh that fluttered and wept and begged.

And all of this was on but one street.

How many more streets are like this?

Sunday lowered the binoculars, because he had seen enough. He looked over at Kat, who nestled Mara in the papoose.

"What do you see?" she asked.

He thought of her there, spread open and pinned with nails, her body peeled. He thought of being next to her, his gut split as it had been in the coma dreams, as they suffered together for eternity.

"Nothing," he said.

He wanted to roll over. Give up, because he could feel the hope draining. What was he thinking? There was no escape.

This child is supposed to make a difference? Here? With this?

But he knew he wouldn't let them get to her. To Kat. And it was then that he understood.

He wasn't doing any of this to save the world. This was not a crusade for God. He was only trying to salvage the small spark inside the two of them, the one that had once burned so bright it would blight the sun. He didn't know how to love, because he'd never been taught, but he would do whatever it took to frame a fortress around them, until hell itself could not breach their shore.

He turned back to the burning city, wondering how to proceed. They had hoped to take a boat from here, but for all he knew, the boats had been burned as well. And if they weren't, who knew if they could even be safely reached. Perhaps they should head farther north, into Syria, or south and back into Israel. But given what he'd seen, the land offered no escape.

No, a boat was the right choice. Hide on the dark waters. There were some uninhabited islands off the coasts of Turkey and Greece. Maybe one of those would have enough food supply to sustain them. For a few months anyway. Maybe a year.

There was a darker section to the north of the burning city. If they could head around that way, then cut back south along the shore, perhaps they could avoid most of the masses. Perhaps. But he would be pressing them between two walls, one made of water, the other of fire.

"We're going to cut through there," he whispered, pointing to the dark path, his mind made up, his decision final.

Or perhaps, he thought, his final decision.

CHAPTER LI

Philadelphia, Pennsylvania
Two Days After Event

Lincoln raced with the others down the snow-covered streets, through the darkness, their heads on pivots. They raced down Spruce to Third Street, passing through a civilization that was no more. An empty postal truck with its doors open, the mail scattered and blowing in the wind, never to be delivered. A restaurant with outdoor seating, the tables and umbrellas toppled and food frozen on plates on the mesh tabletops.

The three who had come to collect him had rapid-fired their names off in the warehouse, but Lincoln hadn't gotten them all. The big Hispanic guy was Miguel. He caught that one. The other two were older, probably sixties, a black man and a white man. Both big guys too. All three carried shotguns.

Before they left Goodwill, Lincoln had asked if he could have a gun.

"No," Miguel answered simply.

They crisscrossed for half an hour, navigated through a park, and stopped in front of a colonial-style church nestled in a row of brick buildings. A white steeple ascended toward the dark sky, but beneath that it was all brick, with dozens of arched windows. A blue hanging sign frosted in snow read *Christ Church, Open Daily 9-5*.

Lincoln followed the three men up the steps, and the big black man banged on the door, a series of knocks in rhythm, a code, which Lincoln thought for sure was him pounding out "Amazing Grace."

The doors were unlocked from the inside, and one of them swung wide, revealing an Asian man with pockmarked cheeks, glasses, and an AR-15. He nodded to the three big men as they stepped inside, and looked askance at Lincoln as he followed.

As soon as they were in he locked the door, sat on a little foldout chair, and laid the rifle across his lap. Lincoln guessed this was his post.

The others knocked the snow off their shoes before stepping into the main sanctuary, which was lit with candles. The church was all white—paneling and pews and balconies on either side. At the front of the church, beneath a giant dark arched window, were several foldout tables loaded with guns. Rifles, shotguns, handguns lined up by caliber, corresponding ammo next to them in boxes… it was all laid out like a parish-hall picnic.

And the place had an actual congregation of sorts, maybe sixty people all told. Old people, homeless people, dirty families and children. Some were in the pews praying, others were giving a church service, while still others just sat and read their Bibles. None of them so much as glanced at Lincoln, his new thrift store boots squeaking on the marble floor.

They walked past the altar, in front of which stood a clawfooted bathtub. For baptisms, perhaps? Lincoln wanted to ask, but he had to hurry to keep up with the men's long strides. Two of them one way, and Miguel went another, gesturing for Lincoln to follow. They departed the sanctuary through a side door and went down a short hall into a kitchen where a woman was stirring something in three large pots on butane burners.

God, it smells good.

They continued on past her too, moving between stacks of canned goods lined up like an aluminum hallway, and finally Miguel stopped at a back door and knocked.

"Yes," said a voice from within.

Miguel turned to Lincoln and nodded toward the door without a word.

Lincoln stepped forward, opened the door, and walked into the room beyond. It was a simple office, lit by a single candle. In the corner, in the shadows, sat a man.

"Hello, Lincoln," the man said.

His voice was weak and strained, but Lincoln recognized it. He had known who was behind this door before he had even opened it.

Daniel Vicario.

"Come. Sit," Daniel said.

Lincoln sat on the only chair in the room, and Daniel rolled forward in his wheelchair, moving from the shadows into the light.

He looks awful.

It had been only a few days since Lincoln had last seen him, but Daniel looked as though he'd aged twenty years. Only a few strands of hair were left on his head, his eyes were deeply withered in his skull, and his bones were prominent through paper-thin skin.

"Thank you for coming," he wheezed.

Resting on his lap was the wooden box. The box was open, the key resting inside. No glow. No bioluminescent golden hum to show its power. Just a cold key in a dark box.

Lincoln wondered how much radiation was now in this room with him.

"How have you been in my head?" Lincoln asked.

Daniel smiled, and it was then that Lincoln noticed his lips were bloody and chapped and most of his teeth were gone.

"You know how. The key is the key."

"How?"

"You want the scientific explanation?"

Lincoln nodded.

"It emits an electromagnetic pulse. A kind of signal, like Wi-Fi. And that is where our science ends. Somehow, I can hear that signal. When I hold the key, I see things in my mind, things beyond these walls. Just glimpses, like I'm looking out a foggy shower door, but enough to sometimes put the pieces together. People emerge. Like you. And when that happens, I can talk to you. Show you things. Put pictures in your mind." He nodded toward the door. "I was able to call all those people out there. That's how I brought them here."

"Why?"

"This is my church. This is where I've come every Sunday since I was a boy. That's my congregation."

He shifted in his seat and pulled a handkerchief from his pocket. He used it to wipe a curd of spit from the corner of his mouth, then continued.

"The problem, Lincoln, is that those things out there... they have their own frequency. They can put things in your head too, things that aren't real. Or... maybe they are. I don't really know what that means anymore. But they can pretend to be people they're not. They like being relatives, particularly dead ones, because it fools you. Like the one you thought was your father. They communicate through that signal, like a hive working in sync. Somewhere out there they have an antenna, broadcasting, keeping them connected. That's the frequency that can show up in your head. Make you see things that aren't there. Make you go crazy, Lincoln."

"How do I know I'm not already crazy?" Lincoln asked. In truth, he'd considered the possibility many times over recent days. "How do I know any of this is real? If what you're saying is true, how do I know that what I'm seeing right now isn't just something that you, or them, is putting in my head?"

Daniel shrugged. "You don't. The crazy rarely know they're crazy. But as for them getting inside your head?" He nodded toward the box in his lap. "The key is like an umbrella. As long as you're here beneath it, within range of its frequency, they can't get to you. Can't find you. Can't get inside our heads." He paused. "At least I think they can't."

None of this, even if it could be believed, answered Lincoln's most pressing question. "What do we do now?"

"We wait," Daniel said.

"For what?"

"For the ones coming for the key. And when they arrive... we fight."

Daniel wheeled in a little closer, and Lincoln could smell traces of rot on him. The man had to know that the key was killing him. Had to know that every time he opened that box, he was irradiating himself. How could he not? But he'd done it anyway, had kept that box unlocked and open on his lap, so he could call all these people here. Including Lincoln.

"Thank you," Lincoln said. "For restoring my sight."

"Don't thank me. The key showed me where you were, helped me hear you crying out in the darkness. I only follow its will. If there is anyone you should thank, it's God. Do you believe that, Lincoln?"

"I... I don't know."

"Would you like to?"

The answer came faster, more easily, than Lincoln expected. "Yes."

Daniel smiled. "Then let's see if you're ready."

"For what?"

"To serve in the Army of God."

* * *

As Lincoln climbed into the tub of ice-cold water, he kept asking himself why he'd agreed to this. But the answer no longer mattered. He was all in.

Daniel stood before the tub, and the congregation gathered around.

"You're a priest?" Lincoln asked. He was still fully clothed, but that did nothing to warm him, and his teeth chattered.

"Just a believer baptizing another believer," Daniel answered.

He gestured for the congregation to come closer, then began.

"Do you, Lincoln, accept that Jesus is the Christ?"

Lincoln was definitely in it now. In the water, and up to his neck. He nodded, hoping that his answer would somehow lead to the end of whatever was going on outside. Or at least, would lead to his acceptance into heaven when the creatures finally came for him. "Yes," he said.

"Do you accept Him as your Lord and Savior?"

"Yes."

"Do you believe that He shall return in our time of need?"

"I do."

"And will you die to protect the Key to the Kingdom of Heaven and the disciple who holds it?"

Lincoln paused. *Disciple? What disciple?* But he nodded, just wanting to get this over with and get out of the freezing water. "Yes."

"Lincoln, I now baptize you in the name of the Father, the Son, and the Holy Spirit, for the forgiveness of your sins and give you the gift of the Holy Spirit."

And with that, Miguel stepped forward and pushed Lincoln's head under the water. It happened so quickly that Lincoln didn't even have a chance to close his eyes, and so it was that there, immersed, under the water, he saw her.

A woman. Young, pretty, white, with long blond hair. She was walking across snow, and behind her followed a man wearing a snow-white hood. Lincoln was walking beside them, as if they were all out for a stroll.

The man stopped, lowered his hood to reveal a scarred face, and he turned his head to stare straight at Lincoln. But then his face changed. His eyes went from blue to green, to gray, to black, those shifting eyes never leaving Lincoln's, though Lincoln knew he wasn't even really there next to him.

The man then cast his gaze behind him, and there stood an army of a thousand of those things. Some looked human, but most were twisted masses of gnarled limbs, and they all marched together, the earth shuddering beneath them.

The man looked back at Lincoln once more.

"See you soon," he said.

Lincoln lifted his head out of the icy water and gasped for air. He looked around the church, at Daniel and Miguel and the congregation that stared down at him.

"What *was* that?" he said.

"That," said Daniel, "is the coming of hell."

CHAPTER LII

Outside Elishama, Israel
Eight Days After Event

Ayelet, Jonah, and Berg followed the interstate to help them make some time. They walked the 481 to the 40, past cars stopped in a forever traffic jam. They'd seen plenty of dead, and at one point found a stack of bodies piled near a bridge. What they had not seen were the things that had done the stacking.

Are they gone? Did they do what they needed to do and then left?

Ayelet knew that was an optimistic thought. More likely they'd just been lucky and had crossed through an area that had already been swept. Everything killed, so they had moved on to the next zone. Perhaps that meant she and the others were actually behind enemy lines. Or maybe it was all just one big enemy line. All she knew for sure as they continued through the cold was that there was leaking in between her legs, and that all this walking had caused some of her stitching to come undone.

In four days, they had traveled only twenty-eight kilometers. Seven kilometers a day. That was about as fast as she was able to go, and now she was getting even slower, her walk more of a scoot. Jonah was patient, but Berg was quick to snap at her. He'd told her to hurry up on several occasions, and she was pretty sure he'd already had at least one private conversation with Jonah about leaving her behind somewhere. Ayelet halfway agreed with the idea. But she knew Jonah wouldn't move on without her, so she kept going.

On the fourth night they camped inside an abandoned RV on the side of the road. They even found some food there, and so dined on that stash instead of their own. And then they sat in silence, listening to the wind outside, each no doubt wondering if they would soon hear something outside the frail aluminum door.

That was when Berg skipped right past Jonah and had the conversation he wanted to have directly with Ayelet. He said to her in no uncertain terms that it would be better for her to stay here. Let them move on. She was ready to do it, because her stitches made it feel like she was slowly coming undone.

But Jonah cut in. "She stays with us."

Ayelet wondered then if Berg would just leave them both in the middle of the night.

She took the back bedroom, while the men took the bunk and couch in the front of the RV. She took off the metal suit pants, though she wasn't supposed to. They'd all had to at least lower them from time to time to relieve themselves, and she'd had to re-dress her wounds before this, and so far no one had gone crazy, so she figured it was fine as long as she didn't do it for too long. She found a lighter and a little makeup mirror in a woman's purse, then unwrapped some of the bandages and pulled them apart from her clinging skin. There was blood on the bandage, but with the mirror she also saw brown in her wound, and she wondered if it was an infection she could overcome.

She cleaned herself as best she could with the baby wipes, and applied some ointment, then rewrapped herself with clean bandages.

She put the pants back on and lay back on the bed. It didn't matter if she closed her eyes; it was dark either way.

Seven kilometers?

A day?

It wasn't much, and she expected tomorrow would be even slower. Berg was right: she was harming the mission, and it made sense for her to stay behind. This abandoned RV on the side of the road in the middle of nowhere was as good a place as any.

There was a little tap on the sliding door.

"Yes?"

"It's me," Jonah said.

"What? What is it?" she sat up, alarmed.

"No. It's okay. We're safe. I just... I just wanted you to say that we're going to do this. Together. Okay?"

"You have a mission. And I'm standing in your way."

He paused. "Can I come in?"

She sat up, a little groan. What was he expecting here? Did he want to talk, or was he expecting something more in return for his good will? He couldn't possibly expect her to somehow pleasure him. Could he? To thank him with her mouth for what she could not do between her legs?

It didn't matter. She'd been with so many men, it just didn't matter anymore. What was one more? Especially now?

She slid open the partition. She couldn't really see him there in the darkness, but she spoke to him anyway.

"Do you want to lie down?"

Her hand found his, and she pulled him forward. He closed the partition behind him, and they lay on the bed together, her fingers on his chest.

She moved her hand down between his legs, but he took her wrist and brought it back up to his chest.

"I'm not here for that," he said.

"Then what do you want?"

"I want you to feel like you're not alone."

She was about to say something more, to tell him it was okay, that she would please him. Instead she lay back in his arms. And that was how she fell asleep.

* * *

She woke to the sound of a child. At first she thought it was the dream, the same dream she'd had the last few nights. In that dream she would see a woman carrying a bundled baby as she walked through a snowy forest. The trees around her were dark, and thick with the chirping of crickets. Then the woman would fall, and a man was there to pick her and the baby up, and she saw him, the man with one eye. John Sunday.

But this was different.

"Ima," the child called.

Mommy.

She drifted awake and heard the child again and realized the shout came from outside the RV. She sat up straight in the bed and wondered again if it was just a dream, but when she scooted slowly off the bed, and felt the twitch of pain between her legs, she knew that she was indeed awake and whatever she happened across now was real.

She parted the blinds for the tiny window and looked out across the snow. It was too dark to see much, but beneath the wind, she heard a whimper. And then, from just below the window, a little foot kicked out into the snow. A foot wearing one of those little blue zip shoes. The foot retreated once more from her view, leaving a drag of blood across the snow.

No.

The boy from the grocery cart. He was dead. Dead as could be. And he was here.

A scratching against the outside skin of the RV, then a little *tap tap* and a soft voice.

"Ima?"

Oh, God.

Before she could put another thought together, the scratching against the RV moved upward, onto the roof, quick and fast like a rat, the scampering of little feet.

She reached over to wake Jonah.

"Jonah," she said, but her voice trailed behind her. "Jonah!" she said again, louder. She pushed him, hard, but he didn't even move an inch. It was like she wasn't actually there to touch him.

She felt a shifting of weight, as if someone lumbered across the RV, and she thought that was a curious sensation for a dream. The feeling of motion. There was more scurrying on the roof, and she moved to the little panel door that separated the bedroom from the rest of the RV. It was already open, and she wondered if someone had come in and watched them while they slept.

She stepped out of the bedroom. Berg was gone. The door to the RV was wide open. And when she moved to the door to close it, fear shot through her.

On his knees in the snow outside, beside a flickering green flare, was Berg. He was naked, the metal suit lying in the snow next to him. In front of him, set in the snow like an altar, was the backpack nuke.

And he bowed repeatedly, banging his head again and again into the ground.

Was this a dream? Was he really out there?

There was more scurrying on the roof. "See, Ima?"

Berg stopped bowing. He reached forward and unzipped the backpack.

Ayelet stumbled back, away from the man with the nuclear bomb, tripped over her own feet. In the flickering green light from the flare outside, she saw one of the guns on the kitchen counter. She picked it up and felt it in her hands. It was heavy. Cold. It was real.

She moved back to the door, fearing the child would jump down on top of her as she stepped outside, and called out to the naked man in the snow.

"Berg!"

He ignored her, all his attention on opening the backpack.

She walked barefoot across the cold, the ice crunching beneath her. The sound of crickets was loud in her ears.

"Berg!" she shouted again, and she wondered if she was real and he was dream, or the other way around.

She came around in front of him so he could see her, and she pointed the gun at him. He was intent on getting to the nuclear device. He was preparing to set it off. Here. In this place. Far from where it could do any harm.

"Berg, stop," she pleaded, her hands shaking from cold and fear. She could sense those things out there, shifting beyond the halo of the flare. They were out there, watching. Clicking and chirping.

Berg finally raised his head to look at her. To her surprise, his eyes were wide with fear, and despite his trained bravado, tears rolled down his face.

"Please," he whispered.

But even as he spoke his hands kept moving, as if he had no control over them, reaching for the central bar on the device. The one that would activate the bomb.

"Berg, don't," she said.

He grabbed the handle, about to pull it up.

She fired.

The round rang out with such cold clarity in the icy silence of the night that it erased any doubt that this was a dream. What followed offered more validity. The round tore through his skull and knocked him backwards and he bled with fierceness into the snow.

What she had done was real. She had killed him.

Jonah appeared in the door of the RV, his expression confused, trying to decipher what had happened. Then he pointed a gun at her.

"Drop it!" he shouted.

She did as he asked, but not because he had asked. If he was possessed too, she just didn't care anymore.

She looked down both sides of the snow road, and she felt them out there. Searching.

Then she heard another voice. This one inside her head, interrupting her own thoughts.

Get inside.

Jonah stepped across the snow, his weapon still trained on her, but his eyes on Berg. "What did you do?"

She kneeled and closed up the backpack. "That wasn't Berg."

She tried to lift the backpack, but it was too heavy, so she began dragging it back across the snow. "We have to get inside," she said. "They're looking for us."

Jonah scanned the dark road. "I don't see anything."

"They're there."

He grabbed the backpack and lifted it over his shoulder. They both got back into the RV. And as they shut the feeble door behind them, Ayelet wondered if she was going crazy.

CHAPTER LIII

Deep Run, Maryland
Thirteen Days After Event

Eve had wanted to wake before him, but as she stirred, she saw him there again by the fire, stoking the embers and feeding another log so that it renewed the heat in the room.

"How'd you sleep?" he asked.

"Good, thanks," she said, sitting up quickly, alarmed that she had been so vulnerable, and he could watch her as she slept.

"I have eggs," he said.

"Um, no. I should get going." She started sliding into her boots.

He turned his head to look at her, the fire shadowing one side of his face. "You're welcome to stay here as long as you want. I'm leaving."

"Where are you going?"

"My wife was on her way to Philadelphia when all this happened. Maybe she's still out there." He paused. "I have to know."

Eve slid on her other boot, debating what she should tell this man. She couldn't tell him why she too was headed to Philly. He'd think she was crazy. But what were they supposed to do? Both head that direction, on the same road, and pretend the other wasn't there? Besides, maybe he could help her get her part of the way there, and then she could split off later.

She kept coming back to the same thought: two guns were better than one.

"What if I go with you?" she said.

He looked at her again. "It's too dangerous. Stay here. Take the house. There's plenty of food."

"But for how long?"

He shrugged. "A few months."

"No, how long before those things come? Storm the house? That little lock isn't going to stop them."

He paused. "No. It won't."

"If there's two of us, maybe we have a better chance of making it," Eve said. "Maybe I can help you find her. After all, I owe you." She scooted forward on the couch and held out a hand. "I'm Eve."

He took it. "Mason. Mason Fin." He took a breath, contemplating. "Thank you, but I can't let you do this. It's too dangerous."

"No more dangerous than if I stay here by myself."

He said nothing. Silence filled the room.

"I'm just…" She focused on tying her laces. "I'm just trying to do the right thing."

After a long moment, he replied. "Me too," he said.

CHAPTER LIV

Sidon, Lebanon
Fourteen Days After Event

The dark street was slick with snow and blood, and the fires in the distance were so bright it made the shadows flicker and move. They were following the course of a river choked with mud and ice and bodies and blood. The priest had said it flowed to the coast, so they traced it as closely as they could, but even in the cold the stench was ripe, the smell of dismembered bodies and open bowels.

As they ran, Sunday couldn't shake a gnawing feeling that something was wrong. Something beyond the terror he could see. He felt like something was watching them, and he was missing something.

And then they were there, on the shore, the dark waters of the Mediterranean lapping the sand. They kept running, Sunday driven by the hope that they'd come across some wayward fishing boat and could cast off right there. But there were only empty lifeguard stands and umbrellas, and the sound of eternal waves hitting the shore, and a cold, howling wind that whistled as it whipped their faces.

And... a castle?

He saw it illuminated from behind by the fires. It stood out in the water, with a bridge leading out to it, two towers on either side.

Then a voice came, over the cold wind, from behind him, only a whisper.

"*Here*," the voice said.

He turned, and there they were. An army of thousands, perhaps more. Teeming masses scurrying and twitching their limbs, some of the bodies moving as if being propelled by a will not their own.

They had been funneled here, toward this place. And in his haste to gain their freedom, Sunday had taken the bait.

The priest raised his gun, but then apparently did the math, and lowered it again. The only shots of any worth here would be into their own skulls.

The masses parted, and a lone figure moved forward, crossing the beach toward them. He was languid in stride, and yet in an instant he was standing in front of them, mere feet away, as if to save time he'd skipped the long walk.

The janitor from the hospital.

"There is no escape here," he said.

And then the janitor shifted, and he was the man who had hunted Sunday since the cave. The man with green eyes. Silas Egin.

"Is this better?" he asked. "Someone more recognizable?"

Sunday answered by raising the rifle and firing. But the bullet passed right through the man. Harmlessly.

Egin smiled and tapped his head. "We're here, John. For each of you."

"What you want," Sunday replied, "will never happen."

"What are you protecting? *Our* seed flows through you, not His," he said, gesturing skyward. "Why does He not come rescue you? Because He has turned His back. Like He has done to us." He pointed to Kat and the baby. "All you carry is false hope."

"So come take it," Sunday said.

Egin smiled again. "You tease. You know well the child must be given. Surrendered like Golgotha. Perhaps you need a small incentive."

Hands emerged from the sand and wrapped around their legs, holding them in place. More hands grabbed their weapons. Sunday looked to Kat, who clutched at her baby. Dead fingers dug into her calves and moved up her body, lengthening their bones and flesh as they traced her torso, and multiplying, until they clawed at her thighs, her chest, her face all at once. Sunday fought to reach her, but he could not move.

"I told you the whore was ours," Egin said. He stepped up to Kat, stopping directly in front of her, and stroked her hair, much like Sunday had done in the boat. "This is our time," he whispered.

The clawed hands sank into her flesh.

Kat screamed, and looked to Sunday—and she was ripped open right in front of him.

It happened so quickly she made no sound, she simply fell limp and Mara fell from her arms onto the sand, screaming and crying, and the hands that had just torn Kat apart, the fingers of the damned, moved on to the infant, scratching at the child's flesh, but though they clutched and grasped, they could not pull her down.

"You motherfucker!" Sunday screamed. "I'll fucking kill you!!"

Egin ignored him.

"Who among you shall give this child?" he said softly. He stepped in front of the priest. "You, Father? To repent for your sins with the children?"

Sunday saw then that the hands from the earth that crawled over the priest were smaller. Children's hands. And they did not claw at him, but caressed him as they held him in place.

Egin's face changed, and the priest's eyes widened. "Father Zula?"

"Do you hear their sobs?" Egin said, leaning in. "Or are you deaf to it?"

The children's hands grabbed the priest's ears, ripped them from his skull, and tossed them onto the sand like dead fish.

Egin moved on to the junkie. The hands spread her arms wide, revealing open mouths in her arms, hungering. Egin became the grandmother, and she touched the junkie gently, soothingly. "Shhh," she said. "I'm here. And look what I have for you…"

The grandmother's fingers became nipples, filling her hungering mouths with some fluid. The junkie's eyes rolled back in her head, and she fell limp in the clutches of the arms, which released her onto the shore next to the baby in the sand.

The junkie rolled on to her side. She started to reach for the baby. And then she stopped herself and looked up at her grandmother.

"I love you, Grandma," she said. "Be with God."

The hands grabbed at her again and filled her veins, and she fattened from the fluids, filling like a tick, until her arms and legs burst and split apart and wept black pus.

Egin stopped before the boy, and turned to the massed creatures. They parted, and from within their mass two figures stepped forward. Sunday recognized them from the photo at the house. The child's mother and little brother. They were not dead and rotten, but as fresh as they had been in that photo.

"Asif," the boy's mother said, stroking his cheek.

The little boy in the blue winter coat wept, and she wiped the tears from his eyes. She nodded at him, and he at her.

And the hands released him.

He stepped past his mother and brother, and approached the baby.

"Don't," Sunday said.

The boy picked up Mara and cradled her in his arms. He returned with her to his mother.

"No," Sunday begged.

The boy looked one last time at the infant... and then he handed her to his mother.

It was done.

The army screamed and hollered, and the hands tore into the others and split them apart on the shore. The priest. The junkie. Even the boy who had just delivered their victory. Their blood soaked the grit, the waves stroking the shore with indifference.

And last of all the hands from the earth tore into Sunday, peeling him apart.

"You are ours," Egin said with a smile. "Again."

"Fuck y—"

But Sunday did not finish, for he was torn apart, his entrails ripped from his body, his vertebrae snapped, his head yanked free. And though he lay there on the bloody sand, he was still aware, and he watched as the creatures feasted upon his open gut. They crawled inside him and occupied him and he could feel all that they were.

He had been in this place before, had been a pilgrim to this very shore. What he had seen in the coma... it was not a dream. It was a vision of what was to come.

Egin stood over his severed head.

"Do you see hell?" he asked.

He produced Kat's head as if from a magician's hat and laid it next to Sunday's own, so that they could be together forever along the dark shore of the Mediterranean.

* * *

Sunday woke then.

He jumped straight up, ready to fight, before realizing he was in the woods. He could hear the horses stirring nearby, and he searched the darkness until he saw the others. Kat and Mara. The priest, the junkie, the boy. Even the dog. All were there. All alive. All asleep.

What was that?

A dream?

He looked once more to the boy in the blue jacket, sleeping near the dog. And he wondered if the dream had been a warning and the boy would betray them.

And what would Sunday have to do to stop him?

CHAPTER LV

Philadelphia, Pennsylvania
Eleven Days After Event

Lincoln entered the low-lit room without waiting for an answer to his knock. He carried a candle through the drifting shadows to the bed where Daniel lay. The man's mouth and eyes were open, but it was hard to tell if he was dead or alive. Lincoln waved the candle flame over Daniel's eyes, and the pupils shrank.

Yes, he was still here.

Over the past week, Daniel had curled up tighter and tighter, his fingers and toes becoming gnarled and twisted. In one of those curled hands he still clutched the key, holding it so tightly the bones would have to be broken in order to release his grip.

Lincoln pulled up a chair next to the bed, placed the candle on the nightstand, picked up the Bible that rested there, and read to himself a passage from Corinthians.

I know a man in Christ who fourteen years ago, whether in the body I do not know, or out of the body I do not know, God knows—such a man caught up to the third heaven. And I know such a man—whether in the body or apart from the body I do not know, God knows—was caught up into Paradise.

Strange, Lincoln thought, that he would return to this book. That he had sought so many other books, modern books, to explain the world to him, not this one that contained answers written by primitive men who did not understand how to transcribe what they were seeing, and therefore their writings were dismissed by skeptics as magic to manipulate men.

He had been one of these skeptics, and had ignored God in all things, because the evidence wasn't concrete and it would have done no good anyway in his pursuit of facts. God was a crutch, not a calculation.

But now…

Now he knew. The things he had seen…

There was much more to the world than science knew. The scientific method might once have been his gospel, but it was God who wrote the book.

What does that mean then for my father?

Daniel seized on the bed, and let out a long gasp. The man's bite guard was now in at all times. Four nights earlier, he had a seizure and bit down on his own tongue. Though he was wasting away, his jaw was still strong, and they'd had to sedate him so they could stitch up his tongue.

Daniel wasn't speaking much anymore anyway; he was almost catatonic. Lincoln wondered how much was even left in there, behind the man's eyes. He believed—or hoped—that Daniel was still in there somewhere. Seeing something. Talking to people. Saving them, directing them, doing whatever it was the key told him to do.

And Lincoln was pretty sure that Daniel was helping the girl somehow. The one he had seen during his baptismal dream. He didn't know why this particular girl was so important—why Daniel was willing to use a radioactive key to kill himself for her—but she was.

In fact, Lincoln still didn't know why Daniel had used the key to bring *him* here. Why, out of all the people out in the world, was Lincoln among the chosen? What was he supposed to do? Just sit here, waiting for Daniel to die, trying to prevent him from biting off the rest of his tongue? There was a whole congregation out there that could do that.

He sat at Daniel's side, his thoughts moving to the rhythm of the flickering candle, until he drifted off to sleep and found himself back in the dark forest, following a woman through the snow. He wanted to call out to her, but he was afraid that somewhere out there in the shadows was the man he had seen before. The man who seemed to know Lincoln was watching him even though Lincoln wasn't really there. So he followed her softly, silently.

His foot crunched in the snow, snapping an old stick, and the woman stopped. She turned, putting her hands behind her back, hiding something from his sight, and he saw that this was not the same woman he had seen in the tub. This was a woman he knew.

"Kat?" he said.

The woman looked at him, or through him, and then Lincoln knew he was not alone. Someone had moved up beside him, and yet they had been there next to him all along. It was the woman from before, the one he'd seen walking with the man in the hood.

She stepped forward, toward Kat, and her face changed. Her hair was brown and curly, then straight and blond, and her skin grew lighter and darker, like a chameleon searching for its match.

As Lincoln watched, a passive observer from afar, a child stepped out from behind Kat. A girl of about six or seven. The woman with the changing faces kneeled, pulled something off her neck, and handed it to the little girl.

From above them came a blinding light, and Lincoln saw then that the woman had handed the child the key, the key from the box, and though the light that shone down upon the women and the little girl was not real, he could feel it warming his dream skin.

* * *

Lincoln opened his eyes, regretting the return to the cold. The single candle, now burnt down to a nub, provided no heat. But Daniel was awake, and was staring at Lincoln, eyes wide, drool leaking from his mouth.

"Is that why I'm here?" Lincoln asked.

Daniel gave no answer.

CHAPTER LVI

Nazareth, Israel
Ten Days After Event

For two days they navigated north, sticking with roads they knew. Ayelet's pace was still slow, but Jonah was slowed too, by the forty pounds of food and the suitcase nuke he carried on his back.

After the RV, after Berg, they had set out again. And she could feel Jonah judging her. She often caught him looking at her, looking thoughtful. She knew what he was thinking. What did this woman do? Why did she kill Berg? Could she be trusted?

On Highway 6 they passed hundreds of cars and trucks lined up for rush hour, with nowhere to rush to. There were some bodies left, filleted and split, but not enough for all the vehicles. She wondered if the others had been taken. Or they'd left on their own dead free will. She hoped some were still alive, safe somewhere, in hiding.

As they walked, she thought about what was to come. What they were going to do when they got to their destination. Were they really going to set off a nuclear bomb? A nuclear bomb designed only to be detonated by someone standing right over it, so when one of them lifted the handle they would face the bright light... and then disappear from existence entirely. Vaporized, as if never there at all.

She wondered what that would be like. Maybe it would be like staring into the Big Bang, or past the edge of a black hole. She wondered too if a soul could ever escape such a cosmic power, or if it would be cut off, like the damned around her, and she would cease to exist in both this life and the next.

It was as she was carrying the weight of her coming death through the passing fog of her exhaled breath that she heard it.

Get off the road.

The voice was so clear that she turned to Jonah. "What?"

"I didn't say anything."

Move.

She darted to the side of the road. Jonah looked at her questioningly, but followed. They tucked themselves in the snow behind a berm, and Ayelet scanned the dark.

"What is it?" Jonah asked.

She didn't answer, just continued to look around for some sign that she wasn't going crazy.

And then it came.

From deep in the eternal night, there was screaming, followed by a low rumble that shook the ground. She might have thought it was the beginning of an earthquake, except there was a cadence and rhythm to it. Was it a herd of animals approaching? Perhaps antelope thrown into chaos like everything else?

Two gruesome creatures emerged from the fog on the road ahead, coming toward Ayelet and Jonah, sniffing the air. Each beast lumbered on four bone-stilt legs, and upon their backs were a dozen heads apiece, mounted like stegosaurus plates, melded right into the backbone. And the heads were alive. They turned from side to side, scanning, searching, sniffing.

Are they looking for us?

Ayelet and Jonah stayed where they were, pressed low into the snow, not even daring to peek as the creatures moved past. When their footsteps receded, Ayelet thought to get up, to keep moving. But the ground continued to tremble, and she heard the voice again.

Don't move.

More creatures appeared. A great, screaming horde. This was the source of the tremors. Hundreds rolled past, moving, stomping, screaming, twisted into grotesque forms. There was an echo in their screams, as if they were between worlds, traveling between this one and the next. And beneath that, or within it, was the roar of something deeper, a bellow, commanding and controlling.

The army passed, and still Ayelet and Jonah lay still.

Go.

Ayelet stood, and Jonah rose to his feet beside her. "How did you know?" he asked.

Ayelet wondered the same. Wondered if God Himself had spoken to her. And if her journey—her journey to detonate a nuclear bomb—was exactly what He wanted.

CHAPTER LVII

Dublin, Maryland
Thirteen Days After Event

Eve followed Mason through woods and over back-country roads, past double-wides and churches, both of which appeared frequently here, though they were now sanctuaries for roaches and rats that feasted on the dead.

They'd been lucky, though. She had expected the monsters to ambush them as they slept, or to be waiting for them in the pines, but all she ever saw was black and gray, and all she ever heard was the cold wind and the faint chirping of crickets.

She and Mason talked little, but she thought about him. Wondered if there was ever going to be such a man in her life—someone so determined to find his love, to save her, or at least try to, even when it was almost certainly too late and all was already lost. Was it too late for her as well? She had assumed one day she'd settle down and raise a family, but that seemed absurd now, like researching 401k plans or wondering what would happen next on her favorite TV show. Here, now, such things were just the noise of a past life. And this man who led her now might be the last man she'd ever know.

That night, he again made a fire. The first time he'd started a fire she worried the light would draw in the creatures, and she said so, and as the fire flickered across his face he checked his rifle and said, "Let them come." He had a tent, but he let her use it, and he slept on a sleeping bag in the snow. She wanted to invite him in out of the cold, but she worried he might have his way with her. So he slept out there, and she in here, and she listened to the sounds of the dark, the cracking of branches and the howl of the wind, and she hoped the zipper between her and the outside would at least give her enough time to grab her rifle before whatever was outside came in.

That night would bring their first encounter since setting out together. She was dozing when gunfire brought her to knees. She unzipped the tent and saw Mason standing feet away, the smoke of his rifle curling around him. She grabbed her own rifle, but before she crawled outside, she saw what he had been shooting at. It was like a large elk, but its flesh was pale and a dozen submerged faces covered its body, their eyes assessing. And its legs... its legs looked like ordinary human legs, but they were attached to this creature, and that was almost more disturbing than anything else.

As the creature raised up as if about to charge, Mason let loose with the M-16. Chunks of the elk-thing blew into the snow, and it retreated into the trees.

Mason calmly switched magazines.

"What if it comes back?" Eve asked, looking up at him from the artificial safety of the tent.

"I'll take care of it."

She wanted to believe his boast, because her stomach was knotted and her heart was pounding and her palms were sweating even in the cold.

"It's okay," he said. "Go back to sleep. You're safe."

She retreated into the tent and lay back down. She heard him rustling around outside—standing guard, then eventually crawling into his sleeping bag. She looked at the open space next to her in the tent. Room for that sleeping bag. Room for him to get in out of the cold.

She started to speak. To invite him into the tent. But maybe he would prefer to stand guard? She lay there some more, breathing slowly, wondering if too much time had passed and he was already asleep.

Then she found the resolve.

"Mason?"

"Yeah?" he said.

"Do you want to sleep in here?"

There was no response. Only the whisper of the pine needles.

Then she heard the zipper. The tent shook slightly as he stepped inside, dragging his sleeping bag.

"You sure?"

She nodded, though it was too dark to see.

"Just for a little bit," he said. "It's cold. Thanks."

That made her feel bad, like she'd been selfish. Which she had.

He situated himself on the tent floor, giving her space, but still near enough that she could feel the heat from his body. She rolled over slightly, so she could see him from the corner of her eye, and even in the darkness she could make out some of the scars on his face.

She wondered how he'd gotten them. Some long-ago fight? Was he abused as a child? As a man?

Well, he was in her now. She'd invited him in. He could roll over on top of her while she was sleeping, and she'd be at his mercy.

And somehow that thought was comforting.

* * *

The next morning they found their way to US 1 and crossed over the Susquehanna River. He was good at directions, and he said he'd been on this road to Philadelphia many times. Just before the town named Rising Sun, they turned north, and soon after they passed a dark-blue sign that read, *Pennsylvania Welcomes You.*

They stopped at a factory that made potato chips, where Eve saw pretzel dough and potatoes just sitting on a conveyer, the machines of man no longer in motion. The doors to the loading docks were open, and long streaks of blood marred the factory floor, as if dead things had been dragged outside. Yet many of the dead lay right where they had worked, many of them older women, working-class women, their white hair nets still about their skulls. They had probably spent their lives in this small town, went to high school here, had their first kisses, and put away their dreams only to work at the local factory bagging and boxing potato chips. That had been their lives. Perhaps in some ways they'd been dead on this floor long before whatever it was barged its way in from the loading docks.

They raided the pre-packaged snacks ready to be shipped out, now bound for nowhere. Eve stuffed a bunch of bags into her backpack, and before leaving she gave a final, almost ceremonial nod to the scattering of dead old ladies who had spent their lives to help feed her.

That night she had another dream, the first one since she'd seen the street sign in the bunker. She was back in the room with the low candle and in the bed was the old man, shriveled and twisted on sheets stained with sweat. The sensations here were fuller, richer than those she'd experienced in other dreams. She could smell the smoke of the candle, the rot of this man in this bed. From outside came the sounds of the snow and the wind blowing. Everything seemed solid, tactile, as real as her daily routine.

"Is this a dream?" she asked.

Although his mouth did not move, he spoke.

"It is a way to talk."

"Who are you?" she asked.

"You know who I am. Do you know why you seek me?"

"My father says you have a key. The key that can open the gate."

"I do."

"Then why don't you use it? Open it? End this."

"I cannot use it to open the door between worlds. That is for you to do."

"Why me?"

"Because the key is meant for Christ. Only He can use it to open the gates. And you carry some of His blood."

"How?"

"You know that too. The man whose blood courses through you—he too carries the blood of Christ within."

She leaned back in her chair as the wind wailed louder outside. Belac carried the blood of *Christ?*

"To wield the key, you must be without sin," he continued. "Do not be tempted. Remain on the path of redemption. And then you shall come to us."

"I don't even know where you are."

"And you won't until you are closer. Keep on the road toward Philadelphia. When you are there, I will show you the way. But you must hurry. Otherwise the dark things will get to us before you do. They will find the key and destroy it. And all of us. Go. See."

He didn't move or gesture, but she knew where he wanted her to go. She rose from her seat and walked to the small window. The storm outside had turned into a full roar, and within its fury were tens of thousands of creatures, crawling over each other, a mass of naked, twisted, broken bodies.

"That is what follows you," the old man said. "You cannot see it, because they have blinded you to it. But where you go, they follow. And they wait."

Eve felt her stomach drop. These things were following her?

She turned to the old man on the bed. "We can be there in a few days."

"The man you travel with. I have tried to speak to him. He does not answer me."

"He's protecting me. Keeping me safe."

"Be careful, Eve. You are followed. You are hunted. You are prey."

* * *

They were crossing a place called Chadds Ford, just past an old Baptist church with cold, gray gravestones in its yard, when Mason stopped. He was staring at a black pickup that had run off the side of the road and into a ditch. Both doors were wide open.

"That's hers," he said with a nod, his voice gritty as gravel.

He approached the driver's side slowly, as if afraid of what he would find. Eve moved around too, so she could see.

She wished she hadn't.

She was there in the driver's seat, Mason's wife, cold and black and dead, propped behind the steering wheel, her neck slit so deeply it looked like her head had been placed back on top afterwards.

He made a single sound.

"Oh."

Eve wondered if she should say something, or reach out. She did neither.

He pulled her body out of the truck and carried her like a bride toward the church. Eve followed him, unsure of her place, as he stepped through the open doors of the sanctuary and walked down the red-carpeted aisle. At the front of the church he laid her body upon the altar. Then he lit some of the candles, kneeled, and lowered his head.

Eve took a seat in the pews and waited, leaving him to his wife and his God and his grief.

Eventually he rose. He picked up one of the candlesticks, walked to a red curtain that ran along the back wall, and used the flame to set the curtain alight. He stepped back. Soon the entire back wall was lit, the fire licking at the ceiling.

And although his face gave no indication, it seemed to Eve that the fire made him happy.

* * *

That night she invited him back into the tent. It was the right thing to do. To be Christianly, as Daniel had suggested, and to offer a warm place to someone in need. Perhaps this was something she needed to do, to be worthy of what lay ahead.

Lying there next to him, she wanted to say something. Get him to open up. She knew he was hurting. But who was she to help? Just some girl, some stranger, who followed him around like a puppy.

"Do you want to talk?" she asked.

"About what?" he said in the darkness.

"Her."

"What do you want to know?"

"How long were you together?"

"Forever." He rolled away from her.

She waited a moment for him to say more. He didn't.

"I'm sorry," she said.

In the darkness, she listened to his breathing. It was slow and deep, and then there was a stutter to it. He wasn't crying, but there was some emotion, maybe some memory, that had gotten caught in his throat. She reached out and placed a hand on his shoulder.

He rolled back over and faced her in the darkness.

Slowly, he reached out too. He touched her face and stroked her hair that still felt strange to her because it was new on her head. Her heart was pounding in her chest, and when he scooted closer and kissed her—gently, a soft touching of his lips to hers—she didn't move away, didn't protest. He pulled away, as if to allow her to decide, and she moved toward him to take in more. His hand moved down her body, and every inch of her reached out to feel his touch.

All she wanted was to not be alone.

All she wanted was someone to watch over her, to protect her, to tell her that the things outside weren't coming to get her.

All she wanted was to be loved.

And so she gave herself to him, in all the ways she could.

* * *

The next morning, he packed up the tent.

"Where are you going now?" she asked.

"South, maybe. Maybe it's warmer."

"You're not coming with me? To Philadelphia?" She tried to make it not sound pathetic and needy, but it came out that way.

He looked at her. "What's in Philadelphia?"

She knew if she started this, it would have to come with more explanation.

"You won't believe me."

He smiled. "Try me."

"A key."

"A key to what?"

"I think to everything."

He listened as she explained to him who her father was, and how this had all happened because her father was part of a group that sought to bring about the end of the world. He listened as she told him that they'd been able to open the gates to hell using a key, which was really the DNA remnants of the Christ, but that there was another key. A key to the gates of heaven.

"And then what?" he asked.

"I don't know. I think maybe that's how we get God's attention, you know. Maybe then, He comes to help. To save us."

Mason didn't speak.

"Well?" she said after a long silence. "Will you go with me?"

He smiled. "Who'd turn down the chance to meet God?"

CHAPTER LVIII

Sidon, Lebanon
Fourteen Days After Event

John Sunday scanned the burning city in the distance. They'd made camp on the outskirts, far enough away that it looked like a candle on the horizon. He watched as something orange shot through the sky over the town, some kind of falling star. It split apart and rained down fire. Some kind of satellite, fallen from orbit and returning to its maker?

The others were still asleep. He was done with sleep for the night. But his mind was still on the dream.

It had been so real, so vivid.

Even now he could smell the sea air in his nose. Could feel the pain in his gut as the creatures tore into his flesh. Could taste the iron in the air from Kat's blood.

Was that really a dream?

He tried to decipher its meaning, because it seemed to hide secrets. The priest—had something happened to him with children? The junkie—would she sell them out for drugs?

And the boy.

Would the boy betray them?

And there had been a castle. Had he conjured that, or was it really there, waiting for them?

Jesus. I'm believing in my dreams now.

Mostly he wondered if the creatures down there in that burning city knew they were coming. If the dream had been sent by those things, to show them what was about to happen.

Steps sounded in the snow behind him, and Kat was standing there, Mara wrapped in a blanket in her arms.

"John?" she said. "Something's wrong."

He turned to face her. "What is it?"

"I had a dream," she said. "About what happens to us on the beach."

Did we have the same dream?

"We died," she continued, her voice choking. "Mara…"

He knew then. These dreams were more than dreams. Someone was talking to them.

"The boy," he said.

Her eyes widened. "Yes."

"I had the same dream."

She tried to speak again, but couldn't get the words out. He wanted to move in and tell her it was going to be okay. To touch her. But he was hesitant, because he had failed her once, and she had been right to rid herself of him. Because he was tainted. And broken men cut with their love.

Instead she moved in toward him, and before he knew it, she was leaning against his chest and he was holding her again, the baby between them. He could smell them both, feel the softness of their skin, the warmth of her, a closeness he had not felt with any other human.

She looked up at him. "Are we going to make it?"

"I think we have a chance."

"What chance?"

"In the dream, they said they couldn't take Mara... she has to be surrendered. They need her to be given. They can't take her. That's why they haven't just come down on top of us." He nodded toward the baby. "Maybe that's the way. If we stay close to her, all of us, and protect her, maybe she can protect us. Maybe we can make it."

"Where?"

"The beach."

"Not the beach!" She looked at him like he was crazy. Maybe he was. Hell, he knew he was.

"I think we have to believe," he said. He was stunned to hear those words coming out of his mouth. Believe? Every institution he'd ever believed in had failed. They were all just intricate lies designed to serve men. Even the one institution he'd thought he could believe in—his own marriage—had failed. And now here he was putting his faith in a baby.

Kat looked down at Mara. She was just as unsure as he was.

"If you don't believe in her," he said, "then believe in me."

She looked back up at him. Hesitated.

"Okay."

* * *

Kat nursed Mara while John and the others packed up the horses. She thought about what he had said. What she was doing. And why. Mara, her daughter, she was just a baby. Nothing more. She wasn't some magic spell or telephone to God. She was just a little girl. A little girl who at this moment needed a diaper change.

If you don't believe in her, then believe in me, John had said.

She looked over at him. His face was tattered in scars, one eye a pit of sealed flesh. This was the man she had fallen in love with once before. The man she had once decided she would cross the universe with, until the universe was done with them both. She had broken that oath, shattered its words, her promise to God before His altar, broken. *She* was the one who left, who nullified her vow.

And now, as she watched the man who had once been her husband and lover, she realized she was forming a new promise. A new testament. She didn't know who the promise was to. God. Herself. John.

But she did know this. No matter what happened, she would be with him now until the end.

CHAPTER LVIX

Philadelphia, Pennsylvania
Fifteen Days After Event

As they walked the final few miles, Eve could hear the inhabitants of the city wailing and screaming in the distance. Fires burned along their path, the houses of old America and the buildings of men now embers to warm the dead. The closer they got the more afraid she became, until even her feet felt heavy, as if they were revolting against her decision to move forward.

It was then she saw the sign. The one from her first dream.

US 1 North. Philadelphia Next Right.

Mason stopped next to her on the road and gauged the burning horizon.

"Which way?" he said.

"I don't know. The man with the key said he'd show me where he was when we got to the city."

"Well, we're here."

"Yeah. We're here."

"So... how is he supposed to show you?"

"Visions, I think."

"Visions? Like in the Bible?"

"More like a dream." She could tell he was frustrated. She should have explained this part sooner.

"Do you need to go to sleep or something?"

"I don't really know."

"Well we can't just wander around the city. Those things will eat us alive."

"I know. Please don't be upset."

"I'm not upset, I'm just giving you the facts. If you're getting visions from God, it would be nice if He could speed up his timetable."

He looked around, then picked up his back and started walking toward an abandoned store.

"Where are you going?" she asked.

"We can't just stand out here waiting for God to show up."

She had just started to follow when she heard a voice inside her skull, clear as a bell. It didn't make any sense.

"Third," she said. "Church."

He turned back. "What?"

"I just heard a voice. It said, 'Third... Church.'"

"What does that mean?"

"Do you have the map?"

He pulled the map from his pack and spread it out on the hood of a snow-covered car. She traced her finger across it until she found what she was looking for.

"Here," she said. "Third Street and Church."

He smiled. "Good girl."

CHAPTER LX

Nabi Yasha Forest, Israel
Thirteen Days After Event

Ayelet and Jonah made camp that night in the cab of an abandoned semi. The voice had said they would come across it, but had failed to mention that its former driver was only a few feet from the rear of the trailer, his face fat and black, his guts a strewn streamer of intestine across the snow. Ayelet was grateful for the freeze; it had frosted the ends of her own toes, but it also meant she could not smell the ripeness of this man.

Jonah checked the cab before letting Ayelet inside. They closed the door and sat in the dark, catching their breath and soaking up the imaginary warmth of a truck heater that no longer worked.

"I miss the stars," he said. "With no electric lights around, it would be beautiful if we could see the stars."

She nodded quietly in the darkness.

He turned to her then. Something on his mind.

"Ayelet, this… this area looks good. Safe. There's a bed back there. A place for you to heal. I'll leave the food. Only one of us needs to go ahead. There's no reason for both of us to go."

Those words were like poetry to her ears. They were words she'd so desperately, secretly wanted to hear, like a lover whispering what he was about to do to her. But she knew it could not be. The voice had told her so.

"He says we both need to go. That it will take two."

"Who says that? The voice in your head?"

She simply nodded. Even saying yes out loud would be too much of an acknowledgment of the possibility she was going crazy.

"Ayelet... do you hear yourself?"

"The voice has guided us this far. Told me what roads to take. Told me where to stay the night. Kept us alive."

"Maybe that's just instinct. Your training."

"It's not *my* voice in my head. It's a man's. And I hear him as clearly as I hear you."

"So why doesn't he talk to me?"

"Maybe he thinks you're boring."

In the darkness, she couldn't tell if he was smiling, but his body relaxed more against the seat. "Really, you don't have to do this. We're only ten, maybe twelve kilometers out. Another day or so. If you stay here, you can live. You'd be outside the blast radius, outside the fallout. You start walking with me tomorrow, and every step you take seals your fate."

"I know."

"So why? Why go?"

Ayelet knew the answer well. Because she'd asked herself the question many times.

"Because I've lived my whole life doing terrible things in the name of my country," she said. "And letting terrible things be done to me. And I know, now, that I was serving the wrong master. And this is my chance to set it right."

"Who is the right master? God? The same God who let all this happen? Where is He now? Why doesn't He stop this?"

"Why should He? Why should God step in and save us when we've done nothing to deserve that? Look at who we are, Jonah. Look at what we've done. We destroyed ourselves long before these things came into the world."

"There's still some good in us."

"Yes. I've seen her."

"Her?"

"A baby."

"What are you talking about?"

"There's a woman out there somewhere right now. She's carrying a little baby. That child is the Savior. That baby *is* the seed of Christ. The one who shall grow, and rise. And with her, I think the light will return."

"I can't believe what you're saying. Aren't you a Jew?"

"I am. As was He. And I know—as a Jew—that I have heard the voice of God. Who am I to ignore Him?"

Jonah said nothing, but she could tell he was frustrated.

"You're right. Maybe it's just wishful thinking," she said. "Maybe there's no woman out there. No baby. Maybe the voice in my head is just me having some

kind of psychological breakdown. But I choose to believe. It's all I have left. And I'm going with you."

That night they slept curled up next to each other
on the mattress behind the seats. Not because there was
love between them, but simply because it was warm
there together as they gave and stole each other's body
heat. And yet, she thought, perhaps this was how all
bonds began in the universe: cold bodies in the night,
seeking warmth and touch, searching for confirmation
that they aren't alone beneath the eternal dark.

CHAPTER LXI

Old City, Philadelphia
Fifteen Days After Event

They traveled along Route 3, then turned on Fifteenth to Chestnut. At each intersection Eve paused, like she was waiting for a GPS to load in her mind. And then she would turn and he would follow her.

Yet when they arrived at their destination, all they saw was a burned-out church. Smoking embers, blackened beams. There was almost nothing left.

"This is it?" Mason asked.

"Yes," she said confidently, moving toward the building.

And as they passed a certain point, there was a sudden shift around them, and the building was whole again. Untouched by fire. It was as if they had stepped through some kind of visual ripple. There were even candles burning somewhere in the sanctuary.

Eve turned to Mason. "He says this is how they keep it hidden."

She walked up to the white door, and tapped out a knock in rhythm, as instructed, and the door was opened by an Asian man with an AR-15. He nodded for them both to enter, then closed the door behind them.

Four other men were waiting for them, each armed with a shotgun. One of them stepped forward.

"Gun," he said to Mason.

Mason hesitated.

"It's okay," Eve said. "We're safe here."

Mason handed over the rifle.

Another of the men turned to Eve. "Eve?" he asked.

"Yes."

"My name is Lincoln."

"Lincoln? Pierce?"

He nodded. "Follow me."

Lincoln led them into a candlelit sanctuary. There had to be more than a hundred people in the pews, waiting as if church was about to begin, except every one of them, man, woman, and child, was armed with a shotgun or rifle.

They walked down the aisle to the altar, where an old man waited for them in a wheelchair. Eve knew this man—she recognized him from her dream. And that smell... it was as if parts of him were dying, but the rest of him hadn't figured it out yet.

Lincoln and three other men formed a semicircle around him.

"Daniel?" she said.

The old man spoke, but his lips barely moved, and his voice was weak. "Eve."

"Yes. I'm Eve."

The old man's gaze drifted to the man standing next to her. "And you. Do you prefer I call you Longinus? Or Belac? Or something else?"

* * *

"You were kept hidden from me," Daniel continued, "but I can see you now."

"What's he talking about?" Eve asked Mason.

Mason ignored her. "Then waste no more time," he said to Daniel. "Give me the key. It can no longer protect you. What waits outside, I cannot hold back. We are billions dead. Billions damned, throughout the whole of the Earth. I promise you, your flock does not have enough bullets."

Eve looked back and forth between the two men. *What's going on here?*

The old man nodded. "We are small. A candle in your darkness. But we light His way."

"*His* way?" Mason laughed. "I will tell you of the way. You are *our* creation, not His. You carry *our* seed. And from it, we have, and shall always, grow."

Eve's face felt flush and her gut churned. *I slept with this man...*

"You... are Belac?" she stammered.

Mason didn't answer. Instead he turned to the congregation and announced, "They have come."

There was a sudden banging on the church doors. Outside, a man screamed, and then that scream was cut short.

There was something out there.

The congregation took cover in the pews, rifles ready, pointed at the back of the church, ready for what was coming.

"You think you can save yourselves in His church," Mason said, mockingly. "There are children among you. You cannot win this. Release the key, and their suffering will be brief."

"Eve, please." Daniel's voice was a whisper. "I can no longer move my hands. Open them, please."

Eve looked down at the twisted, gnarled hands in the old man's lap. He clutched something there. Something metal. Gently, she unfurled his fingers, and as she did, it slipped out.

A key.

It fell from his lap and clanked against the marble floor. She picked it up, and it vibrated in her hands and warmed her fingertips.

"That was a mistake," Mason growled.

The church doors burst open and a horde of dark creatures poured into the aisle, crawling one over the other, twisted human insects moving forth to devour a sea of fresh flesh. The congregation opened fire, and in an instant gunshots and smoke and screams and gore filled the pews, and still the creatures pushed forward, endless, merciless, hurling their broken bodies into their prey, tearing these last chosen survivors apart.

It was a slaughter.

CHAPTER LXII

Sidon, Lebanon
Fifteen Days After Event

Sunday and the others rode their horses along the dark city streets, the dog following behind, his nose sniffing the air, his head turning back and forth because he too knew something was not right.

Sunday felt he'd been here before. Introduced to this place. But now he was in it for real, and he could smell the dead on the streets, and all he wanted to do was get out. In the dream, there had been screaming. The wailing of the dead and dying. Here, those screams were distant, like the flames that licked into the sky from another quarter. The bodies they passed were cold, the buildings dark. Yet he watched closely, constantly expecting something was going to jump out at them.

It couldn't be this easy. Why had this part of the city been spared the torch? Were they once again being funneled forward toward some unknown fate?

The boy.

Sunday couldn't get the dream out of his head.

They turned a corner, and there in front of them stretched the sea—cold, vast, empty.

And before it stood an army.

It was a thousand strong. They were blocking the end of the road and spreading across the beach, fading into the darkness. At their head was Egin, riding a horse. He raised his hand as if to say hello, but then he lowered it in a sweeping motion—and the army charged.

Sunday considered the shotgun, but there weren't nearly enough shells. Not for this.

He spun the horse around. "Go!" he shouted, kicking the horse into a gallop.

The others followed him, riding fast and hard, snow spitting in their wake. The dog had been bringing up the rear, but now he had become the lead, and they raced behind as if chasing him. Sunday overtook him, determined to find a route to safety. They were moving parallel to the shore now, and he veered closer to the sea when he could, hoping that perhaps they could cut over to the shore, find a boat just waiting and ready and they could board and cast off and—

Sunday glanced to his side at an intersection and saw them pouring forth from that direction too. The things bounced off the buildings and each other, a rolling swarm that was far faster than the horses could move.

They weren't going to outrun these things.

Then he saw it up ahead. The long stone bridge. He knew where it led.

The castle.

He shouted for the others to follow, and turned toward it. The long narrow stone path jutted out into the sea just as it had in his dreams, leading to an ancient castle that had stood for all these years even as a modern city sprouted up around it.

"There!" he called.

They raced along the castle path in single file, the ground barely wide enough for a man on foot, let alone a horse. But this worked to their advantage, for the mass of pursuing creatures was subject to the same limitations, only able to cross one or two at a time, and they slowed, allowing Sunday and the others to gain a bit of distance.

Sunday rode straight through an iron gate, the castle's towers on either side crumbling into the sea, and quickly dismounted. Kat and the priest and boy and the junkie followed.

The dog had fallen behind.

It had once been the fastest of them, but it had since slowed, perhaps from living off of canned vegetables. The creatures were right on its heels, and one of them reached out a bone arm and swatted at it, knocking it to the ground.

Sunday raised the shotgun and fired at the pursuing creatures.

"Come on, boy!" he shouted between shots.

As he continued to fire, not yet killing the creatures but at least holding them back, the dog leapt back to its feet and darted past Sunday into the relative safety of the castle. Even then Sunday continued to fire, pausing only to change the mag, hoping to fell one or more and thereby create an obstacle for the others in the narrow path.

The priest and the junkie pushed at the iron gate, trying to close it, but it didn't move.

"It's stuck!" the priest cried.

The boy took Sunday's position at the gate, pulling the shotgun to his shoulder and opening fire, and Sunday moved to help the priest and junkie. Together they slid the heavy door, iron scraping against stone, the creatures coming ever closer. Finally it was shut and Sunday wrapped the heavy chain and around the bars and clicked the padlock in place.

The creatures slammed against the gate, and Sunday fired through the slats, plying their eyes and mouths with rounds.

"Now what?" asked the priest, panting.

"The towers," Sunday said. "You two, take the stairs that tower," he said, pointing to the priest and the junkie and the tower to the east. "You're with us on the other tower," he said to the boy.

Every one of them had their weapons in hand now, including Kat, with Mara still strapped to her. He wondered if Kat knew his thoughts. Knew that he was thinking he had raced them right into a dead end, water on three sides of a castle crumbling into the sea, a bad spot if ever there was one, and this would be their last stand.

He wondered if she knew that he all he really wanted to do was just hold her, even as the creatures pushed aside their dead at the front gate to make room for more and banged against the iron bars. He wondered if she knew he wanted to tell her it would be okay, and that if need be, he would do the thing she had asked him to do after their talk in the woods about the shared dream. That he would kill her first, so she didn't have to watch, and then kill the baby, and finally he would raise the rifle to his own skull and pull the trigger.

He wondered if suicide was a sin or the only way to truly be together.

He guided her up the stone stairs, the dog and the boy already up top, and looked down. Silan Egin had arrived. He'd dismounted his mutant steed at the far end of the bridge and was waiting as the creatures clogged the bridge. And the creatures at the gate were changing tactics. They were piling on top of each other, creating a ramp against the barrier. Soon they would pour into the kingdom of crumbling stone.

The priest and junkie opened fire from their perches on the other tower, and Kat and the boy and Sunday joined in, spraying shot down, knocking stacked beasts into the sea.

It wasn't enough. Some of the creatures piled high enough to scurry over the top, to climb over the gatehouse. Even when one toppled, another would take its place, until the creatures were pouring over the wall like water over a dam.

They had taken the courtyard. Below they could hear the cries of the horses as they were consumed.

And Sunday knew he and the others weren't going to make it.

* * *

Father Simon and the girl were overwhelmed. They had killed untold creatures at the base of the tower, but their ammunition was finite, and these monsters seemed to be infinite.

Tentacled bone arms pulled themselves up and over the stone, and the girl had to back away quickly, still firing, just to avoid its outstretched claws. Her shots filled the creature's flesh, but even as it retreated, another arm fell in its place, and then the girl's gun clicked empty. She sought more mags from the belt on her hip, but there were no more. She was done.

Father Simon kept firing, round after round, until he was empty as well.

Empty except for the two shells he had kept in his pocket.

He loaded them, and turned to the girl.

"Do you repent?" he asked.

"My name is Samiher," she said.

"Do you repent, Samiher?"

"Yes, Father."

He raised the shotgun, and she closed her eyes.

He pulled the trigger.

Sami saw the light then, and she was back again on the stoop in the little stone yard in the back of her house. Her sisters and brothers were playing chase, her father playing the rababa, and the scents of the namourra's orange blossoms drifted through the air. Her grandmother sat next to her and took her wrinkled hand in hers. Her father kissed her cheek and whispered a single word. "Stay."

Father Simon was almost stunned by the blast because the weapon that had done so little against the creatures had destroyed her utterly. And as she dropped, and he looked at his work and felt the weight of it, he wept because he was next.

One of the creature clambered fully over the wall, and what Simon saw next was of the priest's own device.

Father Zula was standing before him, smiling, surrounded by a sea of writhing, naked children. They moaned and wept and called out for help.

"Here they are," said Father Zula. "The ones you have forsaken."

The priest turned the rifle around to insert it into his mouth, but before he could he dropped to his knees and slammed his head over and over into the stone, his will not his own. The children had come for him, and this was *their* will.

"Simon," whispered the children. "Siii-mon."

But there was still some of him left, just enough to put the gun in his mouth and bite down on the barrel and fumble for the trigger. Just enough for that. But no more. Before he could pull the trigger, the children had their stake, and the rifle was tossed over the wall, the shell unfired, his mind fully claimed.

* * *

The boy stood behind to the right of the one-eyed man as both of them, along with the woman, fired on the creatures stacking against the bottom of the west tower. The fight was going to be lost, the boy could see that, they all could, but it was one that they would continue to battle as long as they still had strength to fire.

And then the boy saw something that made his breath catch in his throat.

They were down there, standing in the middle of the courtyard, in the sea of creatures. His mother. His little brother. And they were not the possessed, but as they were in life. Huddled and afraid, creatures swarming around them. His mother clutched his little brother in her arms, to protect him, and looked up at her older son in the tower.

Looked to him for help.

The boy looked over at the woman with the baby, and then at the one-eyed man. Both were occupied with holding back the assault. Neither of them paid attention to the boy.

His sweaty palms gripped his rifle, and he pointed it at the baby in the papoose on the woman's back.

He could do it. Now. It would be quick. Tears formed in his eyes, because he knew this would have to happen. Now. He could not let them suffer anymore.

The shot rang out, and it was over.

CHAPTER LXIII

Caesarea Philippi
Fifteen Days After Event

They started hearing it—and feeling the vibration—about five kilometers out. Like a distant metallic piling being driven into the ground, over and over. It grew louder as they came closer, the vibrations stronger, transforming into a pulsing rhythm, a breathing drum.

And then Ayelet could see it within the darkness: a churning, like the night itself was a storm. It was so inky black that she would not have been able to see it all if not for the forks of lightning that shot from its spin as it hollowed the sky. The sound of the crickets was deafening here, and she wondered if that meant the pulse was creeping into her head, if she was losing the fight for her own mind.

But then it became clear that the chirping of crickets was not organic—it was a high-pitched pulse coming from whatever caused the vibrations, whatever caused the churning blackness in the sky. This was the source of the sounds that radiated across the land.

The chirping was a signal.

She heard the voice again. This time it was very weak, very far away, and nearly drowned out by the pulsing chirp.

You must go without me.

She stopped on the mountain road. "What?" she yelled.

But there was no answer, not when she repeated the question out loud, not when she repeated it in her mind. They were alone.

Whoever had protected her, would do so no longer.

"We have to hurry!" she shouted to Jonah.

She ran as best she could in her metal suit, the friction building heat in the scars between her legs. They reached a nature reserve on the side of the mountain, passed burnt vehicles in the parking lot, and moved on past a visitor center.

Above them the storm throbbed. Ayelet felt like she was staring up at the entire universe.

At the top of a long set of stairs, they found a surgical gurney surrounded by dead women covered in snow. Beyond that was a cave, or what had once been a cave. Its roof, and the top of the mountain, had been blown clear off.

This was the source of the storm.

It poured forth from the mountain, an impossible darkness belching forth like smoke from a volcano.

Ayelet took a step forward...

... and the mountain wasn't there.

In an instant it had shifted, as if it had been rack-focused, and now it was a kilometer away. She stood instead on a giant pockmarked field of granite, dark, black, rocky, and full of holes.

"Jonah?" she called.

But he was a distant aluminum-clad dot on a dark horizon.

Where am I?

Even her thoughts were slowed here.

They emerged then, from the holes. The hands came first, some mere bone, others a mixture of bone and claw and flesh, and behind the hands came people with no eyes. They were naked and pale and new... and they fell to their knees and bowed, over and over, slamming their heads into the rock.

When they rose and came for her, she knew the mountain had gotten inside her head.

She fell to her own knees and bowed. Violently. Her head struck the hard rock. Again. Again. And again. She wanted to stop, to stop, to stop. But she couldn't.

She could feel who she was slipping away, and the creature now possessing her skull. It was bigger than her, bigger than them all, and It shifted her mind away from her, and she was drifting from herself as if she were an island and the world was a boat drifting away from her.

Someone grabbed her hand.

She looked down and tried to focus. A little girl stood next to her, holding her hand. The child was pale as a newt and had no eyes, like a fetus in the womb, but she still looked familiar.

Is that... me?

Her mind was jumbled. And when she looked at the child's hand, she saw it was no longer a child's hand. It was larger, and gloved. And then she saw him next to her.

Jonah.

He pulled her in closer and set the backpack on the ground and kneeled next to it.

The creatures from the holes screamed and swarmed. The ground shook. The mountain itself shuddered. The earth opened where Jonah had placed the backpack, and it started to tumble into the hole. Jonah caught it, but the weight pulled him down and he toppled over with it.

Ayelet grabbed him with both hands.

She lay on her stomach hanging on to his feet, and he dangled below her, the straps of the backpack in his outstretched hands. He was so big, so heavy. And she was so weak. She couldn't hang on.

Below him, the pit seemed to go on forever. Deep below, streams of magma surged, and giant plumes of smoke and gas radiated in bands.

Yet somehow she could see beyond even that. Lower. Deeper. To a giant, throbbing, rotating ball. The core of the earth itself, spinning and rotating. And she knew then that these things were of the earth, and humans could never destroy them without destroying themselves.

"I can't activate it with you holding me!" Jonah yelled.

She felt claw hooks tearing into her calves as the creatures reached her. One way or another, she was going to let Jonah go.

"The stars are still there," he said.

"I know." Her eyes filled with tears.

And she let go.

He dropped into the abyss. As he fell, he pulled the backpack close to his body, cradling it like a baby, and opened it so he could activate the device.

That's when it came upon her.

The light.

It returned to her with such heat and fury, she knew then the world was born of it, and not of the darkness. And as that light engulfed her, she prayed one last time that she would not be lost to these things, or to the nuclear annihilation that was coming. That her soul could somehow rise and not be lost.

CHAPTER LXIV

Old City, Philadelphia
Fifteen Days After Event

The key vibrated in Eve's hand, and as she looked out at the slaughter in the church, everything shook like a ripple on a pond, and colors swirled around her.

"What's happening?" she asked, but her own voice trailed behind her ears, and everything froze, the congregation and the church and the things within it, and it all shifted to shades of red.

And then she was no longer standing in the church. She was in a forest, standing in knee-deep snow. Mason—or Belac, or Longinus, or whatever the hell his name was—was with her too. He had grabbed her arm as... whatever happened, happened.

She looked at the scars on his face. On the face of this man who was both her lover and her own flesh. She wanted to vomit.

"You," she said. "You're him."

He tried to grab the key from her hand, to grab her, and she wasn't fast enough to retreat. Yet his hands didn't touch her; instead they somehow drifted right through her, as if he—or perhaps she—wasn't really there.

"What's happening?" she asked again.

He stopped, looked around, then chuckled as if he'd been in this place before and remembered how it worked.

"This? This is heaven," he said. "Can't you tell?" He turned and held out his arms, as if showing it all off, and shouted into the trees, "Knock, knock! Are you home?"

With a wicked smile that curled up the corner of his mouth, he turned back to Eve. "Ah, Eve. Thank you. You were the only one who could lead us to the key— the only one pure enough to use it. But... not for long. There will be another."

She didn't like the sound of that. "What does that mean?" she asked.

"Two thousand years I've walked this earth. My seed unable to find root." He smiled again. A sly, dirty smile. "Until now."

The words hit her in the gut. Did he mean to say...

I'm pregnant. Oh my God. There's a baby inside me. His baby.

"No..."

At that moment a stiff wind blew and the trees around them rustled, the needles on the pines moving and swaying. But it seemed it was not so much the wind that moved the branches, it was more like... like the trees themselves rippled. It reminded Eve, strangely, of something she'd learned about in science class. A gravity-capillary wave.

And someone was stepping through the trees, through the... disruption. A little girl in a beige tunic. Her bare feet walked on top of the snow, not even leaving footprints.

Ignoring Eve, the girl stopped before Mason.

"The way to me," she said, "is through you."

Mason scowled. "Your words mend nothing."

"Will you not return home, Longinus?"

"It is too late. Save the fatted calf."

The child nodded and turned to Eve.

Eve looked down at the key in her hand. On an impulse, she offered it to the child. "Here. Please. End this."

The girl shook her head. "The time is near. But for now you are the keeper. Protect it."

"What? No!" Eve sputtered. "You—*you* have to save us."

"I did. Now you must wait."

"For what?"

"My return."

"How long will that take?" Eve asked.

"Seven years."

"Seven years!"

"This is only the beginning of sorrows," the girl answered. "Bring the child the key. Those who endure in me until the end shall be saved when the tribulation comes."

"We have already brought it," said Mason. "None shall rise."

The child looked up at him. "You are but servants in the house of the Lord. But keep watch. The master returns."

"Of course, a parable. How *wise*," he said.

The child turned back toward the forest.

"Don't leave us!" Eve said. "What are we supposed to do?"

"Keep the candle. And look to the sky, for the figs of men fall."

And with that the girl disappeared into the trees as if she were a ripple in a pond that simply faded away.

* * *

Eve was back in the church. Gunfire rang out around her, a handful of survivors still able to fight the horde. Mason was there, too, and—

Lincoln tackled her to the ground and covered her eyes with his hands. "Close your eyes!" he yelled.

She was stunned and confused, but she did as he said, and even with his hands covering her closed eyes, she saw the blinding burst of white light.

Lincoln remained on top of her for a few seconds before removing his hands from her eyes and getting up.

"It's done," he said.

She opened her eyes and squinted, and realized Mason was screaming next to her. He was on his knees, howling in agony, clutching at his eyes, and through his fingers she could see the whites of his eyes had been washed in blood while his pupils were singed an opaque white. He had been blinded—and it seemed he was trying to pull his eyes out of his head.

Lincoln raised his rifle and fired, and the round went through Mason's palms into his skull, and he fell backward and landed in a bent-over hump.

"Come on," Lincoln said to Eve, helping her to her feet.

She stood and looked down at Mason. He was dead, but the beasts were not. They overran the remaining resistance, tearing the surviving humans apart. And she, and Lincoln, and Daniel would be next.

From outside the church walls, perhaps somewhere in the sky, came a deafening blast, like a sonic boom. The beams of the church shook, and the beasts and the humans in the pews paused in their mutual slaughter to look toward the rafters. And the voice spoke in Eve's head.

Hide.

* * *

"The altar!" Lincoln shouted.

He grabbed Eve and practically dragged her beneath the altar as the ceiling cracked and collapsed and the entire church came crumbling down around them. They crouched there, huddled together, clinging to one another, the ground shaking, the world turning to destruction and dust.

And then it was done, and the rumble subsided, and the church seemed to settle except for a few groans and creaks of wood. They slipped out of their hiding place and looked over what was left.

The once-proud church looked like it had been bombed. Not just the ceiling but the walls had collapsed, opening the church to the sky. Chunks of wood and mortar covered everything, including the pews where the battle had raged. Nothing moved there—neither beast nor man. All had been crushed, wiped out in one fell swoop.

But Lincoln's attention was elsewhere. His eyes were drawn to the broken wheelchair, and he hurriedly crossed the rafters and pushed the debris aside until he confirmed what he already knew was true.

Daniel was dead.

* * *

Eve looked up at the lights in the sky overhead. For the first time in what felt like forever, it was brightened by what seemed to be tens of thousands of stars.

Only then did she realize that those stars were falling. They sizzled through the air and landed in explosions all around.

It was raining down fire.

"Come on!" Lincoln shouted.

He and Eve climbed over debris to escape what was left of the church, and then they ran together, Lincoln clutching her hand, dodging the raining rocks as they fled into the dark city. In Eve's free hand she could still feel the vibrations of the key, and in her mind she could still hear the child talking to her.

CHAPTER LXV

Sidon, Lebanon
Fifteen Days After Event

The boy fell to his knees. John Sunday had killed him.

He had put a slug in the center of the boy's small skull, blowing brains out the other side, and the boy dropped, dead.

Sunday was damned. He had done it because it had to be done, but he knew his soul would suffer all the same.

The dog sniffed at the boy, nudged his cold dead hand, and whimpered.

Sunday looked to Kat, as if she could somehow cleanse him, and she met his eye, but she said nothing. He had killed the boy in the blue winter coat. To save her. To save the baby. But not himself.

What price was this? What price so this baby could rise?

He turned away from Kat, because he could not face her judgment, and he resumed firing into the beasts below, but in his shots, he was screaming.

And then in the sky, on the distant horizon, it happened. A surge of white light with the strength of a thousand bolts of lightning, followed by a rising plume.

The creatures turned to watch it as well, to watch as the light spread across the dark sky in a ripple, like the Northern Lights, a reverberating orange and white, followed by a rumble of a thousand thunders as if God Himself had woken.

The thunder passed, and there was silence. Stone cold silence all around them. Even the chirping came to a stuttering end.

And then the sound returned. But it wasn't the sounds of crickets, or of battle. It was crying and weeping. Begging and screaming.

Sunday looked down at the base of the tower. The creatures were squirming, convulsing, their melded-together body parts writhing as if trying to move away from each other, as if each was now an individual piece trying to pull away from its host.

A lone voice emerged from below, an unseen woman somewhere among the masses.

"Please! God! Forgive me!"

The other creatures echoed her call, over and over, in their own tongues. "Forgive me! Forgive me!"

The creatures began to circle Egin, who stood now in the courtyard. He spoke words to them Sunday could not hear, but the creatures seemed not to hear either. Or perhaps they simply didn't care. One lashed out with a bone hook and with a single slash ripped out Egin's entrails and brought him to his knees.

And before the creatures tore him to pieces, Silas Egin looked up to the tower, to John Sunday, and smiled.

* * *

When it was done, the creatures turned to face the tower where Sunday stood with Kat. One of the creatures lowered its body and knelt. The others followed. And soon a path was formed with kneeling beasts on either side.

Sunday and Kat descended the stairs, the dog following a few steps behind. As they walked between the kneeling beasts, the faces within the creatures looked up at Kat and the baby, and the mouths spoke, begging forgiveness.

"Please…"

"Please, forgive me."

"God help us."

They were joined in the courtyard by the priest, who had descended from the other tower. The junkie wasn't with him. Sunday didn't ask where she was, and the priest didn't ask after the boy.

They knew.

"Is this real?" the priest asked.

"I think so," said Kat.

They passed Egin. His head and limbs had been removed. His body was split apart. But something moved within his open gut. A darkness, a swirling black pool, as if the corpse itself was a gate.

It began to crawl out of him.

It wasn't done.

Sunday hurried Kat along, and their walk turned into a run as they crossed the stone bridge. From behind them came a roar, and they turned and saw that the darkness had come out of Egin and was moving down the bridge after them. Sunday couldn't see it precisely, couldn't get his eyes to penetrate that inky black, but he knew it was there.

"Go!" Sunday shouted to the others. The docks were nearby. "The boats!"

And as they ran he stood his ground and fired at the thing he could not see.

Then the darkness was around him, and he could feel the tug of it within his mind. And there was a voice he remembered.

"Return..."

He felt the darkness on his flesh, then beneath it, moving into his veins, claiming him from the outside in. He could not resist as it began to seal his thoughts within a tomb, and he felt the love he had for her being drained.

"Kneel," the voice commanded.

He fell to his knees, unable to fight it, and bowed, slamming his head into the ground.

He heard Kat call out to him, and he looked to her, and the last thing he saw before the darkness bound him whole was Kat screaming and sobbing as the priest dragged her away.

* * *

John Sunday rose to his feet. He felt the smile on his face and knew not why. All he knew was that he was going to kill the whore.

He ran after them, full speed, faster than he had ever run, and he closed in, the whore still screaming. He had almost run them down when the dog turned and attacked, leaping, clamping down on his arm. Sunday flung the animal aside with inhuman strength. The dog's jaw tore away a piece of his forearm, but Sunday kept moving.

The fat priest stepped in front of him next. He was unarmed but intended to make some kind of stand anyway.

Sunday bowled right over him.

Behind the priest, the whore had raised her shotgun and aimed it square at him. Sunday should have stopped then. But there was nothing left inside him to tell him to quit. Only to kill. To kill the whore and leave the baby to die on the sands. He saw the gun quivering in her grip, heard the crack as it fired, and felt the burn.

She fired again.

Two shots, one to each leg, blowing out his kneecaps from beneath him. He collapsed to the ground, rolled onto his back, and looked up at her.

The beast would not let him hear her words as she stood over him, but he could see her lips moving, and he understood.

"I love you."

Then she raised the shotgun like a club and brought it down on his skull, and his vision went black.

CHAPTER LXVI

Old City, Philadelphia
Fifteen Days After Event

They eventually made it to the Delaware River, because Eve told him they needed to get away from the land. In a boatyard, Lincoln found a rowboat, and they set out, and he used the oars to take them down the river.

As he paddled, his mind was churning.

What the hell was happening?

He had figured out that the falling sky was not the stars. It was the broken parts of shattered satellites, or maybe even the space station, that showered down all around, many of the pieces no bigger than his fist, but spread out far enough to create a deadly metal hailstorm for a dozen city blocks.

But why? What had caused it? And what on earth had happened back in the church?

More importantly, why had God let all those good people get killed?

Every last one of them. Even Daniel.

Only Lincoln and this girl had survived. And now what was he supposed to do with her? Ferry her around like he was driving Miss Daisy?

She turned to face him.

"It's going to be okay," she said, though he hadn't said a word since getting in the boat. Her eyes were wide, like she was looking at something he couldn't see. "The people in the church. They're going to be okay. There's a better place."

Lincoln said nothing.

"And I'm not Miss Daisy," she added.

What?

"How did you—?"

She held up the key and smiled. "I hear you, like I hear them," she said. "All of them. Your father is there, Lincoln. He says to tell you he's proud of you."

"No. Don't mess with me like that."

"It's true."

What is this girl doing? Making up some damn lies just so I'll take her—

"They're not lies," she said. "They're all there. Even Carol Connors."

He didn't care about Carol Connors.

"Can I talk to him?"

"Of course," she said. "He hears you."

Lincoln looked skyward, toward the falling lights in the heavens, and he said the words he should have said when his father was still alive.

"I love you, Dad. I'm sorry."

He searched the sky, and his mind, for some response. But there was none.

Reluctantly, he looked to Eve for an answer.

She smiled. "He says he loves you too. And everyone wears white in heaven."

The dam in Lincoln's heart broke, and the tears rolled down his face.

* * *

As they floated past the dark city, Eve wrapped herself in a blanket and clutched the key in her hand. Eventually, after some rowing and drifting, she pointed to a marina.

"We need a sailboat," she said. "A big one."

"For what?" Lincoln asked.

"To cross the Atlantic."

"The *Atlantic*? That's three thousand miles!"

"I have to take the key to the child."

"Where is he?"

"She. Greece."

It dawned on him then. The little girl he'd seen in his vision. Still… Greece? They couldn't sail all the way to Greece. How would they navigate with no working equipment? No compass? No stars?

"It'll be okay," she said.

He nodded, not really believing her, and rowed toward the marina.

He settled on a forty-two-foot Hinckley Sou'wester named Solace, but the 'c' and 'e' had partially peeled. They stocked up by raiding the marina bait and tackle, a nearby restaurant, and some of the other yachts for supplies. He found a portable compass, but its needle was spinning wildly as if the earth itself had flipped. Instead he would have to rely on an old sextant—a decoration from the wall of the seafood restaurant. It was real and not a prop, and combined with some navigational charts from one of the yachts, he might be able to manage. Maybe.

He did find one working machine: a wind-up watch left on a desk. He wound it up and it actually started ticking. Though he had no idea of the actual time to set it to.

When he felt they were ready, he raised the sails, and they set off again, and to his relief there was some wind there to fill the canvas. The air was cold, but every so often, he felt gusts of warmer air. Perhaps those gusts came from the fires on the land, but he hoped they signaled that the engine of the earth was restarting.

"Really?" he asked her again as they crossed the rough waters of the bay.

"Really."

Cross-Atlantic sailing trips took years to plan. They had hurriedly grabbed water, snacks, and some scraped-together gear, and had set off within an hour. And they were navigating without GPS or a compass. Dead reckoning, emphasis on dead.

They stayed within sight of the fires on shore until they were off the southern tip of New Jersey. Then Lincoln took a breath, the wind filling his lungs, and pointed the bow toward open water. He wondered where they'd end up. They'd probably just drift haplessly north to Newfoundland, maybe Greenland. They'd pitter around the North Atlantic, getting colder and colder, until they died, the ice forming jewelry on their corpses.

"Look," Eve said from the bow, most of her tucked beneath a blanket. She was pointing to the sky.

The dark clouds had thinned just a bit. Several tiny dots of light peeked through drifts of gray fog and smoke from some distant fire. He thought at first he was looking at another falling satellite. But these lights were steady, and he recognized them.

The Plough. Ursa Major. The Big Dipper.

He peered higher, across the heavens of old, and it was there too.

Polaris. The North Star.

He turned the wheel and felt the rudder head respond.

He knew then. Knew where he was going.

"It'll be okay," she said.

He nodded.

Maybe. Maybe.

CHAPTER LXVII

Sidon, Lebanon
Fifteen Days After Event

Kat found the boat, as she had seen it in the dream. The name on the side read *Fida*.

Behind her, the priest dragged John by a single leg, his head hitting the wood planks and smearing his dripping blood down the ice-frosted dock. She had wanted the priest to carry him over his shoulder, but the priest didn't want him that close. The dog limped along behind.

For once, no one was chasing them. The kneeling creatures at the castle did not follow. Silas Egin was dead. And the darkness that had come from his corpse... it had disappeared inside John.

He had tried to kill her.

So many had already died. The grandmother. The girl. The boy. She wouldn't let them get John too. She wouldn't.

On the sailboat, the priest bound John unconscious to the mast with rope and duct tape he found in the cabin. There was hope in the world—the skies were lightening from black to a mix of gray and orange—but there was still no electricity for the motor, and neither Kat nor the priest had sailed before. They struggled to raise the sails and to decipher the knots.

When they set out, Kat took the wheel, steering much like she would a car. They bumped against the dock, and another boat, and the priest shoved them off each time. They hoped to catch the wind, but they drifted aimlessly on the current. But eventually there was a flap of the sail, and the priest tried the wheel and spun and the sail caught.

After a time John awoke and tried to come undone from his binds, but they'd tied him up with all the rope they could find, and Kat had shot out both of his knee-caps, so he had no muscle to push with. So instead he spat profane things about what he would do to the whore and the baby, and the dog growled at him, and the priest was forced to cover his mouth with duct tape.

Kat had only planned to set sail for a little while, but before they knew it they were far out to sea, with no idea how to get back. Storms came upon them then, and they dropped the sails and huddled below, and the wind lashed them, and Sunday's gag came undone and he screamed and shouted into the night. As the boat rocked, Kat changed the baby, and the infant was as calm as could be despite the storm.

The next morning, Kat saw land. She dreaded docking, because of both the difficulty of the act and what they might find on shore, but they were gaining some basic skill with the boat, and eventually managed it. She saw signs in Greek, and guessed they were somewhere near Cyprus or the mainland. The priest checked John's bonds—he had been re-gagged earlier—then disappeared to find supplies, leaving Kat with the remaining shotgun and a handful of rounds.

He was gone for some time, and Kat worried. Perhaps she should have gone with him. Even if the creatures had ceased their assault here, as they had at the castle, there were other threats in the world of men. But her job was to protect the baby. Mara. So she sat and she held her and she watched John as he slept. He was pale; he'd lost too much blood, and she had no way to dress his wounds.

As she watched him, he woke and stared back. A dark, ominous look. His mouth was sealed with fresh duct tape, but a trail of blood had run down his chin and dried and she wondered if he'd bitten off his tongue.

She moved closer.

She held out the baby and placed Mara's tiny hand on John's forehead, as if to bless him. Instead he merely looked up at her with dark hollow eyes and shook his head at her like she was stupid. She had hoped there would be some miracle here. Some sign that the baby was holy and helpful.

She returned to her seat and cried for what John had become. He was finally here with her now, and yet he had never been farther away.

The priest returned at last with supplies, including some belts that he used to create tourniquets on John's legs to stem the bleeding. Kat wondered if John was going to lose his legs first or his life.

That night she dreamt of a distant shore draped in fog, and she knew then they were not done. Her father waved to her from the beach, beckoning her, and she was worried the things had returned and were using him again as bait.

* * *

They set sail again, following the wind and the currents, at the mercy of their guidance. The sky now stayed gray and orange night or day, and there was no way to gauge time. But it felt like a week had passed before they saw the shore again.

The priest was hesitant, because she had told him of her vision, and the shore was filled with fog just as she had forewarned. He feared such a vision meant something had again gotten hold of their minds. But they had nowhere else to go, and the winds had brought them here, so they approached.

As they drew close, they saw that many figures stood upon the beach. They weren't twisted and broken. They were just people. Men. Women. Children. All apparently waiting for their arrival.

But first they had to dock the boat, and it didn't go so well this time. The boat came in too fast, and instead of hitting the docks as Kat had intended, she simply ran the boat aground on the beach. She hoped she hadn't damaged the hull.

The crowd on the shore came closer, and Kat found herself searching them in the hope that her father might somehow be among them.

An old man with a beard stepped forward and looked up at them.

"*Eísai i Káthrin?*" he said in Greek.

She nodded. "*Eímai i Kát.*"

The old man smiled. "*Eímai o Nikódimos. Eíste as-faleís edó. Eímaste opadoí tou drómou.*"

Kat turned to the priest. "He says they're here to help."

They disembarked, and the crowd kneeled as she passed, the baby in her arms, and she wondered what dream had brought these people to this shore.

EPILOGUE

In time, there was once again a way to gauge the day. In the morning, the sky radiated with orange and rippling gray, and by night it was black again, as if the light still battled for permanence in the skies.

Kat again swaddled the baby and put on her cloak. She shifted the baby on her hip and called out into the cottage for the dog she had named.

"Carrots!"

The dog came running, and together they headed down the cobblestone streets of the small town. The snow had stopped and the air had warmed, but now the air was filled with a constant mist.

She knocked on the door of the small stone building, and a man was there to let her in. They smiled and nodded, but neither spoke as she entered. At the back of the room she unlatched a wooden door, the baby cooing in her arms, and stepped into another room, this one lit by a single guttering candle.

She lit a fresh candle and sat in the rocking chair. She placed the baby in the wooden cradle near her feet and rocked it with her foot, mother and daughter rocking together. The dog took his usual spot near the cradle, settling his head on the stone floor.

Across the room, John lay behind the bars of his cell, his arms and legs shackled to the bed. His mouth was gagged, but he still occasionally wailed and whined beneath it.

She picked up the tattered burgundy Bible and opened it. She began again, from the beginning, translating it from Arabic to English as she read aloud:

"In the beginning was the Word, and the Word was with God, and the Word was God. The same was in the beginning with God. All things were made by Him; and without Him was not anything made that was made. In Him was life; and the life was the light of men. And the light shineth in darkness; and the darkness comprehended it not. There was a man sent from God, whose name was John. The same came for a witness, to bear witness of the Light, that all men through him might believe."

She continued to read, as she had done that morning. And as she would deep into the night. And as she would for all the days to come, for as long as it took.

SPRING 2021
THE END
IS NEAR
jamesholmesauthor.com

THE
LAST
REDEMPTION
JAMES HOLMES

ACKNOWLEDGEMENTS

To all of you who began the journey with *The Last Disciple*, and who continue to come with me on a 'helluva' ride.

To David Gatewood, for editing, but more importantly, for teaching me how to write a better book with your notes and advice.

To Nancy Alvarez, for showing me the depths of what it means to be a true friend.

To Brian Shields, for believing in me and teaching me kindness is cool.

To Chantal Watts, for being a die-hard book nerd and taking that love to market the hell out of these books.

To my Wife, Hannah, Harrison and Hailey, for teaching me patience and unconditional love. On the journey to the light, Everything I do is for you.

ABOUT THE AUTHOR

James Holmes is a journalist who has been writing for television for twenty-five years. He's covered the dark side of human nature for so long he needed a fictional outlet to come to terms with where we're going as a species.

He wakes at 1:30 every morning to write and in this caffeinated haze, his literary monsters are born.

He and his wife homeschool their three children.

The Last Testament is his second novel. The final chapter, *The Last Redemption*, will be available Spring 2021.

Made in the USA
Middletown, DE
05 July 2021

43623991R00241